Two Moons: The Freeman's Captive

TWO MOONS: THE FREEMAN'S CAPTIVE

Book Two

Chelsea Shepard

iUniverse, Inc.

New York Lincoln Shanghai

Two Moons: The Freeman's Captive
Book Two

iUniverse, Inc.

For information address:
iUniverse, Inc.
2021 Pine Lake Road, Suite 100
Lincoln, NE 68512
www.iuniverse.com

ISBN: 0-595-33084-3

Printed in the United States of America

CHAPTER 1

▼

It must have been close to midnight. Hanging in the sky like a Chinese lantern, Plya's white globe brought light into the Khyrian night, its blurry reflection shimmering on the ocean's surface. Under the full moon, the planet was asleep, lulled by waves gently rippling the sand like countless caresses.

Staring at this peaceful nocturnal scene, I remained silent and still, though not by choice. I was spread and chained between two tropical trees, my neck wrapped in a lilk corset that made even nodding impossible. Lilk restraints encased my wrists, shoulders, ankles and hips, all connected to the trunks and branches on both sides and above me. A waist belt, buckled tightly and linked to the trees, completed the harness.

As an elegant touch, Khiru had adorned my feet with high heels, but the spikes, absorbed by the sand, offered no support at all. The extreme stretching of my limbs compensated, keeping me perfectly balanced and immobile. As for being quiet, the neck corset was high enough to cover my lips, and Khiru had reinforced its efficiency with a wad of cotton inside my mouth. Singing under the moonlight was not allowed.

At least he hadn't blindfolded me, and I could enjoy the view.

Plya was my favorite moon. An old Khyrian legend had elected it to be the female satellite; it was therefore my protector and muse. When it was full, Plya also bore a long, white mark—a salt lake, I was told—that looked like a benevolent smile on her face. This, somehow, brought me comfort.

That night, Plya's lunar male companion, Mhô, was behind me on the other side of the sky. When Khiru had brought me outside earlier in the evening, I had observed Mhô's crescent grazing the roof of our cabin. In comparison to Plya's luminous globe, his thin quarter looked very humble, almost nonexistent. I imagined Khyra's male moon spying on his mate, awaiting the proper moment to join her.

In the manner of millions of Khyrians before me, I liked to create allegories based on the moons. They were so omnipresent, so unavoidable. How could you not turn to them for entertainment or support, cast them as characters in the destiny of the planet, or your own? Especially when you had nothing else to do.

Like Plya, I was waiting for my partner to join me, although I knew Khiru might have other intentions, like leaving me to hang alone all night.

Such solitary confinement was not new, but the situation gained intensity every time we played. On the *Noncha*, the starship that had brought us to Khyra from Earth, Khiru had started with bondage sessions that lasted for a couple of hours. After eight months on the planet, we were up to half a day, not counting a long preparation time. Sometimes he would leave me "entertained" with a vibrator, powered clips, or mental teasing programs monitored by a brain controller. Other times, his carefully planned bondage was my sole distraction.

Either way, my torment would start peacefully. I'd long stopped fighting the bonds, as pulling on them often made things worse. Once Khiru was gone, I tested the overall severity of my restraint, then forced my body to relax. When no buzzing, pinching or burning interfered with my yoga-like meditation, I would occasionally drift off to sleep. However, I suspected Khiru knew when to permit it. More frequently, my position was too strenuous to allow such *laisser-aller*. Then, I inevitably became restless and irritated. I longed for action, anything to stop the edginess rising inside me.

But there were sessions when action was amply provided. Prolonged sucking on my nipples, tiny shocks all over my flesh (with particular emphasis on the most tender spots), grinding vibrators inside my rectum, my vagina, or both. Because of the disastrous whipping scene I had provoked on the spaceship and the psychosis I had developed in relation to any kind of pain, Khiru was careful to select torture implements that never truly hurt. To compensate for his clemency, he would keep them going forever, with only one goal in sight: driving me crazy with lust. Khiru always reached his goal, and I would always succumb to bouts of infuriating madness.

Whether I was frantic from too much calm or too much action, I would swear it was the last time. I would talk to him. I couldn't waste my life like this, trapped in lilk or resina, chained or wrapped in sticky tape, my ears plugged, my eyes blinded, my mouth gagged, and my brain exploding with boredom and/or sexual madness. At this stage, tears or furious groans were frequent. Yet they were useless. Khiru never took mercy on me; I would have to endure his predicament until he decided otherwise.

After a frenzied stage that bordered on hysteria, I would reach a hormonal high where I disconnected from my bondage and floated in a world of hot dreams and scary fantasies. That was usually the moment when Khiru would return. At first, his touch was unreal, as if it belonged to my visions; when I recognized it, I welcomed it with rapture. Khiru would slowly bring me to climax. The myriad sensations, escalating in intensity, would leave me stunned with pleasure and gratitude. I couldn't wait to do it again.

My current predicament wasn't really a surprise. During the last few days, Khiru had been with me at all times, so I was due for a solitary scene. But I had never been left in bondage outside, where the sea, the trees, and the wind created a creepy atmosphere. I didn't think I could endure this all night, and wished upon Plya, my only friend in the dark, that Khiru would soon rescue me.

After all, he was officially responsible for me. Should anything bad happen, he would have to report to no less than the Global Council. Such was my importance on Khyra. When the wise men who run the pacified Global Zone realized my Earthling genes were their fastest route to restored Khyrian fertility, they imposed a strict quarantine and gave Khiru the responsibility of implementing it. Although the arrangement proved feasible and hardly as annoying as I'd feared, I reacted poorly at the time it was pronounced. My first day on Khyra wasn't the glorious advent of which I had dreamed.

Before reaching the planet, one of the officers on the *Noncha*, Nur, had confirmed that I would enjoy complete independence on Khyra. Nobody would bother me with public appearances, and I would be spared common duties and work. Pursuing a Khyrian education was, however, high on my list of priorities, as their advanced civilization would give me enough to explore and learn for the next five years. The idea of diving headfirst into a new society was daunting, but Khiru's presence by my side would be a great help.

Ironically, I first had to fight for the right to move in with the man who was later to become my de-facto warden. Nur argued it was too early to settle on one man, especially a Rhysh Master prone to possessiveness and stringent rules. Although lifelong commitment was an absolute goal, Khyrians frowned on the idea of exclusivity too early, preferring extensive trials and inevitable errors. However, Nur finally acknowledged I was entitled to live with the person I loved. I went through the last weeks of the year-long trip with a serene, if somewhat passionate, heart. The green planet, growing bigger every day, seemed more and more inviting.

My arrival was not as smooth as expected. On my first day on Khyra, the official reception at the Space Center ended in a petty confrontation between the Global Council, scientists, Khiru and me. Nur's promise of complete freedom was shattered when Council officers decided I should be kept under high surveillance for safety reason. Basically, they planned to enshrine me in a velvet cage with bodyguards attending my every need and escorting me everywhere. This was unacceptable.

"What could possibly happen to me?" I asked. "Who would harm the one person who can save your race?"

"We can't take any chances," said a tough-looking bald guy. "You're the first alien to set foot on Khyra. Who knows what kind of madness, collective or individual, it could generate?"

"Come on, you're more evolved than that," I replied, averting my eyes from the man's hairless head where the absence of ears was all the more striking. Even after a year, that particular Khyrian feature never ceased to amaze me. "I expect people to be curious, perhaps edgy in my presence, but it's not like I'm some mutant monster from outer space!"

Nobody laughed; Khiru barely smiled. Before he could add his two cents to the debate, another Council officer, a blond giant whose gaze made me feel like a troublesome dwarf, took the floor.

"You're right, Megan," he said. "I don't expect hysterics either. Khyrians have known about Earth for years, and everyone saw the holo-films sent by the *Noncha*. You're hardly a novelty anymore."

"Say that to the freemen," someone sneered.

"However," the officer continued, raising his voice to cover the unwelcome comment, "you are very precious to us. Thanks to your fresh DNA, we can advance our fertility program dozens of years. You are much more useful than all the samples we brought back from Earth. We simply can't lose you, or have you sick or wounded."

"I promise I'll be careful when I cross the street."

"I'm serious, Megan," the blond officer said. "You've already gotten into trouble on the ship."

There were assenting murmurs, and I bit my lip. Of course, he was referring to the whipping accident with Lodel, which had left me in a coma for two days. I couldn't deny I had behaved stupidly, if not dangerously. But at the time, my strategy had made some sense.

After one passionate night at the beginning of the trip, a night that would forever seal my passion for Khiru, the proud, dark-haired officer had seemed to lose interest in me. Aware of my turmoil and confusion, my new Khyrian friends offered contradicting theories. Naari, who had known him since college, explained that Khiru's heart had once been badly broken, and he was reluctant to fall in love again. Myhre argued that, as a Rhysh Master, Khiru required a level of submission and intensity of bondage play that I probably couldn't handle. In the end, I became convinced that if I could show Khiru I was as tough as the next slave, I would revive his interest and ultimately find a way into his heart. Hence my idea of a public whipping scene that I lured him into attending.

In short, the foolish plot of a besotted woman.

"The incident on the *Noncha* was my mistake," I told the Council. "I practically blackmailed Lodel into it. I only wanted to make a good impression."

Khiru smiled encouragingly. In a way, I had gotten what I wanted, although the price was higher than I expected. The drama was poised to haunt me forever.

Lodel, the eccentric exhibitionist who agreed to whip me for a few minutes of glory, was willing but inexperienced. He hit poorly, drawing blood without realizing the inflicted pain didn't yield any rewarding pleasure. Lodel had promised not to stop until I reached orgasm. I was so determined to succeed, I didn't want him to fail me because I whined a little too much. The audience, unaware of my plight, was enthralled, mesmerized by the performance. Only Khiru sensed the absurd drama developing on stage. His anger and pride got in the way of his best instincts, until he, too, finally surrendered. I had already fainted under the lashes when he climbed on stage and rescued me from Lodel's amateur hands. Two days later, Khiru confessed his love to me, and all was well. I had won.

But victory had its price. Since the accident, I had been terrified of pain, even the good kind. The sight of any whipping instrument provoked unbearable nausea. Khiru, who dearly regretted not stopping Lodel more quickly, had been patient and indulging, finding alternative ways to ecstasy. It was hard to tell whether he resented my fears or not. My guess was he did, but he hid his feelings under the sweet coating of love. As did I, although I couldn't fool myself. It was a terrible punishment for someone who'd dreamed of masochism her whole life, to rein back the first man who matched her desires.

"Well, we must avoid a repeat," said the bald Council man. "I'm afraid we can't have you messing around with S/N games when we need you available for scientific experiments."

"What exactly will you demand from her?" Khiru jumped in.

"She will need to donate fresh cells regularly," a scientist answered. "Probably once a month, in four different genetic centers, as we want to use various methods to widen our chances. One is in Mhôakarta; the others are half a day away.

The procedure will be harmless, but the process will be time-consuming. And we can't afford any delays, or omissions."

"I can take care of that," Khiru said. "Megan will live with me, and I'll hold myself responsible for her. I'll organize her life in a way that doesn't jeopardize her health or safety. She will submit to my rules, and only enjoy the freedom I'm willing to grant her. Would that satisfy you?"

The Council members and scientists debated whether Khiru, who was both a Rhysh Master and a respected space officer, could be trusted as my jailor. An older woman wearing a brown lilk bracelet with the Rhysh initial argued that Khiru could not impose full submission on me because I was too inexperienced and could be easily misled. I remembered Nur had made a similar comment on the ship. Khyrians were extremely wary of non-consensual mistreatment. As expected, Khiru readily agreed to moderate discipline, promising to confine our Southie/Northie relationship to the bedroom.

Nobody asked to hear my opinion on the matter.

"There's another problem," said the tall blond man. "We want Megan's whereabouts to remain as secret as possible."

"I was told our address would be private," Khiru said.

"Yes, but there's the matter of public appearances and, er, outdoor activities. They should be restricted to a minimum."

"You can't keep me locked in the house!" I protested, breaking a much-too-long silence.

Khiru motioned for me to stay calm.

"The goal is for her to pass unnoticed," he said. "Her long hair keeps her external ears hidden, but she can wear a hat or a headband to conceal them completely. Her waist and breasts won't show underneath her clothes. And once tanned, her skin will look perfectly normal."

"What about her eyes?" the bald man asked. "They're so round. They don't look Khyrian."

"There are races in the North who have big eyes like hers," the Rhysh woman said. "She will look foreign, but not necessarily alien."

"Also, don't forget, no one's ever seen her face," said the scientist.

A global assent responded to him.

"Morphing her features in every film was a smart move," said the woman. "Wasn't it your idea, Khiru?"

Khiru nodded with false modesty.

Finally, the Council accepted Khiru's proposal to guarantee my safety, keep me incognito, and respect my independence within acceptable limits. They handed me over to him officially until the experiments were completed, which could take a year or more. In the course of an hour, my status on Khyra shifted from honored representative to lab rabbit.

I was of two minds about Khiru's idea. I didn't like being dependent on him, but living under his supervision was better than a custody house. He would probably enjoy plotting schemes to hide my body from public eyes, but he wasn't allowed to turn me into a full-time slave. All in all, it was a good deal.

With my freedom restricted, my life on Khyra wasn't what I had expected, but Khiru made the safety measures entertaining and even thrilling as a natural pretext for bondage and dress-up games.

There was basically one rule I couldn't break: leaving the house on my own. When Khiru took me to a densely public place like a tavern or a theatre, he covered my head with a hood, with or without a gag. A purple bondage hood had been Khiru's first present. Laced tightly in the back of my head, the soft resina, the Khyrian sap that offered extraordinary elasticity, covered my eyes, cheeks and, most importantly, my ears like a second skin. The mask came with an interesting range of options: in front of my eyes, two tiny holes gave me limited vision. Its rubber-like texture was permeable, allowing sweat to evaporate.

Once I got used to the firm wrapping around half my head, I adopted the hood as an essential item, much like shoes or the mediapin I wore on my chest when we were out.

As for the revealing curves of my body—the waist and breasts Khyrian women had lost with their fertility because of genetic mistreatment—he simply covered them with body suits and added chains, belts and other gadgets to hide my hourglass figure.

It was erotic wear in reverse. Usually Northies emphasized the feminine attributes of their partners. With me, Khiru used the opposite technique. The first time, I was afraid somebody would notice the uniqueness of my outfit, but camouflage was actually very popular amongst S/N players. It preserved the anonymity of a relationship, or created a spectacular surprise at a party when the covered person removed his or her clothes. When toys were hidden by the costume, it made it easier for shy Southies to be adorned with erotic jewelry, massaging body gel and dildos.

Khiru exploited the last advantage repeatedly. I've taken many naked walks with clamps chained to a vibrator, all concealed under a black cloak that billowed down to my oft-cuffed ankles.

Things were smoother when we met trustworthy people. Khiru didn't have to conceal my identity in the presence of his family, close friends, officials, or even the local shop owners who knew our secret.

In our travels—a favorite pastime—Khiru rented cabins in isolated locations and let me use a simple hat to cover my ears whenever we joined the crowds. In touristy places, people paid less attention to extraordinary looks, and I could easily pass for a woman belonging to a minority race.

A new sound broke into the tropical night, interrupting my memories. My well-trained ears perceived the flapping of the wings before my eyes caught sight of the pelican-like bird flying across the shore, an impressive shadow cutting through Plya's moonlight. My hearing had become very sharp lately. Prolonged sessions in bondage had led me to pay more attention to noises that were often my sole link to the world.

The presence of a living creature in my surroundings revived my apprehension. I pulled on my arms and fidgeted in the sand, but achieved nothing more than increased nervousness. A bird was harmless, but what if another animal showed up? A poisonous reptile or a deadly meat-eater? Despite the sea breeze, I began to sweat, my sex way ahead of my brow in terms of moisture. I attempted a cry, knowing that the pathetic, muffled sound I produced wouldn't serve any purpose, except inform Khiru that his evil scheme was working satisfactorily. I jerked on my bonds again. I couldn't think of anything but my naked body exposed to the dangers of nature. Fear crept up my spine as I strained my neck to look down and sideways. But the corset gave no slack, so any attacker would approach unseen.

I focused on the sounds. The bird had disappeared, leaving me acutely aware of the wind whistling in the leaves, the waves crashing on the shore, and bugs fluttering here and there. The night was full of murmurs. As I tried to distinguish them, I forgot my fears and calmed down.

Plya was still smiling on me. When it hung in the sky by itself like tonight, I could almost pretend I was on Earth. Stars probably looked different, but I had never paid close attention to constellations. More importantly, the sky was dark, as my instincts would have it, and that put my mind at rest.

When I set foot on Khyra's soil after the bleak reception at the Space Center, I was brutally confronted by a mid-day olive green sky. The color sent wrong signals to my brain, and, losing my balance, I had to lean on Khiru for support.

Vazgor Park, the artificial garden on the spacecraft, should have prepared me for this, but I had always dismissed the fake mint sky on the *Noncha* as a glitch, my mind stubbornly refusing to accept it as an evocation of the real thing.

But once I walked on new terra firma, there it was, daring me with its insolent jealous shade, refusing to turn blue. At dawn, promising peach tones would soon give way to a confusing aquamarine that turned stronger and greener with every passing hour. On cloudy days, watery green patches broke the reassuring whites and grays. When the sandy-gold sun shone high and bright, the sky would boast a glorious lime intensity. At sunset, the ripe-olive shade would be broken by deep coral streaks. It was beautiful, but unnatural. It looked and felt like pollution, or a chemical drama heralding the end of the world. For days, I avoided looking above people's heads.

Gradually I learned to love Khyra's sky and its myriad greens, the intensity the color gives to the oceans and rivers, which merge beautifully amongst meadows and trees. There are fourteen words for "green" in Khyrian.

Once my eyes were familiarized to a sky of a different tint, my acclimation became much easier. Oh, Khyra was a whole new world, but it was no more unusual to me than Africa would seem to a European. Different housing, different fauna, different clothes: those variations were easy to accept as regional peculiarities. Mhôakarta, with its thousands of white cubic houses spread over a gigantic green carpet (parks, gardens, strips of grass between sidewalks) was as exotic to me as it was to an inhabitant of Brega, a city in the north that Khiru and I visited for its famous art galleries. Brega was covered in snow all year long and single-story lodgings were built in grey stone, forming a network of tunnels across the white landscape. Before flying down closer, I had thought Khiru was taking me to a gas extraction plant.

Khyra was, however, resolutely alien. Many details, apparent or subtle, defied my instincts as an Earthling.

One of them was the absence of man-made noise.

Thanks to the use of silent technologies such as levitation for air transport or magnetism for escalators, Mhôakarta, like every other city in the G-Zone, was as peaceful as a country village on a Sunday night. Even in the early afternoon, when Khyrians left the workplace and spilled onto the streets, some of them hurrying to reach the closest underground or Lev-line station, others enjoying a sunny rest on the grass strips separating the sidewalks, it was easy to eavesdrop on conversations. You could also hear birds singing, raindrops splashing on the pavement, or a Lev-bus gently whooshing on take-off, a muffled sound you only noticed if you were standing on the platform.

Speaking of whooshing, an unexpected draft blew up between my legs, returning my thoughts back to my sandy situation. Where did that breeze come from? Just as I thought it was a whim of nature, a puff of cold air landed on my right nipple. The target was perfectly centered and made me suspicious. When my left nipple was teased in the same way, my doubts vanished; Khiru was playing with me. Was he hiding in the dark?

Unsure of how this would progress, I hesitated between anger and joy.

A long breath of air flirted with my labia, and a shockwave rippled up my body like a stroke of lightning in reverse. I knew where this was going to lead me and decided to fight it. The night was young. I might be out here until dawn, and I wasn't going to let Khiru torment me with unfulfilled desire for hours on end. He always said that his tricks worked on me because I allowed them to, because I wanted them to. If that was true, I could use the same willpower to resist. If I couldn't escape physically, I would escape mentally. Boys on Earth thought of baseball; I used similar exercises to curb my arousal.

While tiny needles of cold air pricked my breasts, I forced myself to revive more souvenirs of my first days on Khyra, smiling inwardly at the numerous shocks I'd overcome as I adjusted to the alien-ness of the planet.

One of them derived from the impressive ratio of men over women. My trip on the *Noncha* had done little to prepare me to the shock of being surrounded by such a multitude of males. After all, it was normal, though by no means fair, to find more men than women on a spacecraft.

The stories I'd heard about the genetic degeneration and consequent sterility of the Khyrian race gained much more impact when I was confronted with the reality of the species' number-one problem. Everywhere I visited on the planet, there were four men to one woman: not only in science labs or official administration buildings, but also in shops and beauty salons, in parks and farming grounds.

Slanted eyes, copper skins and a height difference of one or two heads enhanced the glaring sensation of being an intruder. During my first weeks on the planet, the presence of so many Khyrian men made me feel twice as alien, as both an Earthling and a woman.

Fortunately, Khyrians didn't abuse their supremacy. They respected women with the same urgency shown by animal lovers for endangered species. The few men I was allowed to meet were always perfect gentlemen, even though they often obeyed their particularly playful nature and gently teased me, the boldest of them daring Khiru's jealousy with minor flirting.

My fear of being overpowered by hordes of male giants subsided, only to be replaced by a warmth in my loins each time I was in public.

I wasn't very good at this arousal-curbing business. Thinking of a profusion of sexy men had the opposite effect. The wind blowing around and under my body was taking its toll. My nipples had grown hard and needy. With my legs, I pulled at the restraints anchored to the trees and tried to get closer to the source of teasing. Increased dampness between my thighs turned the wind even colder, which in turn created more spasms inside. The cotton gagging my mouth was drenched, but the neck corset held it firmly in place. My breathing accelerated.

How long was he going to leave me here?

As much as I'd learned to appreciate solitary confinement, I liked it better when Khiru played with me. When he entertained me, the scene was always more challenging, but his presence was a powerful aphrodisiac. I felt stronger and braver, not so prone to tears and despair. Alas, as the submissive element in a Southie/Northie couple, the decision was never mine.

Khiru took particular pleasure in complying with the obligations derived from the agreement with the Council. Keeping me away from the public satiated his need for an exclusive relationship with me. But my quarantine also created limits he was looking forward to breaching. He often teased me about how he would rather parade me naked than drape me in a black coat. He would have liked to participate in public scenes, organize our own play parties, and show me off to the world. But for the time being, he was happy to keep me as his secret, private toy because, he said, the delay gave me more time to adjust to my inevitable fate.

When he preached that way, I prayed the genetic experiments would last at least a decade. Between his real threats of public exposure and his underlying desire for more severe discipline, thinking about the future made me edgy.

Khiru insisted that obedience and patience were the first rules for Southies. He made it clear that he would train me relentlessly until even the thought of complaining would no longer occur to me. During the first weeks, complying with his rules was easy. In a world where I didn't know how to turn on the light or shop for bread, I needed his constant guidance and advice. But as I learned to cope with Khyrian ways, my rebellious nature took over.

Submission, I found, was a formidable challenge.

As both my genes and desires testified, I was a Southie by nature, a submissive woman who needed a dominant man to fulfill her, but I was also strong-minded and proud, inspired and occasionally hot-tempered. Come to think of it, there was nothing I resented more than being told what to do. Which was probably why it turned me on. The dichotomy of masochism was something I never quite understood.

Because I liked a good challenge, I resisted Khiru's decisions whenever I felt like it. Not often, but often enough. Khiru probably disapproved. He was not the kind of man who took no for an answer and, in his eyes, resistance was not a game. He was generally a good sport, though. He faked annoyance, punished me in a most pleasurable way, and moved on to other things.

Khiru was smart. He knew he could not claim my complete submission (yet) and had to respect my independence as ruled by the Council. But this moderation wouldn't last forever, and if I couldn't give him pain as a toy, I decided I must at least work on my obedience. Alas, in this case, willing it to happen was simply not enough.

Feeling worthy of Khiru was a recurrent problem. As a Rhysh Master, he was a professional in the art of bondage, discipline and pain for pleasure. I had long considered myself a poor match for a Northie who had taken his dominant traits to their limits, a man who had spent four years at the demanding Rhysh Academy for the sole purpose of turning his sexual heritage into a lifestyle.

Nevertheless, Khiru loved me and lived with me in spite of the contradictions he had to deal with. A skilled expert in the application of discipline, he knew I had become paranoid of any threat of pain. A graduated full-time Master, he couldn't rule my life as severely as his instincts urged him because of the Council's order.

Even though Khiru proved his love to me day and night, I couldn't get rid of the mixture of guilt and fear that he would reconsider his unspoken commitment to me. Making sure that day never happened was on top of my agenda. It was certainly worth a few hours writhing in sexual anguish.

But, by Plya, his hands, even at their naughtiest, would be such a treat compared to the elusive touch of the air.

Another unidentified noise caught my attention. It was close on my left, and sounded like a small animal scratching the sand. My heartbeat quickened while I listened more carefully. It was creeping closer. Without thinking, I pulled violently on my arms. The leaves rustled above me, but the chains held. I tried to lift my feet off the ground, but the sand kept a firm lock around them. Struck by panic, I struggled mightily in my bonds, determined to uproot the trees around me.

I froze when something soft and furry touched my ankle. I held my breath, afraid it would bite me if I moved. Brushing my leg with its paws, sniffing, the animal seemed to hesitate. When it moved away from me, my chest deflated like a balloon. At that very moment, a gush of cold air spurted under me, and a ball of fur on four legs ran next to my leg past my thigh, and gripped my waist belt. I screamed through the gag, and tried to shake the little devil off me. But the animal held on as if its life depended on it. I could feel its body quiver against my hip. The poor creature was as terrified as I was.

Fighting back murderous thoughts against Khiru, I controlled my breathing and regained some composure. I hoped that keeping still would appease whatever was clutching at my belt. Its fluffy tail was brushing against my pubis, and I bit hard on my gag until my jaw hurt. In the end, my patience was rewarded. The furry ball crawled back down my leg, jumped on the beach and scurried off in the night.

I had lost half the water inside me, in every possible fashion. My whole body felt sticky with sweat, and the chilly wind kept tormenting me.

I was tired, I was fed up, I was thirsty and, most of all, I was in need of my man's touch. I longed for Khiru like a castaway longs for a ship. But the ocean in front of me was empty. Even Plya smiled with sympathy.

Will you answer my prayers, Plya? I asked in silence. Did you witness my sacrifice in the temple today? I didn't die, I'll grant you that, but I fainted. Surely worth a wish or two? What paradise awaited the poor slaves who gave their lives on this spit of sand? Khiru had omitted to conclude the historical lecture he'd given me during his live and erotic rendition of a secular ritual.

Pichac Island, where Khiru and I were spending the week, had once been host to a brilliant civilization. Many temples and houses survived as a tourist attraction. Most visitors herded toward the better-preserved ruins, where mediaframes and animated holograms explained their historical meaning and use. Others were more adventurous and went to look for unattended ruins scattered in the woods and rocky plains.

Khiru had insisted on giving me the grand tour. Maximum safety was not required here, but he outfitted me with a funny red cap that looked like a hollow ball cut in half and flattened the top of my hair as well as my ears against my skull. It wasn't very flattering.

"This is a truly indigenous hat," Khiru said when I grumbled. "I want you to live the experience fully. Let's complete your costume."

He wrapped a short animal hide around my waist, buckled a heavy collar around my neck, and adorned my wrists and ankles with bracelets made of shells that clicked whenever I moved.

"Are you sure this is how women used to dress? Bare chest, bare feet, no underwear, and wearing a collar, not to mention a silly hat on their head?" I teased him.

"I never said you were top of the flock. These tribes had slaves, and you're one of them. The cap hiding your hair should make you feel humble. The collar represents ownership. And the noisy jewelry reminds you that you cannot hide, even in your sleep. Oh, I almost forgot one detail."

After fitting a backpack around his shoulders, he connected a leash to my collar and pulled gently.

"Off we go. Let's see how many old rocks we can find."

We wandered among wild plains and small hills for over an hour, then took shelter beneath a tree to have lunch, and resumed our walk. We saw few ruins and met no one. We mostly chatted happily, and I soon forgot my weird outfit. Finally, we came upon a more interesting site on top of a prominence: the remains of a temple, with enough walls and pillars standing straight to indicate what had once been six rooms surrounding a circle.

Along its border, two blocks suggested the presence of statues that had been broken or stolen. Between them rested an odd kind of table. It curved upward, like a tortoise shell, and was supported in its middle by a massive pillar. As Khiru and I approached the table, I noticed a multitude of eyelets screwed into it. They formed the shape of a body with its limbs spread out. They should have been rusty, but they shone brightly in the sunlight.

Without warning, Khiru scooped me up and laid me on the stone table.

"Hush," he said before I could complain. "Spread your arms."

Knowing when to keep silent, I obeyed and watched him pull out ropes from his backpack and lace them around my limbs. He tore the leather skirt off my waist and added more rope between my hips and my armpits, making sure my breasts protruded nicely between two very tight loops. Because of the inclination of the table, my sex stood out as the main point of interest.

"This is a sacrifice stone," Khiru explained. "Imagine the roll of drums, the chant of priests, and a masked sorcerer bending over your virgin body, painting it with sacred symbols, summoning the gods to welcome their offering. Then think of what he would do to you before he drove a knife into your heart."

I have a very good imagination and had no problem seeing the scene as Khiru described it. A recognizable heat radiated throughout my body. I thrashed convincingly.

"Oh, there's no escape. You're a slave. Your only value is a useful death.

"But as the shape of this table indicates," he added, "these people knew how to entertain their victims during their last moments. Let me demonstrate."

I had thought Khiru was just aiming for a bit of bondage thrill and would untie me after a few minutes of make believe. When he produced powered clips and a vibrator, I understood I was in for a real scene and I became anguished.

"Khiru, what if people come?"

He mimicked a sigh. "You never learn, do you?"

Seconds later, he had taped my mouth shut.

Then he started playing with powered clips, tiny suction cups that can be applied anywhere on the body. Once clamped, they emit irregular shocks, tickling, teasing or annoying. The clips Khiru used on me were not powerful enough to hurt, but he compensated intensity by quantity. Our current record was 153 clips.

While he decorated my breasts, I tried to look through the openings in the walls to see if we might expect company. Khiru didn't seem to care, but I did. Being comfortable about all things sex-related, Khyrians wouldn't be shocked at finding us here, but they would probably stop to watch, encourage, even advise. I was still jittery about this kind of intimacy.

Khiru went on fastening clips as if my concerns were unknown to him. My chest and waist were already flickering like a Christmas decoration, and more clips soon pinched my thighs. The electric shocks always took me by surprise, where I least expected them, and their repetition made me frantic. I started to pant, and grabbed the edges of the stone for support.

Once Khiru had covered my legs, he focused on my labia. Fold after fold, each clip created a turmoil of its own. Khiru counted them. He clamped six in total. Then held the last one in front of my pleading eyes.

"We'll keep this one till the end."

My whole body was shuddering frenetically, like a plane caught in turbulence. Again, I fought against the ropes, and pushed on the tape sealing my mouth. I kept banging my head on the stone and was, for once, grateful for the protective bonnet. Khiru had walked out of sight, but I knew he was watching me. I groaned like an enraged animal.

"I bet a knife would almost be a relief, now, wouldn't it?" I heard him say. "Well, I don't have one, but I have something else."

The vibrator found its way between my clamped labia and dug deep. When it roared to life, I lost consciousness of what was going on. My whole life took place in my vagina; nothing else mattered.

Finally, Khiru applied the last clip to my clitoris. Like a rodeo steer trying to buck off its rider, I arched back and forth, banding my muscles as if to loosen all the ropes at once. More spasms followed until I fainted. I came back to my senses in Khiru's arms, in one of the rooms around the stone circle. It was dark and cool. We made love before walking back to the cabin.

After hours of hanging between the trees, I was craving the same conclusion. It was a good thing the restraints were taut and strong, and that my feet were grounded in the sand. I was no longer trying to stand up; instead, I let the bondage support my body. My mind full of wet memories and dreams, I was vaguely aware of my constant humming and languid writhing. I felt drunk and surprisingly happy.

Soon, Khiru would come and ravish me. He was the man of my dreams, the master of my body, the love of my life.

I opened my eyes and wondered how much time had passed. Heavy clouds masked Plya, depriving me of its light, turning the night into frightening darkness.

Surely, it wasn't going to rain?

CHAPTER 2

▼

We flew back to Mhôakarta one day earlier than planned. A tropical shower had interrupted the scene on the beach, and although Khiru had made up for it in bed, much to my satisfaction, he didn't want to be forced to stay inside the cabin all day.

"It's more convenient to play in the house," he said.

He was right, but I feared his attention would shift to other activities once we got home. Like the rest of the *Noncha* crew, Khiru had been on sabbatical for more than eight months. For an active pilot-engineer, it was a long time. He had a certain edginess that made me think he missed work. Before our escapade on the island, he had flown to the Space Center a couple of times "to see how things are going," and I had a hunch he wouldn't wait another half-year to go back as he had been instructed.

Tired from the night's adventure on the beach, I slept most of the way while Khiru flew our private shuttle back home. I woke up as we were descending over the water, with the outskirts of town visible in the distance.

Built on the coast of the Xiu Ocean, Mhôakarta was a four-thousand-year-old city dedicated to Mhô. A member of the Global Alliance, it served as capital of the Nantu state. The city enjoyed sub-tropical weather: hardly any winter, but a short hot summer flanked by two long mild seasons that had done much for its popularity.

Before the Gene War that had devastated the planet centuries ago, Mhôakarta had grown into an overpopulated megapolis, cursed with housing, transportation and pollution problems. The drastic death toll of the war and the rebuilding of the city had restored, even improved, its original charm. With one-tenth of its inhabitants remaining, the surface area was large enough to accommodate every-body in comfortable houses, and offered numerous open spaces.

Mhôakarta had no downtown center. Its neighborhoods, extending from the oceanfront to farming lands, presented a similar share of houses, shops, offices and parks. All industrial plants were built in non-populated areas easily accessible by public shuttles.

As I had observed during my many trips with Khiru, this distribution of living and working units had become standard in major cities all over the G-Zone. Another similarity was the common use of air and underground transportation. Motorized ground vehicles hardly existed anymore. And only qualified persons such as doctors or pilots obtained private air shuttles.

To compensate for their monotonous resemblances, city promoters tried to emphasize their natural and architectural eccentricities, such as Mhôakarta's rec-reational harbor, golden beaches and dazzling, immaculate buildings.

Another attraction was the Space Center, one of the five on the planet, now famous for the prominent role it had played in the Earth mission. It occupied a large meadow by the sea, south of the city, and was only accessible by air. Khiru and I lived within ten-minute's flight from it.

Because we enjoyed private transportation, we were not allowed to live in Mhôakarta itself. The other reason was that the Council wanted to keep me in a discreet area. Our neighborhood looked like other city blocks in every way, but its air-only access had turned it into a restricted enclave for pilots and space offic-ers. Like the military personnel on Earth, these people had an acute sense of belonging to a corps. They could keep secrets buried forever and sentenced any traitor to social exclusion. Despite our precautions, our immediate neighbors had probably figured out who I was, but Khiru was confident none of them would reveal our secret "outside," i.e. to non-officers.

Our house was no exception to the architectural rule of the Nantu state. Built on two floors, it was a small white cube, with a garden in the back and a landing platform on the roof. In front of the house, a strip of grass separated the two side-walks.

After landing on top of the house, we walked down two flights of stairs and entered the L-shaped lounge that took up most of the first floor. In the longer section, three dark purple couches surrounded a low wooden table. On the right, a cooking area overlooked the garden. On the left, large windows offered a clear view of the street. In the smaller section of the L, a neatly arranged desk stood against the wall in front of a large computer frame which, when turned off, posed as the 3-D rendering of a luminous galaxy in the darkness of space. In front of the desk was a black chair with armrests.

The wall by the side of the desk held four mediaframes. They could display images, spreadsheets, or diagrams of the house electronic systems. By pressing their tactile screens, Khiru could monitor the light, the opening or darkening of windows, the heat, and many more interesting appliances. There were similar mediaframes in every room. When they weren't used, they displayed animated paintings or photographs.

From a distance, the wall opposite the office space, between the window and one of the couches, seemed empty. In fact, it was covered with eyelets and hooks, which formed the very distinct shape of an Earth woman's body. Extending between that wall and the desk lay a lilk carpet. Its pale yellow shade nicely balanced the darker colors in the room.

When in the lounge, I spent a considerable amount of time stuck to the wall or kneeling on the carpet. In the evenings, Khiru usually allowed me to sit on a couch. Never in the armchair.

"Take your position," Khiru said behind me, before even entering the room.

While I got undressed and went down on my knees, my hands behind my back, my nose touching my knees, Khiru ordered the lights on. I heard him start the computer-monitored oven in the kitchen and open a few cabinets, no doubt preparing our dinner. Then, he returned and seated himself at his desk.

I stole a swift glance at him. He was probably checking messages and reading the latest news in social and scientific areas. The Data, the official online database, would give him broad and public information. In addition, the exclusive space network he could access with his mediapin would provide more specific details related to his job. As for global events, an account of the last few days was stored in his personalized newsbox.

"Hmm, trouble in NGA 7," I heard him mumble. "Two guys tried to break through the belt but got magnetized. One of them died, the other's in serious condition. Now, they're blaming us for cruel treatment and they're saturating I-nets with calls for rebellion. When are we going to get rid of these rascals?"

His anger sent bad vibes through the room. Any mention of Free Territories always caused him to react more strongly than necessary.

Officially named Non-Global Areas, these territories had lost the Gene War and refused to submit to the winning Alliance and the new Global Federation. They were scattered around the planet, some of them as big as Australia, others a collection of islands. Many, categorized as class-1 territories, were harmless, though fiercely independent. They maintained trade relations with the G-Zone but banned all visitors, official or otherwise.

If all the NGAs had been so peaceful, they would have been a minor problem, easily dismissed. Unfortunately, a number of them, labeled class-2, had chosen violence and mutiny as a way of life, and had become bubbling reservoirs of Khyra's outlaws. A couple of islands were also used as Global prisons for criminals convicted to a life sentence. When the verdict was pronounced, they were given the choice between a confinement unit within the Global Zone or permanent exile on one of those islands.

The Global Council kept a vigilant eye on NGAs through satellite surveillance, and squashed every small outburst that threatened common security. A lethal force field also separated the whole G-Zone from class-2 territories.

Free Territories were a permanent scar that hurt Khyrians' self-esteem and faith. Nobody liked to talk about them, much less hear about troubles at the borders. But Khiru gave the impression he held a personal resentment toward them. I suspected his reasons lay in his troubled past.

Freshly graduated from Rhysh, Khiru had fallen in love in earnest. One night, his girlfriend, Suri, came to him crying that she'd been abused by his best friend, another Rhysh Master named Kalhan. Despite the unlikelihood of her story—Kalhan was an honest and well-trained master, and Suri left town the day after the purported rape without ever reappearing—Khiru denounced his friend. Guilty or not, Kalhan ran away before being taken in custody. I often debated the story with Naari, a witness to it all, and he assumed Kalhan had found shelter in one of the Free Territories.

The drama left Khiru with a bleeding wound. He swore not to love and trust again. But then he met me, and his heart finally gave in. He allowed himself to love again, although trust was another challenge. He spoke to me once about his past, in his most vulnerable moment, after the whipping incident on the ship. He told me about Suri and her betrayal, but didn't mention Kalhan. After that, he seemed to shut down for good. He ignored my questions and became upset when I wanted to learn more about Non-Global Areas.

"There's a reminder for your sampling tomorrow," Khiru said placidly before cheering up considerably with the next message. "Naari's asking if we're going to the Engcamp reunion next week. Absolutely. I'll send him the details of the inn where we stay. Which reminds me, I have to do more shopping for you."

That was good news indeed! The last time I saw Naari was months ago, and I missed him. The even-tempered geologist was the first Khyrian who spoke to me when I stumbled on their secret hideout on Earth. The combination of his short blond hair and dark almond eyes struck me as weird, unnatural. But, unlike Khiru who appeared one moment later with anger and power painted over his handsome face, Naari never made me uncomfortable. He looked strong and brave, but also incredibly friendly and caring. And he proved to be all four.

But what was this reunion thing? Engcamp was the engineering school where Khiru and Naari had studied. Were they going to meet old friends? And why did Khiru have to shop for me? Was I actually invited to one of these forbidden public events? Would he smuggle me in while I wore my customary black costume? I was dying to ask for details, but Khiru hadn't authorized me to speak yet. To catch his attention, I shifted my weight on the carpet.

"Are we getting restless?" he asked without looking back. "Or maybe your neck is getting sore?"

I heard his chair spin around, then saw him kneel by my side. His hands massaged my shoulders.

"Yes, we are a bit tense. I'll remedy that after dinner. Here, get up and make yourself comfortable on a couch."

I stood on my feet but didn't move. Instead, I kept my eyes on his, pleading.

He laughed. "Okay, permission to speak granted."

While he returned in the kitchen, I questioned him about the reunion, but he refused to provide more details than what I had already guessed. Instead, we planned our schedule for the next day. Because Khiru had a few errands to run in the city, I would call the medical lab to organize a pick-up for my bi-monthly DNA sampling. This week, I was scheduled to visit the Mhôakarta genetic unit; the procedure would only keep me busy half the day.

"Why don't you spend the rest of the day with Myhre?" Khiru suggested. "The med-shuttle could drop you at her place."

Although I felt like a child who needed a nanny for the afternoon, I welcomed the idea of meeting my friend. She always had great gossip to share.

After dinner, Khiru led me to the bedroom.

"You need a long rest from last night," he said behind me as we walked up the stairs.

When we reached the landing, he made me stop. His hands came to rest on my naked hips, and I shivered with pleasure. I leaned back against him, pressing my bottom against his legs. I wasn't quite ready to sleep yet.

For a brief moment, I hoped Khiru would take me to the second room, at the end of the corridor, but he gently pushed me toward the door on our right. No dungeon tonight. Khiru either meant to make love gently—that is, he would only cuff my limbs, possibly gag me—or he would leave me in sleep bondage for the night.

Sleeping in restraints was another major trial for me. I tossed a lot in my sleep and highly resented any impediment to my nocturnal gymnastics. I was game for night scenes, as my latest adventure on the beach showed, but couldn't reconcile the notion of sleep with that of bondage. When I explained this to Khiru, he argued that he'd already watched me fall asleep in confinement.

"Not if I know it's for a whole night," I protested. "What if I need to stretch, drink, pee?"

All I got was a sympathetic smile. The next night, Khiru tied my hands in front of me, then chained my ankles together to the footboard, and prompted me to have sweet dreams.

Anger and frustration played a worse part in my torment than the lilk cuffs. I dozed off in the middle of the night and slept until noon, when a triumphant Khiru woke me up with a kiss.

"See, I knew you could do it."

I had to let the man win once in a while.

Since that first time, I had spent more nights in relatively easy bondage, but I still hated it. Sleep was sacred. Any attempt to defy it was a direct abuse. But Khiru's purported goal was to keep me in restraints *every* night. He loved to know I was lying helpless by his side, unable to escape him or the bed. I tried my best to accommodate his will, finding comfort in the knowledge that it satiated his needs and made him happy, but I was always nervous when Khiru accompanied me to the bedroom to "tuck me in."

As I stepped forward, the door to the bedroom slid open.

The bed, high and magnificent, was the central piece in the room. The only other equipment was a built-in cabinet taking up most of the left wall, barely leaving enough space for an open passage leading to the bathroom. On the right side of the bed, a large window overlooked the garden. It was programmed to turn opaque at sunset, then recover its translucence gradually in the morning to let the light in. A vocal command could change those settings instantly.

Finally, the fourth wall, by the door, held two mediaframes. One was hooked on external data and file transfer; the other controlled house appliances. When unused, they usually represented two complementary views of a stormy sea at night, with lightning strokes hitting the foamed edges of the waves.

Our large poster bed was, in itself, a tribute to bondage. It was built of kauchu, a solid metal coated in a thick paste that gave it the appearance and touch of rubber. Kauchu had a strong resistance to traction and offered a smooth and comfortable surface to lean on. Thanks to the coating, it wasn't cold to the touch and didn't twang when in contact with other types of metal. Kauchu beds, chairs and dungeon contraptions were very fashionable on Khyra.

Our bed had a maritime theme, a favorite of Khiru's. It had a dark finish with subtle emerald touches that glittered when sunrays hit them. The grids making up the headboard and footboard represented waves, and sea shrubs and shells decorated the lower sides of the bed. The four posts were finely carved as tropical trunks and ended in a fan of kauchu leaves that met in the center of the canopy.

A slot ran around the bed, just under the mattress, where Khiru had inserted various cuffs and hooks that could be slid into an infinity of positions. More permanent restraints hung from the posts and canopy, like strange fruits growing from the trees.

That night, he asked me to lie on my belly and raise my arms over my head. Before dinner, he had vaguely hinted at a massage, and my apprehension of a worse fate vanished behind a large smile.

Khiru maneuvered heavy metal cuffs to the middle of the headboard and footboard, and locked my wrists and ankles inside them, stretching my body as tautly as the cable of a tightrope walker. From a closed alcove carved in the wall, he withdrew a penis gag and buckled the heavy leather strap around my mouth. Next, he went to the bathroom and returned with a jar of unctuous cream.

Instead of starting with my shoulders, Khiru first worked on my bottom, conscientiously applying the cream on my cheeks, then between them. His fingers probed my vagina and teased my clitoris. Then he spread my folds apart and, with his other hand, entered my rectum, screwing his fingers in, forcing me open until I moaned. He withdrew a little, but continued to massage me. I was panting, willing myself to open up to him, yet resisting the intrusion.

Khiru scooped up more cream and returned to the hole that wouldn't surrender. Oblivious to my sighs and useless attempts at squirming away, he coaxed, rubbed and pressed. And coaxed, rubbed and pressed.

All I could do was bite into the leather penis with a vengeance. And prepare myself for worse.

Khiru straddled me. In a reflex, I contracted my anus, closing the passage he had taken such a long time to widen.

"Pointless, my girl," he said. "I will take you this way, and there's nothing you can do about it."

The tip of his penis was already pushing its way in. Khiru grabbed my cheeks and split them open. Then he forced himself into me. Once inside, he gave me a moment to catch my breath, then fucked me.

Pleasure came instantly. Instead of fighting back, I tried to suck him deeper inside. I was also very aware of my other hole gaping wide and demanding the same attention.

Maintaining a constant rhythm, Khiru slid one hand underneath me and pinched my clit. It caught fire like a match, and Khiru kept the flame growing by stroking it.

Trapped between the cuffs, my body tensed and arched like a bow, ready for the trigger.

Khiru launched his load with a brutal thrust of his hips against mine, and squeezed my clit with the same urgency. I buckled under his weight and shook violently for a minute or two.

I hardly felt him slide out of me, but exhaled deep and long when he lay by my side and placed a soothing hand on my back.

"Don't talk," he said as he began to remove the gag after a long and restful break. "I'm not done with your massage."

While I continued to rest, Khiru sat on my thighs and resumed his work where he'd left off. This time, he didn't try to arouse me, but applied the cream in firm but tender strokes on my back all the way up to my shoulders. My muscles relaxed one after the other, and I soon felt ready for sleep.

However, when Khiru kissed me goodnight and walked away from the bed without unlocking my restraints, I raised my head and disobeyed his order.

"You're not going to leave me like this, are you?"

He didn't bother to answer. Instead, he came back to me, re-buckled the penis gag where it belonged, then left the room.

I fell asleep long after he had joined me in bed, a few hours before the first sunrays pierced the window.

In the morning, I wasn't in a good mood, even when I realized my mouth was gag-free. Did it mean I could call out to him? Khiru had already gotten up, and I was unable to leave the bed without his help. But I knew where screaming could get me...

Besides, I was due for sampling at the medical center, and Khiru would never let me be late for an official duty. He would come and free me soon.

By the time I heard his footsteps on the stairs, my patience had grown thin. But instead of stopping behind the bedroom door as I expected him to, Khiru continued up the second flight to the roof. When he walked out, a deadly silence fell upon the house. One minute later, the shuttle engine started, but its familiar drone was interrupted by a series of clicks above my head and at my feet. While Khiru took off, I pulled out of the cuffs, which he had opened with his remote.

Ha, I grinned to myself, he knew he'd better avoid me this morning.

Curious to see if he'd left a message, I hurried down the stairs naked. Just in case, I yelled an order for all windows to refract the light from outside so that nobody could see through them, then called at the mediaframe built in one of the kitchen cabinets.

"Any message for Megan?"

A portrait of Khiru and I having a picnic in a wood dissolved, to be replaced by a close-up of Khiru.

"Good morning, sweetie," he said. "I had to leave early today, and I figured you wanted to sleep in. Breakfast's ready, and the med-shuttle will pick you up at 11. I've also arranged for your transfer to Myhre's. I'll join you there for dinner. Have a nice day. I love you."

The computer asked if I wanted to reply. I declined, and the picnic photograph came back.

Not a word about last night. Typical. And probably for the better as there was truly nothing to say. He knew I hated night bondage, but that wasn't going to stop him. And he probably also knew I was horny as hell this morning, a direct consequence of his devious scheme. But at least there was something I could do about that.

Breakfast was delayed a few minutes.

One hour later, I was reporting for duty at the lab after a short flight with Sertee, the young pilot who flew me to each of my sampling obligations, even outside Mhôakarta. We hardly had a chance to talk that day, but we had gotten to know each other better on longer trips. Sertee had obtained his pilot license the year before and been assigned to an official airtaxi unit that organized the transfer of important dignitaries in the city. It had been a boring job until he was made responsible for my trips to the DNA labs. For safety reasons, the Council had insisted that the same pilot fly me everywhere. Whenever Khiru or I called for him, Sertee was supposed to abandon any other assignment and give me priority.

In other words, Sertee was my personal chauffeur.

He was also a cute, shy Southie who was only at peace with himself in the middle of heavy humiliation scenes. Although he had a few recurrent partners— male and female, but he admitted a slight preference for women—he was a regular at Mhôakarta's scenemats, public clubs where individuals or groups could enact their sexual fantasies.

"You see, when I get there, my only request is to wear a blinding hood so I don't see who's going to top me," he had explained on our second flight together.

"After that, I don't care. I'm in for anything. I don't even want to choose a theme."

"What happens next? Do you get whipped? Is there an audience?"

Khiru had never taken me to a scenemat; the Council would not approve of the idea. I knew there were hundreds of them, specializing in every possible genre of erotic activity, offering the best fantasy set-ups and costumes, and a wide range of play partners. My only experience with organized scenes dated back to the Twilight, the erotic playground aboard the *Noncha*. In one of its thematic dungeons, Myhre had organized a circus party for the birthday of her second lifepartner, Jova. I had also attended various shows at the Cabaret where, green with envy, I had watched Khiru whip a Rhysh slave to ecstasy. And a few weeks later, I had taken the stage myself, with Lodel.

Perhaps that was another reason why Khiru and I avoided public play houses. Our last memory of them was not a happy one.

But I still enjoyed hearing about people's experiences. I didn't share Sertee's kink for humiliation—and was grateful that Khiru didn't seem to care much for it either—but I liked to think I improved my sexual education by listening to his stories, of which he had dozens.

Once we reached the medical lab and registered at the electronic booth on top of the roof, Sertee went down a floor to the lounge where he would wait for me. I stayed in the elevator all the way to the ground floor and the sampling unit. The lab spread across four floors divided into four or five rooms, but there were just six scientists on the staff, with only half of them working at any given time.

Their task was as intricate as it was confidential. Months ago, they had started by studying my Earthling genome and the differences with its Khyrian counterpart. Next, they had isolated the genes responsible for sexual hormones and fertility. Now scientists tested whether they could incorporate my cells into Khyrian DNA without compromising other genetic attributes. Finally, they would establish a protocol for mass production. Four labs were working full-time on the trial phase. Even then, it would take many more months before completion. No risk would be taken so as not to repeat or worsen the genetic disaster provoked centuries before.

At that time, overpopulation had become a threat, and scientists thought they were wise to manipulate Khyrian genes to limit fertility. At first, they appeared to be right. In those states that allowed genetic therapy, population dropped and wealth was restored. In the others, poverty struck hard. Inevitably, war broke out between the wealthier countries and the rest of the planet. Excited by their earlier success, scientists went back to their labs to alter the gender gene so that women would give birth to a majority of boys destined to become soldiers. After three decades, the Gene War ended, and the losers were forced to submit to a genetic program eradicating diseases, but also controlling reproduction. All in all, it took a couple of hundred years to cause Khyrian DNA to deteriorate irrevocably.

People got scared, and the Global Council passed the Gene Law forbidding any kind of genetic manipulation. However, while it stopped the process, it didn't reverse it. Most men and women were still sterile, and when they could conceive, generally thanks to elaborate external procedures, their chance of having a girl was one in four. At that rate, the Khyrian race was doomed to become extinct.

My healthy genes, so close to theirs, offered Khyrians a chance at survival. You could say I was always warmly welcomed each time I entered a lab.

Tyrko, the oldest scientist in the center, hugged me affectionately when I stepped inside the sampling room. His assistant, Larm, looked up from his 3-D computer hologram and waved.

"Hello, Megan. Nice to see you again."

"How's everything at home? How's Khiru?"

While we chatted, I lay down on a reclining chair and pulled my shirt up to expose my belly.

Tyrko tied a braincontroller around my forehead so I wouldn't feel any pain, or even the slightest discomfort. Then he adjusted what looked like a heavy movie projector, but was really a sophisticated camera, above me. Its light hit a small spot next to my navel. After disinfecting my skin, Tyrko inserted a long thin needle inside my abdomen down to one of my ovaries. We all followed its progress on the holo-image hanging in the air above Larm's desk.

When the needle hit my walnut-size ovary, Tyrko collected a few cells inside and removed the needle. Larm checked the data sent by the beecee; when he was satisfied I was unharmed, he untied it.

That was it. I could leave. My next sampling would be taken five weeks later, in another center.

Because I had time to spare, I accompanied Larm to another room and watched him place my cells in a multiplier. He tried to explain the results of the combination trials they had carried out since my last visit, but the technicalities were beyond my comprehension. All I understood was that the Khyrian genome reacted too vehemently to the introduction of my DNA, and they were going to try a new procedure with the fresh samples.

The sun was still high in the sky when Sertee and I flew back downtown, and he left me on top of Myhre's white house.

The door—which, like every other roof door, looked like a chimney to me—slid open, and my red-haired friend burst out.

"Darling, it's been a while! Come on, what's new with you?"

Myhre had made me smile from the first time I met her, a few hours after boarding the *Noncha*. By Khyrian standards, she was a short woman, but her energy equalled that of two men. A good thing too, since she was a Northie with two lifepartners, Liu and Jova, who loved to put their fates in her very capable hands.

Enthusiastic and generous, Myhre was also prudent and thoughtful. With me, she acted like an older sister, providing explanations and advice when I needed them, or not. She had warned me against falling in love with Khiru, but had then become our most fervent supporter.

I hadn't seen her much in the last eight months, but we stayed in touch. While Khiru and I traveled across the planet, she had gone on a romantic trip with her two lovers. She had prolonged her stay with Liu who, as a teacher, had stayed on Khyra while Jova and Myhre had set off on the four-year mission to Earth.

When they returned to Mhôakarta, we visited them a couple of times, and Myhre took me shopping once, an activity she favored amongst many others. But Khiru was worried about my rambling around in the city without his personal protection, and asked us to avoid all public places.

"Weren't you supposed to be on Pichac Island?" she asked as we walked through the house and out to the garden where Myhre had already installed two sunbeds.

"We flew back yesterday. The rain."

"You mean, Khiru couldn't entertain you indoors?"

She grinned maliciously, and I hated myself for blushing, a bad Earth habit I couldn't lose.

"We have better toys here. And anyway, I was due for my sampling."

"Sure. And where's your master now?"

She pronounced "master" with a hint of malice. Myhre, who wasn't shy with a whip, didn't approve of Rhysh ways. She thought they were too extreme and missed the real goal in life: to have fun. But she was fond of Khiru and knew he loved me as much as I loved him.

"My master," I replied using the same tone, "is out shopping for me. We're going to the Engcamp reunion next week."

"Lucky you! I never had a chance to attend one, but I heard they're particularly entertaining."

"Really?" I was both interested and apprehensive. "Do they, er, play or something?"

She looked at me as if she just remembered I had landed from another planet.

"Khiru didn't tell you anything, did he?" she asked rhetorically. "Then, you'll find out by yourself."

She closed her eyes and offered her face to the sun, as if she intended to do nothing else for the next hour. I protested that as my best friend, she was supposed to be on my side, but solidarity between Northies demanded she kept silent.

"Besides," she added, "we have better things to talk about. What are you doing for Seisha Day?"

I had no idea, but would definitely come up with one. Seisha Day was a holiday in honor of a Southie who once saved the lives of several Northies. On that day, Southies were exceptionally allowed to make requests to their dominant partners. It was also a big occasion for parties of all kinds, as well as street parades and family events. I asked Myhre the exact date.

"It's in two weeks, dear. With this long sabbatical, I've lost sense of time myself, but my two beloved slaves reminded me of their rights."

Rights that were mine, too. Last year, Seisha Day had been a sad experience, as I'd had to watch Khiru whip another woman—a request he had been unable to refuse. This year, I intended to make up for it. Khiru would have to indulge me. What could I possibly ask him?

"I haven't thought about it," I said, my mind already elsewhere.

"Then ask Khiru to spend it with us. I'll rent a dungeon by the beach, and we can all party! I'm going to invite Naari, too."

"Great idea. I will definitely ask Khiru. And I'll ask Naari at the Engcamp reunion."

"Yes, if you can talk. I'd better call him myself."

Myhre and I chatted until the men, first hers, then mine, joined us. We had dinner together, then Khiru and I flew back home. That night, he let me sleep unrestrained.

CHAPTER 3

▼

For Khiru and me, the trip to Pichac Island was the last moment of carefree happiness. The Engcamp reunion marked the beginning of troubles.

We met Naari at the secluded inn Khiru had chosen for our sleepover before the event. To Khyrian eyes, Naari was a friend who'd had sex with me. No more, no less. In mine, he was an ex-lover with whom I could have fallen in love if my heart hadn't been already obsessed with Khiru. Naari's feelings for me also went beyond friendship. He had hinted at the possibility of becoming my second partner, and always had that glitter in his eyes, both hopeful and nostalgic, that made me feel embarrassingly self-conscious.

After a cheerful dinner and a quiet night, the three of us flew to the Campus of Engineering, a modern-looking piece of architecture where bright young men and women studied the state of the art in advanced technologies. The roofs held enough parking spaces for hundreds of shuttles, but when we landed, only half of Roof One was occupied.

Before stepping out, Khiru adjusted my hood, checked whether I could see through the fine mesh in front of my eyes, and held my hand all the way inside the building. Naari was on the other side, as if the two of them were guarding me from unknown dangers. I couldn't help smiling behind the lilk veil. With the dark heavy mantle covering me from head to toes, nobody would recognize me.

Underneath the protective cloth, I was naked, save for three metal cuffs around my arms and four around my legs.

After walking through a bright glass dome that served as the main entrance to the school, we proceeded down a long corridor, then up to the first floor and finally to a formidable laboratory transformed for the occasion into a party room.

We met few people on our way as Khiru had decided to arrive early to avoid unnecessary complications with the crowd. No one looked at my hidden figure with the slightest curiosity or concern.

The laboratory must have been dedicated to physics or similar sciences. Various holograms showcased complicated patterns and diagrams, and shelves supported instruments that must have given headaches to many students. A giant mediaframe took up one wall, the Khyrian equivalent of our chalkboard. The desks that usually stood in lines in front of it had been pulled into the corridor, leaving a large open space for the party.

A space that was now being filled with bodies in bondage.

Two groups were already at work when we entered the room. On our left, near the wall, three men were tying two naked girls and one boy around a post. There was much giggling and fake cursing. On our right, in the middle of the room, four persons were trying to create a suspension bondage. The Southie, a man as far as I could judge, was adorned in various lilk implements, with a sturdy harness wrapping him completely. The Northies were struggling to hook him onto a cable extending from one wall to another, but each time they let go, the poor guy tilted headfirst and balanced awkwardly.

Khiru and Naari led me to the wall across the room where a clear space seemed to be waiting for me. Khiru went to get a folding screen, which he used to hide us from the rest of the room.

Naari kept a vigilant eye on potential spectators while Khiru fixed a strange metallic plate to the wall. Then he asked me to stand in front of it. The plate went from my shoulders to just under my crotch, and was slightly wider than I was. Its sides were curved, and the lower edge was grazing my thighs through the cloak.

"Perfect," he said.

In one swift move, Khiru unzipped the mantle to separate it from the hood, and pulled it down to reveal my naked body and its fourteen shiny bracelets.

"Place your arms in the holes, there. Now spread your legs a little. Feel the holes there too? That's it. Don't move. Naari, will you watch the top while I fix the bottom?"

Khiru lifted a plate similar to the first one and brought it close to my body. With Naari guiding it into position at chest level, the two men connected the plates together, and a clear snap confirmed that the contraption was properly installed.

It now looked like a magician's box, the kind in which you put a woman before you cut it in half. My limbs and head extended from holes in the box, and there was enough room inside to squirm a little.

"Megan, place your arms and legs firmly against the wall," Khiru ordered.

As I obeyed, he keyed in a command on a mediaframe. A series of clicks resonated behind the cuffs I was wearing, and I found I was unable to move my arms and legs from the wall.

"Aren't you afraid someone will want to tear off her hood?" Naari asked.

"I've thought about that. Open her mouth hole, will you? Thanks. Now, darling, bite on this."

Khiru presented me a resina mouthpiece with two metallic straps fitting around my head and connecting to the plate behind me.

"That's my girl," he approved when I opened my mouth. "This gag will not only hold the hood in place around her head, but also glue her head to the wall. Isn't that clever?"

The two men took a step back to admire their work. I always hated that moment, when Khiru knew what was going to happen to me and already reveled at the thought, while I was left with scary speculations.

"Nothing bad will happen to you today, Megan," he said as if he'd read my mind. "Just a lot of fun and excitement. And not only by yourself. You'll be able to watch what's going on in the room, too."

On that cheerful note, he removed the screen and let me appreciate the full meaning of his words.

There was going to be a lot of action indeed. The harnessed man was now hanging from the ceiling in a very neat hogtie, like a wing-less bird frozen in its flight. He was not the only suspended person either. A girl hung in a similar fashion on the other side of the room.

The three naked Southies tied up to the post were no longer giggling. They were all heavily gagged and blindfolded. Their legs were slightly apart, and their arms were pulled above their heads, with their six hands forming a big mess of entwined fingers. Loops and loops of wires circled their bodies in random fashion, digging into arms and thighs, snaking between legs, enveloping the boy's erection and the girls' breasts. This human sculpture looked magnificent.

Many other people had entered the room since our early arrival. Some of them were chatting, drinks in hand; others were adding a final touch to their scenes. The alumni, men or women, wore conventional suits in a variety of colors. Khiru was in black, a favorite of mine; Naari wore cinnamon, a tone that nicely enhanced his blond hair. Their respectable, almost too formal, appearance clashed with the nudity of their victims.

In front of me, one man was spreadeagled on a table, with a large transparent cone hovering above his sex. Further away, a girl was bent over a bench, her vagina obscenely plugged with a prod extending from a machine. Further still, two men were wrapped together in layers of black tape. A strong cable connected them to the ceiling, forcing them to stand on tiptoe.

All things considered, I wasn't too uncomfortable in my big box.

While I observed the room, Khiru and Naari walked away. They joined friends I didn't know and were probably having a good time remembering the old days.

As the room buzzed heavily with conversations, a group of new people appeared, and silence spontaneously returned. The school board, I guessed.

Speeches followed, but they were mercifully short. A particularly brilliant student was awarded a merit medal. Two older teachers announced their retirements, which prompted the audience to cheer and applaud, although I couldn't tell whether they were honoring the teachers or mocking them.

When the official part was over, a sudden thrill blew across the room. It was time to launch the party. Those engineers had suffered through years of heavy studies that had often kept them away from the pleasures of life. When they reunited, they made it a point of honor to reverse the trend, and devoted their acquired knowledge to the humblest sport of all, sex.

A red-haired man stepped up onto a chair and loudly announced the different experiments on the day's program. He referred to me as the "Dayrifa cage," and all heads turned in my direction.

I learned a lot about the Dayrifa cage that day. The sealed device creates a void through which oscillating currents pass rapidly once you turn the power on. These electromagnetic waves provoke erotic tingles, like bubbles fizzing over the skin. At their maximum intensity, they may also create sharp shocks, but Khiru had limited the scope of the cage to a painless level. It felt like a giant vibrator teasing my body from chest to crotch.

"Side-effects are even more intriguing," a tall woman in a red suit explained to a group of falsely curious men. "Watch the limbs shake, particularly the legs. If they weren't glued to the wall, they would get out of control. With this simple precaution, the subject is immobile, and the experiment may go on for hours, unperturbed."

I made another observation, unknown to external observers. Even when drenched, the cage worked.

Thanks to the control mediaframe next to me, people could adjust the intensity of the waves inside the box. At their lowest, the vibrations massaged me like a hot tub device. At their worse, they made me climax nicely. Between groups of visitors, I studied the other victims.

The two Southies hanging in the air were free flying. I couldn't see what triggered their movements, but watched as they were launched along the cable from one wall to the other. Sometimes they stopped halfway, closer to the ground, and a group of alumni teased their bodies until they jerked violently. Then, they were sent flying again.

The trio tied to the post was glittering like a window display. An electric current traveled through the wires, lightening them up on its way. Red and blue flashes sparkled here and there, provoking many spasms in all three bodies.

The man lying in front of me was in greater pain. When the cone descended upon his crotch, his penis seemed to triple in size. Judging from the moans coming through his gag, the man was dying to come. I don't think he ever did.

The girl on the bench was resting. Several times already, I had watched the plug fuck her vagina until she buckled and passed out. A man had whispered to her, and she had shaken her head vehemently. He had left her in bondage, but had removed the prod. Now the man was talking to Khiru.

So far, I had paid scant attention to Khiru. He chatted happily, if somewhat distractedly, more with teachers than fellow graduates, and I supposed they were questioning him about the mission to Earth. But now he was frowning. He looked at the woman bent over on the bench, then returned to the man, but not without stealing a quick glance at me, as if considering options. He talked some more, and his features relaxed. He had made a decision.

While the man went back to his girlfriend, Khiru left the room. He returned with a thick rod in hand and headed straight to the bench. When he took position behind it and stared at the bare bottom in front of him, a fever invaded my head.

Khiru shook the rod once, and several beams of blue light spurted out of it, like the straps of a flogger. He aimed and hit the girl's ass.

Trapped in my box, I had no chance to react. I wanted to run, grab the whip, throw it out, and lead Khiru outside. As it were, I was grateful for the bondage that prevented me from acting so stupidly in front of a crowd. But how was I to deal with an anger mounting as fast as boiling milk? This scene was awfully reminiscent of the whipping Khiru had administered to a Rhysh slave on the *Noncha*. Seeing him top another woman had made me envious and vengeful; it had ultimately led to my own fateful performance with Lodel.

That Khiru repeated the insolent act when he was my confirmed lover added insult to injury. If I confronted him, he would argue he was only playing, that it didn't mean anything. But it did. The girl, who was sensually squirming on the bench, obviously enjoyed the whipping. Soon she would climax. I couldn't allow Khiru to make another woman come. Especially when he also took pleasure in it, as the passion in his eyes seemed to indicate.

The crowd around Khiru's scene became too dense, and I lost sight of him. Frustration and sadness built up. My own physical torment, not so much the dying Dayrifa waves but the confinement to the wall, seemed unfair and unjustified. I wanted to get out. Of the box, the room, the school. The velvety lining of my hood was soon soaked in tears.

By the time the scene ended, I had fallen in a blank daze, which Khiru mistook for physical exhaustion. I didn't talk until much later, back home. By then, my feelings seemed absurd. Khiru would never understand. He was acting as any Khyrian Northie would. I was the one who needed adjustment.

At least I knew what I was going to request for Seisha Day.

CHAPTER 4

▼

Neither Khiru nor I were in a good mood when we joined Myhre, Jova and Liu at the dungeon our friend had rented on one of Mhôakarta's beaches. The two-story cottage was a shiny white spot in the middle of trees. Between the house and the sea, a carpet of sand defined our private beach. Our three hosts were already exposing their bodies to the sun. We stripped and joined them.

It was late in the morning, and we had the place to ourselves until the next day. The plan was to enjoy the outdoors until dinner, and celebrate Seisha until bedtime.

Khiru had agreed to my request, but only reluctantly. He looked worried, and I considered calling it off. It would certainly make for a better day at the beach for both of us. I was tense and absent-minded, unable to focus on any conversation. He was nervous and spoke too loud. But I needed to go through with this.

As the scene at the Engcamp reunion party had once again proved, Khiru needed to dominate and inflict pain the same way a sailor needs to tame the ocean. I had similar fantasies once; my recent fears all derived from one unfortunate incident. If I tried harder, I might overcome them. And Khiru would never have to whip another woman again.

Naari flew in after lunch. He had brought Kenia, a young girl barely out of college, who was a distant cousin and therefore could be trusted with meeting me. For a Khyrian woman, Kenia had nice firm breasts and the beginning of a waist. She had no pubic hair, but that was an evolutionary process that affected both men and women, and had little to do with the deterioration of the Khyrian genome. Kenia's female hormones visibly worked; there was hope for the race.

Kenia was shy and easily impressed. She told me she wasn't very experienced with S/N games and that this was her first Seisha Day as a participant. But she was looking forward to playing with Naari, whom she had always secretly admired. With her ingenuous kindness, Kenia somewhat mollified my mood and gave me confidence to pursue my goal.

After a quiet, though not peaceful afternoon, followed by a light dinner, Myhre set the wheels in motion. We were three women for four men, a remarkable ratio on the male-dominated planet. Four of us were Southies, and the night was ours.

The weather was warm, and we chose to play outside. We would retrieve material from the dungeon if needed.

Myhre decided Naari and Kenia would open the show. Following the girl's prior request, Naari dressed her up in an elegant corset, long gloves and thigh-high boots, all in bright red resina. Then he tied her to a trunk, using conventional ropes and making sure she wasn't too uncomfortable. Once she was secured, he decorated her nipples with clamps and small weights, and strapped a vibrator inside her.

"She just wants to watch and be nicely entertained," he explained when he took his seat back in our circle.

"No need to go too far too fast," Khiru approved.

Myhre nodded and looked at me. In the afternoon, she and I had a discussion over who should play last. Myhre wished for intimacy with her lovers. In addition, she didn't think I would enjoy their common scene. I, for one, believed she wanted Khiru and I to play first because she would be in a more alert state to watch and care. Always the big sister.

"Want to go next, Megan?" she asked, respecting Seisha's protocol by addressing me, not Khiru, as she would have on any other day.

Nervously, I stood up. I first had a speech to give.

"Myhre, Jova, Naari, last year you witnessed the whipping scene with Lodel and its disastrous consequences."

Myhre was already questioning Khiru with wide-open eyes.

"Since then," I continued, "I've been terrified by the prospect of pain, even for pleasure. I want to change that. Deep inside, my desires for masochist games are intact, and tonight, I would like to revive them. I've asked Khiru to whip me until I come. Of course, if things go wrong, he will stop. But I want him to try hard."

I directed the last words to Khiru, and he closed his eyes in agreement. I tried not to notice how disconsolate he looked.

From the corner of my eyes, I saw Myhre struggling with herself. Was she going to try to prevent the scene? Naari looked equally uncomfortable, but both he and Myhre kept calm.

Because bondage helps create a submissive mindset, I had requested severe restraints and a gag. However, I had accepted wearing a beecee, a concession I couldn't refuse. Khiru, who could read body signals better than anyone, would have an additional safety net by reading my brain waves.

He got up.

"Megan, kneel and wait for me." His voice was steady and controlled. "You're not allowed to talk. Naari, will you come help me fetch a few things inside? Myhre, could you make room over there? Thanks."

Sparkles of excitement warmed up my body, obliterating any lingering doubt. I want this, I repeated to myself. I want Khiru to whip me.

Khiru and Naari brought out heavy wooden stocks. Both men were banding their muscles, and I reacted favorably to their act of strength.

The contraption presented five big openings, for my head, wrists and ankles. Dozens of smaller holes, just wide enough for ropes, drew the rough contour of a torso across the panels. It looked like a connect-the-dots puzzle.

"Stand up, Megan."

Feeling submissive to the core, I kept my eyes low while Khiru adjusted the beecee around my head and checked its settings. He also wrapped a leather cincher around my waist, ostensibly to protect my kidneys and other sensitive organs. His training and skill were all the insurance I needed, but Khiru was taking extreme precautions. Oddly, it increased my own nervousness.

When I took my position in front of the stocks, Khiru lifted the upper panel and lowered it back around my head and hands. Then he opened the lower panel and snapped it around my feet. The stocks were slightly tilted and offered good support for my weight.

Satisfied that I couldn't escape, I closed my eyes, controlled my breathing and realized Khiru had forgotten to gag me.

I scraped my throat to alert him, but no sound came out, not even a moan. I tried again, this time opening my mouth and forming a clear and distinct "ah." I was mute; I couldn't even groan. The only feeble sound I could produce was by exhaling deeply. Then I understood Khiru was controlling my vocal cords through the beecee. This was a first. This was exciting.

While I was blowing air on one side of the stocks, Khiru was seriously busy on the other. Loop after loop, he patiently threaded a tight web of rope around my body through the wooden panels. Only my bottom remained free of restraints.

When he was finished, he paused.

Around us, only the sea breeze and the waves broke the silence. Anxiety was palpable in the air.

His first stroke hit me without warning. I let out an inaudible gasp, more out of surprise than pain. A warm glow spread through my cheek. It hadn't yet diffused when a second blow landed on the other cheek. After two more strikes, Khiru found his rhythm and proceeded to drum on my bottom with fascinating regularity: left, right, right, left, right. I was warming up nicely, in more ways than one. And there was no pain to frighten me yet. It didn't feel like a whipping, more like a severe rubbing that left a very sensual fire on my flesh.

My hips began to writhe with pleasure, and I dropped my guard. I felt safe, ready for more.

Khiru picked up another implement. When the straps connected with my ass, wrapping it like the arms of an octopus, they pricked like a thousand needles. It hurt. I tensed, constricting my jaw and clenching my hands into tight fists. My heartbeat doubled, and I began to hyperventilate. But I couldn't fail this time.

Khiru, who must have been carefully monitoring the reactions both on my body and the beecee, seemed to hesitate. I tried to send happy thoughts through the brain controller.

Another stroke impacted my cheeks, but Khiru had opted for another instrument. It left an aching dent from my thigh up to my hip, which sent wrong signals to my brain again. I knew the pain was minimal, practically irrelevant, even for an inexperienced Southie, but I couldn't control the absurd mechanism inside me. Pain meant fear meant panic meant nausea. Tears welled up in my eyes at the thought of losing Khiru over a failed whipping scene. I braced myself again, determined to fight my demons if it was the last thing I did.

Khiru hit several more times with various tools, even reverting to the first paddle he had used to warm me up. It was a complete disaster. Each stroke turned my body into a mass of tense muscles. I was shivering uncontrollably, sobbing more and more. When Khiru placed his hands on my waist and massaged gently, murmuring soft words to calm me down, I collapsed with grief and guilt.

Nothing would ever be the same.

CHAPTER 5

▼

I confronted Khiru two weeks later. Until then, both of us acted as if nothing had happened, not Khiru's successful whipping scene at the Engcamp reunion, nor my breakdown on Seisha Day. Khiru was twice as tender and loving; I was submitting to his orders with exaggerated enthusiasm. It was a masquerade of happiness. We were living with a monster in the house, and it was time one of us killed it. I thought talking about it would do the trick.

It was morning. Khyra's orange sun darted its rays through the window and onto our bed, daring us to resist its call. We had just made love and were delaying the beginning of the day as long as we could. This was as good a moment as any.

I mentioned his performance at the Campus.

"I was afraid you'd whine about it," Khiru sighed.

"I'm not whining," I said too sharply. "I'm just saying it hurt my feelings."

"And of course this is why you asked to be whipped on Seisha Day."

It wasn't a question.

"Megan," he continued gently, "don't you understand you don't need to do this? I love you, no matter what."

And to prove his feelings, he kissed me possessively, overwhelming my heart with passion.

"But will you do it again?" I insisted, slightly breathless.

"What? Whip another woman?"

I went to the bathroom to give him time to answer. When I returned, he was sitting on the bed, leaning against the headboard, his arms folded against his chest. With the light bouncing off his bare chest, he looked like a Greek god. Who had just given a verdict.

As I hesitated, he patted the sheet next to him, and I hurried to cuddle up in his arms.

"Megan," he said, his voice as soft as an angel's, "when I whip another woman, I don't get emotional about it. It's like a sport. It relieves the tension in me."

"But you give them pleasure, you make them come, and you enjoy it."

"Of course I do, but not at a sentimental level. I enjoy it the way you enjoy a massage at the Therms."

I tried to be rational, accept his justification as any Khyrian woman would, but my love was too passionate, too demanding.

"It's not the same to me," I whispered. "I don't think I can ever accept it. I'm sorry."

Khiru got up and paced back and forth by the bed.

"I can't give it all up, Megan. I respect the fact that you're a moderate player—"

It sounded like an insult.

"—but I'm a Rhysh Master, and I wouldn't have made it through Rhysh if I didn't have special needs, needs you can't begin to comprehend. It's purely physical; it's like a hormone rush, a fire in me. If I don't deal with it, I go crazy."

"You've dealt with it perfectly during the mission to Earth and these last months."

"No, I haven't." He was facing the window, looking away from me. "I had regular sessions on the ship, on both trips. Even on Earth, Swomi made a very willing partner."

He turned around and confronted my eyes. "On the way back, I stopped once we became lovers, and the scene on the Campus was my first since we returned. But abstinence is hard, darling. It makes me nervous, irritable."

"What about our love, our passion, the games we play?" I asked. "It's not like you don't have your way with me. You even got me to sleep in bondage!"

He smiled, but his eyes were somber.

"If I truly had my way with you, you wouldn't leave the playroom for days on end, and your body would bear my marks permanently, without any respite for healing."

"Is that supposed to make me feel better?" I sneered.

"No." He banged his fist into the canopy above him. He was getting upset, too. "It's supposed to make you see that I do my best to match your needs and forget about mine. But you've got to give me some slack here."

"On Earth, this would be unacceptable," I said, almost to myself and feeling I was losing the fight.

"You're on Khyra."

"I know."

And that was the end of it. We had breakfast in silence, and I wished I could have told him he was right. In my heart, I knew he was, but each time I pictured him whipping the bare bottom of a girl, I saw red flashes of anger. I chose not to say another word on the subject, hoping he would change, fearing he wouldn't.

A few days later, we flew out of Mhôakarta to visit friends of Khiru's in a neighboring town. All signs of the unsolved fight had vanished, and we looked like a happy couple again. We had played—moderately—and I had had enough orgasms in a week to make me feel light-headed for a month.

This social call wasn't as trivial as I thought. A man, Perhy, opened the roof-door. Older than Khiru, he had a crew cut and rough features that made him look like a cartoonesque villain. But his eyes darted a power that I recognized well. It was the self-assurance and dominance only Rhysh Masters conveyed. To welcome me, he extended his hand palm down, a symbolic gesture only used by Academy graduates. Remembering Khiru's lessons in Rhysh etiquette, I placed my hand palm up underneath Perhy's and instinctively lowered my eyes.

In the living room, another man, younger and more conventional, stood up to greet us.

"Ordan is courting Nah," Perhy explained to Khiru, without looking at me.

"Then I'm honored to meet you, Ordan. You must be a special man if you obtained Perhy's approval."

"Don't mock, Khiru," Perhy said. "I knew the time would come. As much as I would have liked to, I can't keep Nah to myself forever."

"How long have you been partners again?" Khiru asked as we all sat on black lilk couches.

"Nine years and counting."

"You kept her off the game as long as you could, my friend. So, Ordan, what do you do?"

While the men caught up with each other's lives, oblivious to my existence, I scanned the room. The disposition and furniture resembled ours, as social rules would have dictated, but I observed many more S/N elements: hooks in the walls, metal bars on the floor, leather straps hanging from one chair, and a collection of whips neatly hanging next to a book shelf. These people were serious players. Of course the thick bracelet around Perhy's wrist was a giveaway. The cobalt-green lilk band bore the Rhysh initial, which was entwined with Nah's name. Without seeing it, I knew the woman's bracelet would feature the same color and design, with Perhy's name carved on it. She would also bear the Rhysh initial if she had graduated from the Academy. They were lifepartners, and their bracelets testified to their official commitment.

If Nah took Ordan as a second partner, she would wear his bracelet on the other arm. Some women wore as many as four bracelets.

I stared at Khiru's indigo bracelet with envy, dreaming of the moment I would receive its twin, although without the ornate "Rh."

When Perhy offered drinks and went to get them in the kitchen, I wondered whether Nah would join us. I felt uncomfortable amongst three clearly domineering Northies, and wished for more submissive company.

Perhy gave me a glass of plio juice, and I turned to set it down on the low black table next to me.

As the glass touched a surface that wasn't as solid and flat as I expected, I realized, too late, what I was doing. Shocked, I gave a start and spilled the contents of my glass all over me.

"I'm sorry," I stammered, reddening with confusion, "I hadn't seen, I..."

"It's okay, Megan," Perhy said while Khiru held my glass, and Ordan went to pick up a towel. "I should have warned you."

The black shiny heap wasn't a table; it was Nah, curled down onto her knees and totally covered in lustrous resina. As still as a...well, piece of furniture, she didn't react to the commotion I had just created.

"How, how long has she been like this?" I managed to ask.

"Since early this morning," Ordan said as he handed me a towel.

The afternoon was well on its way.

I felt dizzy as I rubbed my mini-dress with more vigor than necessary, hesitant to say one more word for fear they would turn me into a lamp or a carpet for the rest of the day.

"Well, since you're here," Ordan said, "I suppose Nah can be allowed a short break."

He bent over the shapeless body and worked at clasps on her sides and front. As he helped her redress, I saw her body suit came with a hood that completely cut her off from the world. She was breathing through a tube.

Nah sat on her knees, her arms still trapped behind her.

Ordan unzipped the hood at its base around the neck and removed it. The woman's eyes were covered with black patches, and the tiny protuberances standing for ears were sealed with some sort of plaster. And she was bald. Even her eyebrows were gone.

I moved closer to Khiru.

While I fought to keep my vision clear, Ordan peeled off the eye bandages. Nah blinked a few times and looked down. Then Ordan lifted her chin and gave her a long and tender kiss.

"You may look up," he said as their lips parted.

As I met her eyes, I read humility, contentment, and the cheerfulness you would find in a child. She looked beautiful.

Perhy let her sip at his glass, then Ordan came back with big powered pins. Through two openings he undid at chest level, he pulled out her small breasts, and pinched the pins on her nipples. She couldn't refrain a shudder and a frown, but stayed still and quiet. Her eyes were slightly wet when she reopened them.

Khiru and I stayed until dinnertime, at which point Perhy insisted that we join them, but we didn't. While the men resumed their conversation, and I did a lot of daydreaming, Nah knelt in silence. Whenever one of her lovers focused their attention on her, whether with a stare, a smile, or additional pins around her breasts, she gazed back with an expression full of love and respect. I had never seen a woman who found so much happiness in submission.

When we left, Ordan was already bringing back new eye patches and the hood.

"Do you think they're going to leave her in that state for much longer?" I asked Khiru as he maneuvered the shuttle off the roof.

"Probably until bedtime, yes."

"Won't she have dinner with them?"

"Apparently not. Are you worried about her?"

I was more worried about myself. Was she a model I had to emulate?

"Not really," I said. "I saw she was happy. And they care a great deal about her."

"You're right. Perhy and she have been together for fifteen years. They sealed their union nine years ago, and signed a Full Submission contract. I was one of his witnesses. I believe they've been living in bliss ever since."

A pause, and then I had to ask: "Is there a reason why you brought me to their place?"

"They invited us."

Why couldn't I believe him?

In the following weeks, Khiru's edginess increased, and he paid several visits to the Space Center. I spent my free time with Myhre or entertaining myself at home, but I began to seriously resent the restrictions imposed by the Council and so severely applied by Khiru. Why couldn't I take a walk by myself?

And was he really going to the Space Center?

My concerns were legitimate. He never mentioned his "special needs" again, and yet he was more relaxed, almost too much. A mere trip to the office couldn't work such wonders.

I decided to spy on him and called the only person who could help, my personal chauffeur.

It took some coaxing to convince Sertee to fly me to the Space Center, but he finally did. Khiru's shuttle wasn't there.

This was the signal I needed to carry out an extensive search. If he cheated, I could cheat, too. I searched his pockets, his files, his mail, even his mediapin, and found nothing. I staved off my impatience by gardening and enjoying the sun, or abusing my unlimited quotas to buy clothes and shoes online with Myhre.

The worst part was submitting to a man who was lying to me. I started to invoke headaches and cramps to avoid playing. Khiru expressed concern about my health, but didn't complain about the abstinence I was forcing on him. To me, it was another clue.

One day I finally got lucky. I had spent the whole afternoon in the garden while Khiru was supposedly out shopping for sex toys. Before he was due back, I checked his mail and found the confirmation of a rendezvous at a scenemat the next day.

Sure enough, when I woke up, he said he would go to the Center for a few hours. But I was ready.

Sertee, who had sworn it was the last time, was waiting for me a few blocks from the house. On my signal, he picked me up in the med-shuttle, flew me to the other side of Mhôakarta, deep into the industrial suburbs, and left me within walking distance of the scenemat where Khiru was probably testing whips. He would wait an hour, then leave. I expected to be back after twenty minutes.

I took the elevator down to the parking lot. Once on the street, I followed the map I had printed. I had never been in an industrial center on Khyra before, and it struck me as exceptionally quiet. I was walking beside a big white building with no windows, probably a factory. On the other side of the street was an impressive storage facility. Unlike the streets in living or office neighborhoods, this one wasn't made of grass and gravel, but concrete.

As I kept walking, I heard faint machinery sounds, but saw no one. At this time of the day, everyone would be working.

I walked across an intersection, double-checking my map, and didn't see the men hiding behind the corner.

The next thing I knew, someone was dragging me backward, and a cupping mask was forced against my nose and mouth. With my arms tugged back, I couldn't reach my mediapin and call for help. I breathed once into the mask and passed out.

CHAPTER 6

▼

A door banging on its frame woke me up. It was an odd sound on Khyra, where most doors slid in and out silently.

As my brain cleared, I went through a quick check of my body parts and their degree of confinement. At that stage, I still hoped Khiru had planned a surprise scene and pretended to kidnap me. If that was the case, he had done a very good job in the fear department. Not so much in bondage, however.

I was lying on a cold, hard floor, next to a wall. My hands and feet were tied up in a hogtie and wrapped with wires that were shearing off my flesh. My mouth was filled with a sour-tasting hankie and taped shut, and a filthy bag had been dropped over my head. It was poorly executed bondage, as far as professional standards go. It was uncomfortable in a non-sexy way and hurt unnecessarily. My hands were already numb. And I was still wearing all my clothes, except the shoes. Was this supposed to set me off balance, make the scene more real?

A loud, unknown voice came through from another room and it startled me. The man spoke a dialect I didn't understand, and that detail freaked me out. Khiru would never involve a stranger in a scene.

A very bad feeling grew inside me.

I worried and fidgeted on the floor for a long time. Nobody came to look after me, give me water or check my restraints, another sign that this wasn't a regular scene. I had long lost all sensations in my limbs, and I was getting faint from a lack of food.

Finally, heavy steps shook the floor, and four hands grabbed my shoulders and knees and lifted me face down. My whimpers were useless. After a brief walk, the men lowered me on a floor that smelled strongly of chemicals. They pushed me against a wall, then locked me to it with a series of chains.

I thought they were going to leave me there, but before they did, they filled the space around me with boxes or containers, heavy pieces that touched me on all sides and provoked a short burst of claustrophobia. I fought to stay clear-headed. I needed as much information as possible if I planned on escaping.

At that last thought, I gave in to a blend of anger and despair. This wasn't for show; I was being kidnapped. I thrashed against the chains and moaned hard. A deep clang answered me from the other side of the boxes. Like a door closing.

A few minutes later, the room moved forward, and the chains held me back before my face connected with the nearest container. No engine was roaring, but the horizontal traction and the air blowing on the other side of the wall were evident clues. I was in a ground vehicle, probably a truck that was only authorized in the countryside to connect industrial sites.

I cried a long time as I thought of Khiru and how I was being carried away from him. Then I imagined how he would search for me. He would find the message that had lured me to the scenemat (I had obviously fallen into an easy trap), talk to Sertee, and alert the Council and local authorities. Perhaps they would react quickly enough to stop the truck?

Poor Khiru. He would be devastated by the sense of failure for losing me. Guilt increased my misery, but also strengthened my will to fight.

After a long, but smooth drive, the vehicle came to a halt, and another clang indicated the opening of the back door.

The space around me became chillier as it was emptied of its load. Someone unlocked the chains so I could be carried outside, then into a building where the air was warmer, up two flights of stairs into a room, and down on something soft. A mattress?

Moving was bringing blood and pain back inside my arms and legs, and I groaned.

A new voice—another man—rose angrily in the same unknown language. My abductors gave nervous explanations until the new guy interrupted them sharply. They all left the room, and I heard them fight until they were out of listening range.

They hadn't secured me to anything, but my dead limbs were useless to attempt any maneuver. There was nothing I could do but lie on the bed and wait until one of the men returned.

I didn't have to wait long. A man came in, and immediately worked on my restraints.

"Don't try anything stupid," he said with a voice that left no doubt to the implied threat. He was clearly a man used to giving orders and being obeyed without hesitation.

He cut the wires behind me, and helped me lie on my back with my arms at the sides. While the pain kicked in and grew worse with every cell of blood flowing past my elbows and knees, the man wrapped cuffs where the wires had been and connected them to the sides of the bed, effectively immobilizing limbs that had a hard time coming back to life. I tried to protest, but all he did was rub my arms, then my legs, until I calmed down.

"Now, if you want to eat and drink, stay silent. One word, and I'll gag you."

I nodded.

First, he pulled the bag off my head. I expected to see a face; all I got was a black mask covering his head, leaving only tiny holes for his eyes. It reminded me of the hood I'd worn at the Engcamp reunion, a memory that sent a sharp arrow through my heart, as if that happy past was forever out of reach now.

I made an effort to hold back tears, but when the masked man peeled the layers of tape off my chin, I let a few run down.

At least I was glad to spit the hanky out.

In silence my jailor fed me. When I had finished the plate and drunk a glass of water, he gagged me again, albeit with a more comfortable bit gag.

Then he walked out and locked the door, leaving me in darkness, silence and terror.

Weeks of practice helped me sleep despite the restraints, and I was reasonably rested when I woke up the next day. But then, the lack of action and permanent fear seriously undermined my mood.

I stayed in the empty bedroom for five days, tied to the bed and gagged. I never saw the masked man again. Instead, a younger boy, in his early twenties, brought me food every morning and evening. He was cute in a savage kind of way: long blond hair running down his neck, skin tanned and roughed from a life in the outdoors, eyes that reflected the innocence and hopes of childhood, yet had witnessed enough drama to broadcast sparkles of distrust and bitterness. His nose was abnormally flat, practically pushed into his face. In flagrant contradiction with Khyrian fashion as I knew it, his pants and shirt were twice too large, and had seen better days. His name was Leeham. He didn't speak much, but would smile once in a while, as if to apologize for the treatment inflicted upon me.

Every morning and evening, Leeham unlocked one of my wrists so I could eat on my own while he watched me from a distance. Then he had me lie back down and relocked the cuff. Once a day, he brought a pot of cold water so I could wash and relieve myself, with one hand still cuffed to the bed.

Outsmarting him was impossible. The boy was tall and strong, and never took his eyes off me. Without the full use of my hands, I was as helpless as a caged snake.

One morning, I tested his dedication.

"Do you realize what you're doing?" I asked him. "When you're caught, you'll end up in jail for the rest of your life. But if you help me now, I'll make sure it doesn't happen."

Leeham looked at me as if I had risen from the dead. Then he caught himself and gave me a pitiful stare. "How can you possibly disobey the rule?" he seemed to think.

He left me without a word and didn't come back until the next day. I was starving and ate in silence without meeting his eyes.

On the evening of the fifth day, things took a different turn, not for the better. After taking care of my various body needs, Leeham cuffed both hands in front of me, pushed the usual gag into my mouth, and blindfolded me with a large lilk band that he laced tightly at the back of my head. Then he led me out of the room and down the stairs until we got to a chillier place.

After locking my bound wrists to a chain above my head, he went to get his boss. I heard him call "Shoan," then the stairs creaked under determined footsteps.

I immediately recognized the touch of his expert hand when the man verified the tightness of the blindfold and the gag. Without a word, Shoan, the masked man—who, I wagered, was probably unmasked now that I couldn't see him—began to cut through my clothes.

When I tried to kick him, he pulled my arms further up, forcing me to stand on tiptoe. I stayed put until he stripped me naked.

I feared he would torture me, maybe rape me, but he pressed my legs together and proceeded to bind them with layer after layer of smooth, nonetheless resistant lilk that soon extended from my toes to my thighs. Once my legs were perfectly still and useless, he called to Leeham to help him.

Following directions I didn't understand, the boy unlocked the cuffs around my wrists, brought me down to the floor and held my arms to my sides. Quickly, Shoan looped more layers of lilk around my hips and waist, imprisoning my hands, and continued more slowly over my chest until he reached my neck.

I was now confident he wouldn't touch me, but this certainty didn't ease my fears about what he was going to do next.

Like lift me up and place me inside a box, a coffin, that was filled with hard foam cut exactly to my shape, without any slack on either side. Then close the lid.

I panicked to the point of fainting. When I came back to my senses, I was on the move again, but not on the ground. Slight moves up and down indicated another means of transportation. An air shuttle. Where were they taking me?

I generally don't suffer from claustrophobia, but those long hours trapped like a living corpse made me look at life from a new angle. I swore I would be a better woman if I came out of this unscathed. There would be no jealousy, no envy, no impatience. I would cherish every breath, every ray of sunshine, every parcel of green sky. I would be good to my friends, and better yet with Khiru.

Khiru. Was he on my tracks? Would the Khyrian equivalent of the FBI lie in ambush at the airport? I had never seen a weapon on the planet, but on Earth I had seen Naari disintegrate rocks with a single light beam. Would there be any shooting? A laser-fire massacre?

Making up action movie scripts kept me sane during most of the flight. When the plane landed, I paid attention to all the sensatory details I was able to process. My box was unloaded, then wheeled to a quiet room. There, when all movements stopped, silence filled the air like an oppressive blanket, and I lost my precarious calm. My heart pounded too much blood, and I sucked on the stale air as if I was drowning. Sweating and in tears, I clenched all my muscles at once, trying to break free like superheroes are supposed to do.

"I don't want to die," echoed a terrified voice in my head as I redoubled my efforts to crack the box.

My useless outburst gave way to general exhaustion. I was going to die, but if I did, let it be quick and painless. And preferably now. Could I just fall asleep and never wake up?

But my final day hadn't arrived yet. When I came around, I was on the move again, and a surreal feeling of joy overwhelmed me for a few seconds. They hadn't abandoned me. I wouldn't be buried alive.

In rapid succession, I felt hungry, thirsty, hot, dirty, and excessively jittery. My struggles had increased the nuisance of the bondage.

Although it has the glossy look and pungent smell of leather, lilk also has textile properties. It may be sliced in thin, almost transparent layers, like silk, and is wonderfully malleable. When worn as clothes, lilk is soft to the touch, light and supple. I have beautiful dresses made in lilk. In bondage gear, the synthetic material allows for precise adjustments to body curves. There is no "working" on lilk, like with leather. But lilk is most surprising when wet, when its internal layer fills with water and adheres to any surface.

As a result of my abundant sweating, the tapes were now sticking to my body like a second skin, filling every crease, covering every minute bump. The large blindfold coated my face between my nostrils and forehead. The strap securing the now well-bitten gag compressed my mouth and chin in a tight hold.

And I'm ashamed to say the pressure between my legs and on my pubis sent awfully wrong ideas to my mind. I fought them off, resisting the mere concept of pleasure in such an abject situation.

When I was incapable of meeting any of my physical needs and various discomforts, anger took over. It kept my mind focused for a long time.

The road on which we were traveling was unusually bumpy, as if made of gravel or uneven dirt. Soon we ascended a hill, and gravity pushed me down to my feet. At regular intervals, the vehicle, silent save for the wheels scraping the ground, slowed down and turned sharply. After reaching the summit, I tilted the other way and praised the foam that was protecting my head from too much pressure.

We drove up and down several peaks, and the heat, which had been stifling all day long, dropped to a more temperate level. My thirst eased slightly.

I had lolled into a semi-sleep when the wheels ground to a halt. I was immediately alert.

Again, the casket was lifted and carried through what seemed to be a maze of corridors. When the lid finally opened, a cool breeze permeated the layers of lilk. Someone pulled me out of the box, laid me next to it, and began to unwrap my cocoon. One nightmare was over; another one was probably about to start.

Slow, heavy footsteps came closer, and the voice of an old woman broke the silence. She spoke in dialect.

Then the man working on my bondage talked to me. I recognized Leeham.

"You must be thirsty. I'm going to ungag you, but you'd better stay calm. Understood?"

Water had never tasted so fresh. I gulped down a full glass, then asked for another.

"Later," he replied. "Maori will fix you something to eat, too. But I want to finish unwrapping you first."

I shivered as he peeled off the last length of tape, and my sweaty legs came in contact with the cold air. Before I could bend them, Leeham grabbed one ankle and locked it inside a shackle. When I pulled, a chain clicked and held my leg still. I couldn't suppress a sigh of irritation. I had just about had enough of bondage.

"Be nice," Leeham said as he started working on the layers around my hips and hands, "and this will be your only restraint for the night. If you fight, I have plenty more I can use, from your neck down to your toes."

He sounded like he was repeating a line, but he wasn't kidding, and I let him finish the unrolling process. Finally, he unlaced the blindfold.

Night had already fallen, and the light from the ceiling was dim, but after hours in the dark, it felt like bright sunshine. I squinted for a few minutes before scanning my new abode. It was a small cell, with bare brick walls painted white. It had two openings: a door on the right, and a small, wired window on the left. I couldn't judge the view, as the window opened on utter blackness.

In the corner next to the window stood a wooden table with a matching chair. The other piece of furniture was the bed where I sat. It was narrow, but robust. The headboard and footboard were tall grids of metal, perhaps even kauchu. Low railings ran along the sides, offering many anchoring points.

The décor and what it implied was utterly depressing.

Leeham got up to leave. I watched him hesitate as he broke away from his domineering character.

"Maori will take care of you," he said gently. "Be brave, Earth girl."

Leeham walked out the room just as an old woman came in with a wooden tray in her hands. They exchanged a few words in their language, and Leeham stepped out, letting a heavy metallic door slide shut behind him. I heard the heartbreaking sound of bolts being pushed in place and noted that my best chance of escaping the room was to break the code on the digit pad on the wall.

Without a word, Maori placed the tray on my lap, then stood back and waited, her hands joined in front of her. I was too stunned to speak and ate under her vigilant stare. She was a strongly built woman, with broad shoulders and broader hips, but she was small and obviously old. Her hair, tied up in a bun, was gray with streaks of white. Her face was wrinkled, her cheeks too red on ghastly pale skin. Only her eyes, vivid and smart, indicated she was someone with whom to be reckoned.

She had the same flat nose as Leeham, and I wondered whether they were related.

A boy barely an adult and an ancient woman. If these were my jailers, my hopes were high.

Sated and more comfortable than I'd been for days, I slept relatively well, confident that morning would mark the beginning of my retaliation.

CHAPTER 7

▼

When I woke up, a bright streak of sunshine was hitting the table by the window, as if to introduce the breakfast tray that was lying on it. However, food wasn't as inviting as the world outside.

I rushed out of bed, careful not to stumble on the metal rings connecting my ankle to the footboard. Dismissing the appetizing smell, I walked as close to the window as the chain would allow, my leg bent backward toward the bed. Behind the glass was a tight mesh of rusty bars. Behind the bars was a wall of rocks. I skeptically punched the button on the wall and watched the window slowly slide down with a sense of freedom in my heart.

But the sensation didn't last.

As I leaned forward, standing on one foot and touching the cold grid with my nose, I realized I faced a mountain, not a wall. It was tall and broad, with no end in sight. High above the bare rocks that formed its base was a dense forest, with imposing emerald trees and clusters of brighter bushes. The thin slice of sky I could make out was a cloudless faded green.

There was much dampness around, but the air was brisk and clear, and strongly smelling of the wild. I breathed deeply and offered my face to the morning sun. At this early hour, the light rays pierced through a narrow crevice between the rocky mass and the house, but they would soon disappear behind the mountain, not to return again until the late evening when they would strike from the opposite side.

I took another long breath, enjoying the cold rush into my lungs and the scent of nature filling my head.

"But the view sucks," I said out loud, breaking the spell.

For good measure, I inserted three fingers between the tiny grid squares and pulled. I wasn't going to get out that way.

The chilly draft on my naked body made me shiver, and I closed the window half way. Despite the cold, I needed an opening to the world to maintain the illusion of freedom. Then I turned around to face the door and crawled across the bed. Unfortunately, the chain yanked me back before I could reach the digit pad.

Hopping back on the bed, I checked the shackle around my ankle. Despite its antique look, it was a modern device, with a fingerprint lock. Only one person would be able to open it.

I prayed that person was the old woman.

Determined to go to war, I turned to the table and sat on the chair, my leg twisted by the chain. I devoured the fresh, cake-tasting bread and washed it down with half the mild infusion.

As I stared at the wired window, a faint smile lightened my face. It reminded me of the first setting Khiru had used in what he called our playroom.

Because I wasn't allowed to see it until the twentieth day, a whole Khyrian month after we moved in our new house, I referred to our second room as the secret dungeon. When I finally walked through the door, ahead of Khiru, I reckoned my description was more appropriate than his.

All four walls were built of dark bricks, bare and damp, with irregular cracks giving the impression the room was going to tumble down soon. The floor was rough concrete, cold under my naked feet. In front of us, a small grid acted as a depressing window. And in the middle of the room stood a metallic cage into which Khiru ordered me to crawl.

He asked me to sit with my back against the railings and my legs spread out so that my toes touched the opposite corners. My head, wrapped in a resina trainer, raked the ceiling of the cage. The contraption was a perfect fit, which came as no surprise since Khiru had sent my measurements to the cage manufacturer.

Khiru chained and locked the various cuffs he had previously adorned me with to rings welded on all sides of the cage. Two for my ankles, two for my knees, two for my thighs. Six for my thick corset. Two for my collar. Another four for my trainer, on the sides and above my head. Finally a series of six for each arm from shoulders to wrists.

When he was certain I couldn't move, he left me alone and only returned when I had reached both the bottom of despair and the peak of arousal.

Was I really going to spend days in here? In a cold, dreary cell where even the light refused to enter? With only this uncomfortable cage to play with? Where was the mahogany furniture I had fantasized about? The wooden panels supporting lilk accessories? The tall mirror where I would parade in erotic wear and the detested high heels? The Spartan theme of a prison, while undoubtedly effective, was way below my romantic expectations.

I felt abandoned and miserable.

I also felt completely at Khiru's mercy, and, as usual, my helplessness aroused me.

When Khiru came back, he presented me a new tool: a thin torch that produced a straight beam of light, the kind an Earth doctor would use to check the throat of a patient. He pointed the ray at my belly and moved it all over my body, experimenting with the intensity of the light as he went along. The sensations ranged from tickling to burning, none of which were recommended when applied to highly responsive spots. Khiru admitted he had never played with such a toy before, but he planned to become an expert by the end of the day.

Sure enough, when the feeble light in the dungeon had transformed into the bright orange of sunset, Khiru hit a bull's eye whether he aimed at my nipple, my earlobe or my clitoris.

When night fell, Khiru carried me, half-conscious, to our poster bed in the adjacent room. I was happy to be out of the cell, and fearful of going back.

My reprieve didn't exceed a few hours. The next morning, Khiru gagged and blindfolded me before leading me into the playroom. Instead of asking me to kneel down and enter the cage, he had me lie down on a swivel chair, with my legs resting on elevated pads on either side. Good, I remember thinking, he brought more furniture.

When I was secured with a collection of heavy straps, he removed the blindfold.

The cell was gone. I was in a white, clean medical unit, with shelves supporting potions and prodding tools, a mediaframe displaying numbers and diagrams, and a bright spotlight above me.

Khiru laughed at my confusion. "I guessed you didn't like the dungeon, so I renovated the room. I hope you appreciate all the hard work?"

Unable to speak, I shook my head in disbelief, and he explained.

The whole room, from floor to ceiling, was paneled in mediaframes that could display hundreds of different settings. Once you knew the trick, it was easy to spot artificial glitches, but when taken unaware, like I'd been, the illusion was close to perfect.

I was delighted. Each time I entered the playroom, I looked forward to discovering a new environment. Khiru never managed to recreate the stupor of the first day, except maybe once, when he hung me above a bird's-eye view, as if I was falling from the sky, but confronting an unknown setting certainly helped me get in the mood for whatever scene he had in mind.

I was still staring at my now all-too-real meshed window when the three bolts behind the door banged out of their sockets one by one.

Maori, my short, gray-haired warden, ambled into the room. She wore a long burgundy dress, clean but worn out, protected by a black apron. Her shoes were coarse and shabby. She looked like an old cook or a farmer. Or a hard-working, tough-tempered nanny.

Before I could attempt a smile and a welcoming word, she showed me the flogger protruding from a side pocket and pointed at the ceiling. A pair of heavy cuffs I hadn't noticed dangled from a very solid ring. I had no problem comprehending her warning to hang me like a piece of meat, but I failed to see how she could implement it. She would have to stretch to reach the restraints and would be in no position to hold me still.

On the other hand, I probably could return the threat to her.

"Okay, Maori," I said gently, emphasizing her name, "I'll behave. Thank you for breakfast, by the way. It was truly good."

Without any sign of understanding, she motioned me to get back on the bed. I moved to obey her, but at the last second I grabbed the mug, threw its contents in the direction of her face and jumped for her hands.

A violent flash of pain pushed me back, and I fell on the floor, holding my wounded hip. An unpleasant sensation irradiated through my body, turning my limbs into jelly. I felt like a rag doll, unable to move. Maori was standing in front of me, one hand on her hip, the other holding up the whip. There was a big wet stain on her belly.

Paralyzed, I watched her reach for the cuffs and drag them down to my level. With a firm hand, she snatched my lifeless wrists and locked them in. Then, she walked to the control box by the door and, as she dialed, I was hauled up until my fingers touched the ceiling and my feet scraped the floor. One of them was still chained to the footboard.

What had I been thinking?

Maori removed the breakfast tray and left the room, irritation still perceptible in her nervous stride.

Are you completely stupid? I admonished myself, on the brink of tears. Why couldn't I just wait and plot a safer escape? Had I become so desperate?

The door opened again, this time to let in Leeham. He didn't look happy, but I was under the impression he was forcing himself into character.

"How dare you attack an old lady?" he yelled in a theatrical way. "She's here to take care of you. What an ungrateful brat you are!"

"Leeham, please," I pleaded, "I'm tired, I'm scared, I'm hurt. I'm a prisoner, for Plya's sake, I have a right to escape."

"What are you talking about? You have a right to shut up, that's all."

And to illustrate his words, he forced a pump gag in my mouth and inflated it until my jaw threatened to break.

"Ah, this is what you like, isn't it?" Leeham said with a strange, Northie-wan-nabe voice that was as unnatural to him as pleading was to a Rhysh Master. "I know your kind. You like to rebel so you can get more, huh? Well I hope these will entertain you."

The heavy clamps bit my nipples and pulled them down.

"What else would a naughty girl want? A good spanking perhaps?"

His blows were ridiculously feeble, but I cried of despair. Did he think this was all a game? Or was he just being sarcastic?

When Leeham left after another lecture he seemed to have learned from a book, my spirits sank in a deep black hole. My body was stretched to its limit, and I was getting awfully hot. The window was still half-opened and, although the sunlight had long deserted my cell, the air had become gradually warmer until it turned the room into an oven. I was thirsty. Unable to swallow, I dribbled on the floor while my throat got drier. Several times, I pulled with all my weight on the restraints, but the pulley was securely locked. I eventually stopped trying. I was too hot anyway.

Much later that day, I had one last visitor. I was facing the window, holding my head down, too depressed to turn and look up. When I felt male hands around my waist, I sprang back to life and spun around.

Our eyes locked for a minute, and I couldn't read him. Was he mad, amused or interested? His brown almond-shaped eyes pierced through me and seemed to make a statement, then turned away.

"Don't direct your wrath onto Maori, Megan," he said calmly.

I knew that voice: he was Shoan, the masked man. He was as tall as any Khyrian man, but more muscular than most I knew. The sun had darkened his copper skin, and he had a pale scar running up his arm from wrist to elbow. His tousled, brown hair fell loose on his shoulders. His forehead indicated intelligence; his chin, determination. But the wrinkles around his mouth showed he was a man who loved to laugh.

Dressed in a baggy shirt and rough, well-worn pants, Shoan was the kind of man you easily pictured hiking through the jungle with a backpack, and enjoying every scary minute of it. Perhaps he was some sort of treasure hunter, and I was his latest bounty?

"Nor onto Leeham," he added. "They're good people. Kind and devoted."

Yeah, right. One of them whipped me with the devil's toy; the other damaged my nipples.

"But they have strict orders," he went on, "from me. And they will kill you if I ask them to."

So I'm just supposed to hang here like a good girl, and wait for what?

"Now that you've arrived safely, I can explain a few things." He moved behind me and whispered, "I'm going to deflate this, but don't you dare interrupt me."

Once the gag had shrunk down to a tiny lollypop, he went to lean on the footboard, facing me.

"We mean you no harm."

He had a nerve to say that without batting an eyelid.

"You're in a class-1 territory," he continued, "and we intend to keep you here until we obtain what we want from the Global Council. You're so valuable to them, I'm certain it won't be long. Then you'll be free to go. In the meantime, you may either fight and stay bound in your room, or accept your situation, in which case I'll make your life much more comfortable."

I questioned him with my eyes.

"You'll be allowed to walk around the house," he explained. "Take showers, enjoy the garden, read."

I nodded, my hopes rising dramatically.

"But another trick of yours, another attempt to escape, and I'll show no mercy. Are we clear?"

My head went up and down in a frenzy.

"Good. I'm going to untie you, then Maori will bring you dinner. Don't blame her if she's still mad at you. She's a brave woman, but can't take disobedience."

At that moment, Shoan unclipped one clamp, and pain made me jerk like a dislocated puppet. He pressed his lips on my nipple and sucked. I stood still, lost in the moment, fighting back the spasm building in my loins. When he removed the second one, once again using his tongue and mouth to ease the pain, I secretly swooned and let my body rest against his hand holding my back.

While I regained a more respectable composure, he unstrapped the pump gag, freed my arms, and carried me to the bed, leaving only the ankle restraint as a reminder of my status.

"Don't forget my warning," he said before leaving. "I won't repeat it."

I could have sworn I saw him wink. His mouth—so warm and soft—had definitely curved upward.

The next day, I was as docile as a lamb, and my proper behavior was rewarded after lunch when Maori allowed me to venture out of the cell for the first time. After cuffing my wrists in front of me and keeping one hand on her flogger, she led me down a narrow corridor, parallel to the mountain, and let me enjoy a prolonged and extensive use of the bathroom.

The shower was a far cry from the computer-controlled, dry-blowing massage unit to which I had so quickly become accustomed in Mhôakarta, but the water was warm, the soap as unctuous as honey, and the smooth towel smelled like wilderness.

When I came out of the bathroom, Maori unlocked my wrists so I could put on the one piece of clothing I was allowed: a long dress cut in a light gray fabric similar to transparent linen. Then she relocked the cuffs, added a wide leather belt around my waist and chained my wrists to a ring in front. Thus restrained, I preceded her further down the corridor to an open door into the garden.

Compared to the cool temperature in the house, the heat outside was stifling. But the garden looked like a haven of peace. Framed by the mountain, the house and a wooden fence on the two open sides, it was four times the size of my cell. Dense trees around the fence blocked most of the view from the terrain below, but they provided a most welcome shade.

The view above me was magnificent. I squinted to look up at the verdant peaks poking through the emerald sky, brighter than ever. I admired the mosaic of greens, only broken by purple and white floral stains.

A dirt path, crackled by the heat, slithered around the perimeter of the yard, with bushes of wildflowers seemingly planted at random. In the middle, a miniature fountain spurted clear water over moss-covered rocks. Two stone benches, one set against the mountain, the other against the white brick wall of the house, were an invitation to rest and meditate.

After walking a complete and careful tour and tasting the icy-cold water from the fountain, I sat on the bench next to the house, in the shade, and ignored Maori who chose the other bench, obviously determined to keep a vigilant watch on me all day.

Through the frail dress, the stone felt cold on my ass. I leaned against the wall, feeling its coolness soothe me. I began to meditate in a very practical way.

There was no escape from this garden. Behind the fence and the row of trees, the mountain dropped abysmally. The house was probably built on a promontory, with only one access at the front. I would have to check all the rooms to find a way out. That would be tricky.

But did I really need to escape? Should I trust Shoan, this ruthless adventurer I had come to nickname Indiana in a modest attempt to cheer myself up? If he spoke the truth, I would only have to wait a few more days. And maybe he and his people had a valid reason to act so ruthlessly. Maybe I was helping a righteous cause. Evidently, Indiana, Tough Mamma and Little Dom-wannabe were hardly a gang of murderers.

Then I remembered the two goons who had kidnapped me in the first place. These members of the gang had freaked me out. They were definitely up to no good.

So maybe it wasn't all that clean and simple.

I sighed and got up to sit on the dirt path close to the fountain. I splashed water on my face and neck, then held my hand under the cool tiny cascade, sending drops all around.

Maori wasn't moving an eyelid.

The hell with her, I thought. Why can't I spend more time with Leeham? For all his rehearsed authority and his blind obedience to his boss, he looked like a friendly person I could chat with.

And where was the boss anyway? Was he in the house? Would I only see him in case of trouble?

I blushed at the recollection of my reaction the day before. His lips on my breasts, his hand in my back…I didn't think I would have fought if he had tried to take it further.

But how could I surrender to a vile impulse when I had already found the man of my dreams, and was practically committed to living with him forever?

As I thought of Khiru, my heart clenched in grief. Was he looking for me? Was he flying around the planet in search of a clue? The poor man must be crazy with anger and helplessness.

Changing position for the second time, I went to stand in front of the fence, my back to Maori, my eyes guessing at the daunting void underneath me. I mouthed my decision to the trees.

I will escape.

CHAPTER 8

▼

I spent the next two days in relative quiet between my room and the garden, with Maori following me like my shadow. As I walked back and forth between the only two locations I was allowed to visit, I noted as many details as I could.

The corridor leading to the back yard ended on the other side with a small, unwired window. A Khyrian man couldn't have slipped through, but I might. There was no dial by its side, which seemed to indicate it couldn't be opened. But if it was made of glass, it could be broken.

It took me a full day to discover the door that opened onto the front of the house. It was carved in the stone wall opposite my cell, further to the right. Its outline coincided with the slits between the rocks and was hardly noticeable. After paying close attention to Maori's noises before she opened my door, I figured it all out. I even spotted the tiny control panel camouflaged at knee level.

If the opening of the secret door was coded, the window remained my best option. Provided it didn't lead onto another rocky abyss, a prospect that I was unable to verify under Maori's constant watch.

Of course, there was always a nagging question at the back of the mind: even if I managed to slip out of the house, where would I go next?

The complexities of escaping kept me at bay for two days. Then a horrifying incident set my course of action on a definite path.

It was the early afternoon. I was in the garden, leaning against the damp stones surrounding the fountain, trying to cool myself from another hot day. With my hands still bound in front of me, I was reading a historic novel Maori had dug up for me. The old woman sat on her favorite bench against the mountain and looked on the verge of dozing off.

I heard voices coming from the hidden front of the house, probably through an open window. And standing close to it, a man was yelling in Khyrian.

"You can't keep her here longer. She's got to be transferred to Gahra."

Then Shoan's voice, calm but with a nervous edge: "It's too risky. They've doubled all controls at the borders. Leaving Sweendi would be madness. Talk about reentering a class-2!"

"You know it's feasible by boat."

"Not with the Globals scanning the planet in search of Megan. You'll be on the open sea for three days, with nowhere to hide."

"Our boat's covered with sheets of harilium. Completely undetectable, even by G-radars."

Shoan produced a funny whistle of surprise.

"Harilium? How did you get hold of harilium?"

"That's another story, none of your concern. So when can I start wrapping up the girl?"

At that point, I started to feel nauseous and had goosebumps all over my body. I peeked at Maori, but her eyes were closed. She didn't seem to be aware of the conversation inside the house.

"Hang on, Smit," Shoan was saying. "What happens when you reach Gahra's coast? There's a class-2 field all around your charming neck of the woods."

"Vogh creates a diversion at the Global border. Some people are going to get stuck in the field again. They'll have to turn it off, and the ship, still invisible under its harilium cloak, will sail through."

"That requires exact timing."

"No problem."

"People will die in the field."

"Not the first time. What do you think happened when you and the boy sailed to Gahra and crossed the border to the G-Zone? You didn't seem too concerned back then. So, any other questions?" Smit was getting impatient.

"Why do you have to bring her to Gahra?" Shoan insisted, for which I was ultimately grateful. "Isn't she safer here? The Globals are looking for her in all class-2 territories. They trust us here."

"They'll find her sooner or later. You don't have any militia, nor radar-proof shelter."

"That's precisely why they don't look for her in these parts."

"Look, enough talking. The plan was for you to kidnap the Earthling and deliver her to us. Now, Vogh needs the girl. He has plans for her, and besides, he doesn't trust you. Prepare her to be transported tonight."

Smit's voice was fading. He must have been walking away from the window.

"What plans?" I heard Shoan ask in shock before silence returned.

I exhaled deeply and dropped the petals of the flower I had unconsciously plucked and destroyed while eavesdropping. My palm was purple, and I washed off the stain under the water, rubbing harder than necessary.

My lips were quaking, and my legs felt weak. Focus, I yelled at myself. You have a few hours ahead of you. There is still time for action.

But just as I was planning to jump on Maori and kick her unconscious before she could reach for her whip, the door slid open. Shoan stomped out on the dirt path, shaking the old woman from her daydreaming and sending me on full alert.

Not now, I silently pleaded. Don't let them take me now. Don't do this to me.

He looked at me once, and I resisted his stare. Then he turned to Maori and gave orders in her dialect. He sounded angry and determined.

I wondered if this was a good moment for tears.

When the boss left like a hurricane, Maori motioned for me to walk back inside. She had removed the whip out of her pocket and was ready to fire.

Once I was in the cell, she instructed me to lie on the bed. She quickly chained my still-shackled ankle to the footboard, and added a similar restraint on the other leg. Then she produced two chains from under the sides of the bed and connected them to my waist belt. I noticed the locks were finger-activated like the one used around my ankle.

At dinnertime, Maori returned with a full meal. She wouldn't allow me to sit at the table, and fed me each spoonful while I still lay on the bed, my head propped up by the pillow. Despite the fear cramping my stomach, I forced myself to eat. For strength.

When Maori left, it was dark outside. Night had come. And with it, my worst nightmare.

Smit entered the room alone. He was a tall, heavy man, with long black hair and a small beard, a very unusual feature on Khyra. His face was bloated, his eyes, evil. He looked like the ogre from a child's tale.

The chains jingled around me as I instinctively jerked away.

"I knew the bastard couldn't be trusted," Smit said. "Look at this. He says you're safe, and here I am, past two coded doors and into your cell. Outrageously easy.

"And of course, he didn't prepare you," he added as he stepped closer.

A foul smell of alcohol reached my nostrils.

"Vogh will have him pay for this. Now, what do we have here?"

He fiddled with one of the locks securing my waist belt to the bed.

"Fingerprint? How did he get these? Seems like we all have our little secrets."

Still trying to keep my body away from Smit's foul hands, I realized the locks were now protecting me. Perhaps Shoan was going to have it his way after all.

"Well, Earth girl, seems I won't be able to take you with me tonight. I'll have to ask your treacherous protector to undo these for me. And he will, trust me."

He smirked, then press his hand on my thigh, his fingers diving between my wide-open legs. I tried to stop him with my hands, but the chain connected to the belt held them back.

"Don't you dare, or I'll scream," I said, realizing I could at least speak.

"You will, huh? Well, why don't you try?"

He covered my mouth with his hand while he straddled me with his disgusting weight resting on my hips and hands. His other fingers rubbed my sex.

"See? Maybe I *can* take you tonight after all."

I moaned and kicked my chained legs to produce as much sound as possible. Seemingly undisturbed, Smit tore up a length of fabric off the bed sheet, stuffed it into my mouth and secured it with another strip he knotted around my head.

Next, he got off me and the bed, and removed his pants.

I began to thrash like a madwoman. Where was Maori and her whip when I needed them?

With a satisfied grin, Smit lay on top of me. He was already hard, but instead of forcing his way into me, he lowered himself to suck my nipple, grabbing the other breast with his hand.

"My, they're so round," he said between one slurp and a nibble. "Do all women have breasts like yours on your planet? And this waist. So curvy."

His hands were all over my body, soiling it, degrading it, and his mouth ate my breasts with rage. Sweat dribbled from his forehead down my chest.

I tried to free my hands so I could at least pinch him, but they were trapped under his chest.

"Let's see what's inside you now," he said, panting.

"Oh no, you won't."

Smit and I both turned our heads to the door. Shoan was standing in its frame, raising Maori's flogger.

I watched with incredible relief as the straps hit Smit's fat bottom.

"Fuck!" he yelled. "What do you think...aaaah."

Smit collapsed on me like a corpse.

"Get off her, bastard."

"I can't. I can't move my legs."

Paralyzed from the waist down, Smit was squirming like a stranded whale. Gripping one arm and one leg, Shoan dragged him to the floor and kicked him in the waist. At that moment, Leeham burst into the room, his eyes going from me to Smit. He couldn't comprehend what he saw.

"Leeham, here," Shoan said. "Take the whip. Make sure our guest finds the way out and never comes back."

"Sure thing, Shoan."

Leeham left, hauling Smit out by his arms.

I stopped paying attention to Smit's curses and growls when Shoan sat by my side.

"I'm sorry. This shouldn't have happened." He untied the strap around my mouth and removed the ball of fabric from it. "I thought I was smart to lock you up so he wouldn't kidnap you, but I never thought he would try to rape you instead."

I didn't know what to think or say. Hadn't he kidnapped me in the first place? What did he care if another guy took over?

"Anyway, this won't happen again," he continued. "I'll post guards at the door. Poor Maori is in no better shape than you are. Smit assailed her and threatened to cut off her fingers if she didn't give him the code for the doors."

Shoan placed his index finger on a lock in the side of my belt, and it snapped open.

"I'm sure she would have resisted," he continued while unclasping the other three locks, "but, like me, she knew you were safely restrained to the bed. So she gave him what he wanted. After that, he knocked her out."

He seemed to hesitate before unlocking the last cuff, the one around my left ankle.

"I suppose you'll want to shower," he said, partly to me, partly to himself, and applied his magic finger one last time.

Grateful, I stretched and sat on the bed.

"How is she now?" I asked, feeling unexpected mercy for the old woman.

"I sent her off to bed with orders to sleep. She'll be fine tomorrow. She's a tough one."

Somehow I knew that.

Shoan helped me get up, then accompanied me to the bathroom where he waited until I was done. Back in the room, he repositioned the shackle around my ankle.

"For precaution," he said.

Whether he meant precaution against any attempt to escape or any attempt to kidnap me was unclear.

"Why didn't you let him take me?" I asked.

He thought about it for a second.

"Because they've changed the plan, and I don't trust them."

They didn't trust him either, I recalled.

"I need to talk to their leader before I send you away," he added.

"You said you were just using me as a hostage to obtain favors from the Council. That I would be free to go soon. That I wouldn't get hurt."

"Well, that's what I want. But I'm not alone in this. Like I said, I need a discussion."

"But this Smit guy is a criminal. You can't let him take me!"

He sighed, then got up and walked to the door.

"I'll do my best. I promise."

"That's not enough. Wait."

The three bolts were in place, and I was alone again.

Unable to sleep, I went to the window and opened it. The night's chilled air rushed inside the room, caressing my skin on its way. Although the sun had long set, it wasn't completely dark. A misty white light inundated the night. I leaned forward and looked up along the wedge between the house and the mountain. Mhô, the male moon, was hanging halfway between the ground and the summit. It was full and glitzy.

Unsurprisingly in that tiny section of sky, I couldn't see Plya. She was out there, somewhere. And that certainty made me feel better.

I lay down on the bed. With Mhô's light bathing my body, I finally fell asleep.

CHAPTER 9

▼

The day after the attempted rape was nerve-wracking for everyone in the house. Despite the four villagers posted outside, both Maori and I feared an intrusion. Our misadventure had somewhat smoothed the vibes between us, although we still didn't speak to each other. I suspected Maori felt guilty for giving the lock codes to Smit, and I felt bad for being the cause of her mistreatment. No one should hurt an old woman, I thought illogically, given I had planned to assault her myself.

We decided not to go in the garden, for fear our enemy would climb up or down the mountain, and I was allowed in the front quarters for the first time.

As I followed Maori through the forbidden door, my hands remained chained to the belt and locked in front of me.

There were only two rooms on the other side of the corridor: a large living area on the left, and a kitchen on the right. The bolted door opened in the middle of the first room. When it slid back into place, I noted it was carefully concealed in the white stone wall. When Maori moved a tall plant in front of it, the door became invisible to the unsuspecting eye. Unfortunately, Smit had known what to look for.

The living room was sparsely furnished: a low table flanked by two armchairs upholstered in navy blue velvet, shelves on one wall, everything in dark wood. It looked rustic and manly, the den of a lonely hermit. The only extravagant piece was a large woven carpet covering the floor from behind the table to the room's only window on the opposite wall. It had elaborate, somewhat esoteric motifs in bright orange and crimson colors. Time, and many footsteps, had given it a respectable patina.

Behind the armchair on the left was a steep flight of stairs that went up to a second floor I wasn't invited to visit.

On the right, an opening led into the kitchen with cupboards on three sides and a square work table in the middle, all handcrafted in dark wood. But the appliances were high-tech, controlled through a mediaframe on the wall. This was the first electronic display I saw in the house.

The front door to the house was in the kitchen. It was a sturdy item, with three deadbolts in addition to the coded lock. Next to it was a wired window, through which I caught sight of one of the guards.

I had expected uniformed officers. The man, well in his fifties, looked like a farmer, which did nothing to reassure me.

I spent most of the day reading in an armchair. I volunteered to cook, but Maori wouldn't let me. She had retrieved her whip, and I knew that, despite her newfound sympathy, she wouldn't hesitate to use it should I try something inappropriate.

While Maori was busy in the kitchen, I checked the window in the living room to see if it would provide an escape route. Alas, while it wasn't grid-protected, it led onto the same abysmal drop I had stared at from the garden and was therefore of no use to me. The only way to access—and leave—the house was the path that ended at the kitchen corner.

Judging the front door too risky, I decided my best option was the small unwired window in the back corridor. Any normal person would draw the same conclusion, and that was all I needed.

Young Leeham came to visit us in the morning, inquiring about our well-being. He had given up trying to act like a Northie with me. Instead, he was kind and subdued, and amenable to a chat. We first talked about his favorite subject, Shoan. Leeham had met him a good ten years ago. He wouldn't tell me from where he originated, but confirmed that he'd always been living in the cabin up the mountain. When I commented how strange this was for an active, smart man, Leeham shrugged. The only additional detail I was able to get out of him was that in all those years, Shoan had never had a girlfriend.

Not giving Leeham time to regret the confidence, I asked him about his village and how far it was. When he refused to answer beyond vague postcard descriptions—it was a quiet place to live—I tried a more provoking approach.

"What about Smit?" I asked. "Do you know what 'plans' they have in mind for me?"

He didn't hesitate.

"Besides trading you for goods, no, I don't."

But he wished he did.

We were standing by the window in the living room. Leeham looked preoccupied and kept his eyes on the view outside, avoiding me.

"Has your boss talked to that other guy, their leader?" I asked.

He checked on Maori, who observed us from an armchair. She sat on the edge of it, with her spine straight, as if it would hurt to lean back.

"Is he going to let them take me?" I insisted.

"I don't know, Megan. I'm sorry." With a pitiful look on his face, he started to walk toward the kitchen. "I must return to the village. I'll come back tomorrow."

It was as if he, too, was afraid of staying in the house. But at least he could run away.

Maori rose to let Leeham out, then returned to her seat.

I sat opposite her, slumping as far back as I could, and pretended to continue reading. But my brain couldn't even decipher the letters. All I could think of was the imminent threat of another attack.

At the end of the afternoon, Maori brought me back to the rear section of the house where I took a shower before I was confined in my room, my ankle duly shackled.

Two hours later, after sunset, I expected Maori to return with dinner, but Shoan came instead.

"Everything's quiet. I thought you would enjoy dining out tonight."

My eyes widened.

"Yes, sure," I replied quickly before he could change his mind. "What am I going to wear?"

He laughed. "Your see-through dress will be just fine."

Then he unlocked the shackle with his finger.

"Will you uncuff my hands, too? Please?"

He considered it, then removed the restraints from my wrists.

I became very excited. Perhaps this was the opportunity I'd been waiting for. Were we going in the village?

At the thought of socializing, I became very conscious of my nipples protruding beneath the fabric and the visible cleavage between my legs.

Smiling as though he'd read my thoughts, Shoan motioned me out of the room, and I walked toward the coded door.

"No, not that way. Left. To the garden."

"Oh."

So that was his idea of dining out. The garden. Trapped again.

But when I stepped outside, my disappointment subsided. Old-fashioned candles, placed at random on the ground, up the wall and against the mountain, lit up the darkness like tiny stars. Their reflection glittered in the fountain pool and on the wet stones around it.

I looked up and saw Mhô, his left side clipped by the shadow of the planet, trying to cast his moonlight through a veil of clouds. Further aside, on a lower and much more distant orbit, Plya was reduced to a thin slice of light, like an apostrophe hooked to the side of the mountain.

"This way," Shoan whispered, gently pushing me toward the bench against the house.

A tray with a variety of dishes, a jar and two glasses lay in the center of the stone seat.

We sat on the dirt path in front of it, face to face, and started eating.

Confused by the romantic setting and the intimate proximity of my captor, I waited for him to talk. The purpose of this dinner eluded me. Was he trying to make up for last night? Was it a farewell treat before a new nightmare began? Did he have good news or bad intentions?

When we both dipped our spoons in the same bowl, our wrists touched, and I withdrew mine instantly, as if struck by an electric shock. He didn't laugh, as I expected, but poured his helping into my plate, then scooped more for himself.

In silence, he also filled our glasses with the violet contents of the jar. I took a large gulp, and the fruity wine went straight to my head.

"Careful," Shoan said, "it's sweet but treacherous."

Like you, I thought. I was slowly falling into a warm erotic daze. It would have been nice to surrender and succumb to this man. I was longing for tenderness and comfort. And the night was so inviting.

But I caught myself.

"Is the bad guy gone?" I asked as I scooped up more yellow vegetables.

"He went back to his boat," Shoan answered in an even voice, "but they haven't weighed anchor yet. Don't worry. I've got men keeping an eye on them; they won't walk up to the village unnoticed."

I did worry. Shoan didn't seem prepared to confront allies who had turned into fierce enemies. His army was made up of villagers who, as far as I could judge that morning, would be better off farming their lands. I didn't doubt their commitment, but did they really have the skills to fight cold-blooded bandits? Who knew how many were hiding on that boat?

Choosing my words carefully, I shared my concerns with him.

"Their leader, Vogh, cannot risk heavy combat in this zone," Shoan replied. "It would immediately attract the Globals' attention, and that's the last thing he wants."

"You think he'll give up, just because you don't cooperate?" I scorned.

"No, but he can't do much here in Sweendi. And all I want is to discuss his new ideas. Before I deliver you, I must make sure they'll treat you right."

I choked on the implied threat.

"*Before* you deliver me? You're going to let these mad rapists take me?" I yelled, standing up in one brisk move. "What kind of a man are you?"

I eyed the collection of bowls, resisting the temptation of breaking one on his head. Instead, I turned to look for the door. He caught my arm before I could take a step forward.

"Don't," he ordered, forcing me to sit down again. "Let me explain."

Yanking my arm free, I grabbed my glass and drained it. The night felt immediately warmer.

"All Free Territories want access to the new DNA that will be worked out with your genes," he started. "We know the Global Council has no intention of giving it to us, because all they want is our extinction, pure and simple. I personally wouldn't mind if all class-2 people died without lineage, but without their help, we wouldn't have been able to kidnap you in the first place. So Vogh and I made a deal."

"Vogh being the leader of class-2 territories?" I asked.

"No. He's a convict on the island of Gahra. The Globals use the territory as a garbage disposal for their worst criminals. In a few years, Vogh has managed to become their leader."

"Charming friends you have."

"Yes. Anyway, Gahra's convicts are all tagged electronically. They can't enter the G-Zone without leaving a trace on the surveillance computers."

"But Smit entered Sweendi, didn't he?"

"Not the same thing. Sweendi is an independent NGA that doesn't belong to the G-Zone. The Globals may monitor our borders, but not the whole territory. The only way they could have caught Smit was when he crossed Gahra's magnetized belt."

"And they didn't?"

"No. Months ago," Shoan explained, "Vogh created a diversion on Gahra's border. Some of his guys died in the magnetic field. To remove the bodies, the G-guards had to turn the power off for a few minutes. That's when Leeham and I entered the Global Zone. And presumably when Smit's crew left the island."

"I know what happened next. But how did you find me?"

"I hacked into Khiru's computer."

A new surge of anger went up my throat upon hearing my lover's name in Shoan's mouth.

"I didn't know it was so easy," I said, controlling myself better this time.

"It isn't. I just did it. It was interesting to see how having you was not enough for him. How he still needed to attend Rhysh clubs."

There was definite sarcasm in his voice. But instead of retaliating, I found myself speechless. Only the truth hurts, and Shoan's pique had hit deeply. In a few words, he had carelessly confirmed my suspicions: I couldn't satisfy Khiru, probably never would, and he would continue to play with other women. Between his needs and my jealousy, our relationship suddenly appeared very fragile. Shaken, I would have liked to retreat to my room and stay alone, but the situation wasn't propitious to grieving. Drawing strength from my determination to escape, I forced myself to listen to Shoan's explanations with desperate interest.

"My job became very easy once Leeham, who was spying on you, told me you'd finally broken the rule and left the house without a proper escort. I only had to bait you with a false rendezvous, and you were mine."

I stared blindly at his victorious smile. Modesty was not in the man's vocabulary. He hadn't even noticed how withdrawn I'd become.

"Then you re-entered Sweendi with me in a box," I said as a matter of fact.

"Yes, accessing a class-1 territory is authorized, though by no means recommended, under Global law. Freemen don't admit many people and keep official records of all visitors, but here they conveniently forgot to scan our pins."

I nodded. While Shoan went on, I moved closer to the fountain. I plunged both hands in the basin and splashed my face. The coolness of the water revived me. Whether Khiru needed me or not, I wasn't going to sacrifice myself to a bunch of terrorists.

"So now that I'm yours," I said with recovered spite, "why does Vogh want me away from you?"

"He thinks you'll be safer in Gahra, but I disagree. The Globals won't look for you in peaceful Sweendi, where they have no reason to fear any rebellion or crime."

He took another mouthful and munched heartily. I looked down at my bowl, half-filled, and decided I couldn't swallow another chunk.

"Vogh won't let you keep me," I contended "You said he had new ideas. What did you mean?"

He dropped his spoon in his empty dish and looked at me.

"My best guess is that he wants to do some sampling on his own. Perhaps he found a way to build a lab and wants to experiment."

He was thinking out loud.

"But if that's the reason, I'm surprised he never mentioned it. Anyway, I want to accompany you there, with my most trusted Sweendi friends. Then I'm sure we can all come to an agreement."

The topic appeared to be closed, and Shoan asked me if I was still hungry. I ate a juicy red fruit, but declined to help him finish the wine.

He drank his glass and piled all the dishes on the tray. His face was at peace, but his hands showed signs of nervousness. Avoiding his piercing eyes or his full lips, I stared at his aquiline nose.

"You're not originally from Sweendi, are you?" I asked.

He rearranged one bowl, then looked up.

"No, I'm not."

"So why did you leave the G-Zone?" I attempted, knowing he could have come from another Free Territory, but betting my life he didn't.

"Some people don't like to live by the rules, and I'm one of them."

His answer was not entirely unfounded. I had made a similar comment, a long time ago, when I was on the *Noncha*, learning about Khyra and its peculiar customs. Myhre had explained how official regulations and counseling carefully organized their lives, from the school they would attend to the house they would live in and the job for which they would be best suited. She had contended it was in the interest of all, but I had argued that not everyone enjoyed following the herd, even when the destination was green and flourishing. I understood why a man like Shoan would run away from common standards to live under his own command.

Nonetheless, a man like him needed a better reason to choose to live like a hermit, without family, without a career, without a woman.

CHAPTER 10

▼

"Do you think I could take a quick shower before going to bed?" I asked on our way back to my cell.

Shoan's answer would determine whether I would run away tonight or never. The time and conditions were ideal. I was free of any restraint, spurred by contained anger, and desperate enough to try anything. I had no faith in Shoan's ability to defeat Vogh and his goons. Even if Gahra's leader allowed him to accompany me to his crime-infested den, Shoan was naïve to think that his presence would guarantee my safety.

I had also given up my hope of seeing Khiru burst into my prison with one hundred armed guards. With two dozen NGAs to search and scan, it could take months for the Globals to find me in these remote mountains, in a region where peace prevailed. Besides, I wasn't sure I wanted to return to Mhôakarta, where another cage awaited me, attended by a jailor who was losing interest in me.

I was weary of Khyrian maneuvers to control my life, whether for good or bad. I could take care of myself. If I managed to escape, I would find another class-1 territory and see how its independent spirit suited me.

There were numerous obstacles to overcome before achieving freedom, but as I stopped by the bathroom door, I dismissed them. One step at a time, as any counselor would advise. And the first step was to get rid of one man, which was precisely my intention.

"Go ahead," Shoan answered as he pushed the door open. "But make it fast. I'll be waiting here."

Once inside, I stripped and carefully placed my dress over a rack on top of a towel. Then I stepped inside the cubicle where I checked how far the showerhead extended. Satisfied I could take it an arm-length out of the booth, I turned on the water jet and let it run at my feet, careful not to get too wet. This time, I was relieved to be in an old-fashioned bathroom. In the G-Zone, all showers were electronically processed. Thanks to a finger-touch screen inside the cubicle, you could practically draw the outline of the streams coming out of the shower walls. Higher, colder, softer, one jet or ten, from one side or three, all the parameters were computer-activated. There was no hose to play with, no showerhead to manipulate.

Thank Plya, not today.

With one hand holding the showerhead down, the other on the temperature switch, I stamped on the floor, bumped the wall hard with my ass, and yelled. The sounds echoed loudly in the tiled room.

The door immediately opened, and Shoan slid the shower panel sideway.

"What the...argh!"

The gush of boiling water hit his face, and he stumbled back with his hands covering his eyes. Jumping out of the booth, I slugged his right temple with the showerhead and watched him fall. I dropped my still-spurting weapon, grabbed my dress and the towel from the rack, and ran out of the bathroom where hot water cascaded in all directions.

With my brain clearly focused on the series of actions I had mentally rehearsed ten times, I sprinted past my room to the tiny window at the end of the corridor. I protected my elbow with the towel and cracked the glass with a violent push. I gave two more furious thrusts, and the whole pane shattered. I cleared the frame of most shards, but kept one in my hand. With its sharp edge, I cut the fleshy tip of my thumb and wiped the blood on my dress. Then I ripped off the stained section and threw it out the window.

After a quick glance outside, I walked back to my cell and, using my dress as a pillow, hid under the bed. There I tried to stop my frenetic panting while I listened to the chaotic sounds in the house.

Barely one minute had elapsed since I'd left Shoan lying in the bathroom, but all the noise must have alerted whoever was guarding the house. Someone was unlocking the door coming from the front. While it opened, a drenched Shoan, his hair sticking to his cheeks, came running past my bedroom.

"The window," he shouted, "she slipped through the window."

The man who had just walked in cursed in his language, then dashed back into the living room. I heard him yell to other guards and imagined them launching an extensive search around the house. Meanwhile, Shoan was still in the corridor. He had picked up the towel I had dropped underneath the broken window, and, oblivious to the general turmoil, was placidly wiping himself in the doorframe of my cell.

Sweat glistened on my forehead. If he didn't buy my trick, he would immediately know where to find me, and the game was over.

When he bent down to dry his legs, I was ready to concede defeat. Two minutes later, he was following his friends outside, and I let the air out of my lungs.

There was no time to waste. I crawled out from under the bed, then put on the dress and peeked out of the room. As I hoped, the door to the living room was still open, and nobody guarded it. I walked through.

With sounds of the search party resonating in the distance, I tiptoed in the dark and found my way to the stairs leading to the first floor. I hesitated before climbing the steps. I hated staying in the house longer than necessary, but with a whole village looking for me outside, this remained the safest place for the next hour. They wouldn't think of searching the house until they knew for sure I wasn't hiding in a tree or a cave.

The door was unlocked and opened onto the master's bedroom, bathed in the moonlight coming through a window on the left side. While the panel shut behind me, I soundlessly stepped forward into the private chamber.

Like the rest of the house, it was sparsely furnished, with a single bed in the left corner, a cabinet, a desk and a chair, all in the same dark wood I had noticed in the living room. On the right, a door opened onto a bathroom similar to the one downstairs.

More interesting was the equipment on the desk and the wall behind it. I recognized the black cube in the middle of the table as a 3-D computer generator. It was probably networked with the mediaframe that presently displayed a desert of maroon rock dunes.

I sat at the desk and studied the mysterious cube. Khiru had one at his office in the space center, but at home, where he only needed to access the Data, news networks and his mail, he preferred to use a touch-screen mediaframe. I wagered that Shoan required such sophisticated equipment to hack into the Global network. Accessing his files might prove very useful.

I worked one dial after the other and finally generated a hologramic page in front of me. It looked like a compact white cloud, the size of a monitor. Its edges were blurred, but most of its mass was clearly defined. I touched the cloud and created a maelstrom of panicked pixels around my finger. Then the image stabilized.

I had used a 3-D computer more than a year before, with the engineers aboard the *Noncha*. They had let me fumble with their pages of graphics, laughing at my pathetic attempts to finger-drop the representation of our spacecraft onto the right trajectory. That first lesson hardly helped now; I couldn't get past the start page. There had to be a menu somewhere, but I couldn't summon it. I tried to touch, talk, and even blow. All I managed was to provoke more hologramic storms, with my highest achievement being to turn the cloud a bright red. Afraid it would self-combust, I pressed the on/off dial and watched the image disappear instantly with a pop.

Next, I tried to activate the mediaframe, a device with which I was more familiar. I closed the desert view, and another photograph filled the screen. A petite brown-haired woman surrounded by three tall men smiled at the camera. She had Shoan's high brow and straight nose, and her cheerful face shone like his when he laughed. She must have been his mother posing next to her lifepartners.

The family picture reminded me of Khiru's parents. I had met them twice, the first time two days after our return from Earth. Having recently retired, they lived in farmland on the edge of the Nantu state, a two-hour flight from Mhôakarta. Their standalone house stood amidst the fields, but a nearby Lev-line stop connected them to the closest city.

Moirinha, Khiru's mother, had been delighted to meet me. Like any female who was protective of her child, she had worried that Khiru would never love a woman again, and told me how much happier he looked now. Unlike her son, she was cheerful and talkative. Khiru had inherited his mother's dark hair and penetrating eyes, but his introverted temperament took more after his genetic father, Argel, who was Moirinha's second lifepartner.

Before landing on the roof of the white, U-shaped house, Khiru had reminded me that, like a majority of Khyrians, he had more than one father. In his case, two: Moirinha had met Argel six years after committing to her first lifepartner, Lahri. The three of them had lived together for two years when they decided to try to conceive a child.

On Khyra, where only one couple out of two is able to procreate, conception is a highly advanced technological act. The nine-month procedure starts with in-vitro fertilization and, when successful, continues with the placement of the egg inside an artificial uterus where it will develop until birth. At first, I was horrified to learn that babies were born in sophisticated aquariums, but my first visit to a fetus ward left me filled with emotions.

Each tank was placed in a small, dimly lit room. Doctors have access to the fetus on one side while parents and other visitors may see the soon-to-be-born baby on the other side. In addition to the couches and table standard to every unit, parents are welcome to decorate the room to their liking. And they may spend as much time as want near their little one, watching him or her grow, talking, singing nursery rhymes, getting to know each other.

Thanks to the elaborate care the fetus receives throughout the extra-corpus pregnancy, the success ratio is extremely high. And birth is the easiest part of the process, with the mother cutting the umbilical cord connecting the child to a homegrown placenta.

Moirinha and Lahri had failed to conceive. So Argel took over and delivered his sperm. They tried twice and succeeded the second time. When Khiru was born, both Argel and Lahri acted as his fathers. This complicated pregnancy story, alien to my ears, was very common on Khyra. Having more than one partner increased the odds to have a child, and, ultimately, preserve the Khyrian race.

For lunch, Moirinha had cooked her son's favorite recipe, gonsha, a viscous affair on a bed of blue leaves which Khiru had once forced me to eat. Trying hard to make a good impression, I munched and swallowed without complaint under Khiru's amused stare. After listening to our lively account of the mission to Earth, Khiru's mother suggested to go for a walk in the surrounding meadows and woods. She placed a special emphasis on "walk" and winked at Khiru, who nodded his agreement.

"Then, we're going to get ready," she said before gesturing at Argel and Lahri to get up and follow her. "Khiru, meet us in the patio in twenty minutes."

"What's all the mystery about?" I asked Khiru when they were gone.

"Oh, they're just looking for excitement. Playing a bit, you know."

And because I still didn't understand, he added: "Mom's a Northie, and her favorite fetish is argali dress-up. This is why they live in the middle of nowhere. She says it feels more authentic here than in a city."

Authentic made sense when I stepped onto the lilk-covered black coach and sat on the padded seat, next to Moirinha. She had swapped her comfortable summer dress for a tight corset exposing her firm breasts, and thigh-high boots. Her garments were cut in the softest red lilk and made her look twenty years younger. Dressed in a casual blue mini-dress, I was humbled and in awe of her glamorous elegance.

Aware of my mute admiration, she smiled and patted my knee. Then she pulled on the leather reins in her hands and yelled the order to move forward.

The wheels screeched in the gravel, and the coach ran slowly out of the patio and onto a path separating a pasture from a wood. Khiru walked by our side. There wasn't enough room for three on the seat, and his additional weight would have compromised the success of our ride.

I felt guilty enough as it was.

In front of us, pulling the coach, Argel and Lahri panted as they tried to find a suitable gait. With each turn of the wheels, their shoulders muscles, enhanced by body harnesses, tensed violently, and their thighs swelled up. Long tails jutted out of their asses and swung from left to right like slow metronomes.

Moirinha grabbed a long whip on the side of the cart and snapped it twice over their heads.

"Come on, boys," she taunted, "don't be lazy."

Our human mounts grunted behind their gags, but combined their efforts to increase our speed. And soon, they were trotting gaily, their heads and tails upright, as if indulging in a healthy morning jog. Khiru had to take long strides to keep up with us.

"Do you often go on rides like this?" I asked.

"Not as often as we used to," Moirinha said, "but we try to do it once a week, if not twice. We're getting old, you know."

I knew, and the fact that they were Khiru's parents increased my discomfort. Mothers and fathers should be post-sexual, I thought. It was bad enough to imagine them having sex, but watching them engage in erotic games was beyond sanity. Yet, they were all so easygoing about it, I locked my Earth taboos in a corner of my mind and enjoyed the ride. At least, for once, I was on the dominant side of the scene.

"You've never tried a flogger?" Khiru asked his mother as she was whirling her whip above her partners to goad them up a small hill. "And hit them for real?"

"No, you know we're not really into pain. None of us." Moirinha then turned to me. "I was quite surprised when Khiru applied for Rhysh," she said. "We've always been light players in the family, and I don't know where he got that taste for extreme games. But he's definitely talented. We were all so proud when he graduated as a Rhysh Master."

I gave her the smile she expected, and refrained from voicing my concerns about Khiru's extreme talents.

We had completed a long tour of the rural neighborhood when Argel and Lohri showed signs of fatigue. The house had appeared in the distance, about two fields away, but I doubted they were going to make it.

Moirinha, however, knew how to stimulate them; since I was her special guest that day, she gave me the honor.

"Here, darling," she said as she handed me a small box with two sets of identical dials, "have fun. And let them have some, too."

She didn't need to explain what the box controlled; the men's reactions were explicit enough. They jolted, clenched their buttocks, shook their tails and groaned, but they found enough energy to lead us back home.

Khiru and I sipped sodas in the garden while Moirinha was rewarding her faithful braves in the bedroom. Then the three of them joined us for a late supper.

Before we prepared to leave, I asked Moirinha why she had called her son Khiru, which sounded so much like the name of the planet. I obviously wasn't the first person to ask, and she smiled knowingly as she repeated the answer she must have given so many times before.

"The day Khiru was born," she said, "the Council announced that a spaceship would be built for a mission to Earth. It was the dawn of a new age, where space travelers would become our ambassadors to another race. I decided that my child should represent our planet in the hypothetical event that he would meet Earthlings. Fate proved me right."

Back then, I had agreed wholeheartedly. Now, months later, I felt like crying at the recollection of those happy days. I was no longer sure fate had planned for Khiru and me to be together.

Focusing back on Shoan's mediaframe, I tried to guess who among the three men was his genetic father, but no resemblance was striking like his mother. It didn't matter anyway. I closed the picture and searched for more helpful files. The only titles I accessed were fingerprint-protected. I finally called back the desert photograph and turned away from the wall.

A long-suppressed yawn made me realize that more than an hour had passed. The room had become much darker, and still no sound came from outside.

I looked out the window, which opened above the small one I'd broken earlier. Thanks to Mhô's light, I saw, on my left, a gravel road that started close to the kitchen door and ran down along the slope of the mountain. A profusion of tall trees and bushes bordered it on the hillside. On the valley side, there was nothing but dark emptiness.

The wilderness called out to me, and I decided not to stay in the house one minute longer. Throwing caution to the wind, I charged down the stairs and out of the house, aiming for the trees between the road and the mountain.

CHAPTER 11

▼

"Caught."

His arms wrapped mine around my chest just as he whispered his victory in my ear. I had been zigzagging from one trunk to another when Shoan suddenly materialized behind me, as if he'd jumped from an overhead branch.

His breath warmed my head, and his chest heaved in my back. Further down, his sex poked through my dress. Deep inside, I responded with unwanted fervor.

"I was wondering when you'd come out," Shoan said. "I suppose you've been visiting my bedroom. Tried to access my computer. Any luck?"

I shook my head, mortified he had known where I was all along.

"See, I could have caught you up there, but it was more fun waiting for you here. Besides, I didn't want to expose myself to another trick of yours."

Glancing up and sideways, I noticed his face was abnormally red, but I was relieved to see I hadn't scorched him for life.

"Well," he continued as I averted my eyes from his, "I've sent all the guards and Maori home. It's just between you and me now. Time for your punishment."

His voice was strangely composed, seducing instead of chastising. Yet, it sent bolts of panic through my body. Especially when he yanked my hands behind my back and tied them with rope.

"Let's go. Back to the house."

As I hesitated, he pressed me forward with his knees. On shaky legs, I walked back the way I came, wondering what kind of punishment he had in mind.

Shoan led me straight to my cell. After stripping off my dress and untying the rope, he locked my wrists in the cuffs hanging from the ceiling. Then he turned my body so I would face the footboard of the bed, and spread my legs wide. He shackled each ankle and chained the restraints to the bed. After that, he left me hanging while he fetched more material in another room.

Feeling impending signs of nausea, I began to beg him to forgive me as soon as he returned to the room.

"Oh, I'll have none of that," he said, forcing a huge penis gag into my mouth. "Hmm, as the partner of a Rhysh Master, you're probably used to fancy devices. I will try to accommodate you, but you'll have to forgive the inadequacy of my supplies. In this part of the world, toys are hard to get, and mail delivery is a pain. We'll have to make do with the basics."

His humor only made me more nervous and spastic. I jerked around and groaned violently.

"I see," he went on with the same playful tone, "you like to resist. Does Khiru enjoy it? Does he hit harder? Do you come quicker?"

While he talked to me, his hands did all the heavy work. He wrapped a large leather belt around my waist and connected both sides to the footboard, restricting my swinging most effectively. Next, he blindfolded me with a mask covering half my head. And finally, he placed a wide collar around my neck, and chained its back to the hook in the ceiling.

Talk about "basics."

"I'm afraid I'm equally limited in terms of whipping implements. I only have the most common floggers and paddles. Oh, and a wonderful cane I built myself. Quite an accomplishment, you'll see."

Upon hearing the dreadful names of whips, my stomach contracted violently and…I peed.

My unexpected reaction silenced Shoan for an instant, then he recovered his wits.

"I suppose this is a good sign. Let's see if we can get you to leak from another hole, shall we?"

No. He couldn't do this to me. Not a whipping. He didn't know, he had to know, how could I let him know? But even if he heard me, why would he stop? He was just pretending to play. He was my jailor; I'd tried to escape, and he was punishing me. For real. My paranoia would only increase his satisfaction.

I hoped to faint quickly.

"One."

The paddle impacted my cheek with a loud thud, and heat spread across my bottom.

I exhaled violently and hadn't caught my breath when Shoan counted "two." My whole body tensed, unwilling to take any blow, and my jaw clenched around the gag. I remained prostrated and rigid during the next thirty hits, trying to escape mentally, to manage the fear, which was ten times worse than the pain. But my throat had begun to choke, and shivers spread through my spine.

The paddle was moving up and down my thighs, with an obvious preference for my bottom. Each blow hurt more than the previous one.

At "fifty," I started crying. I didn't want to go through all this again. The pain, the suffocation, the fainting.

The next blows were less stringent, more like teasing than torment, but they never stopped. Through my tears, they continued, with mathematical regularity and precision.

Before I knew it, I was becoming obsessed with their rhythm, the way the "thuds" chanted in my mind. "Sixty-four, sixty-five, sixty-six." I momentarily forgot the pain, which had eased considerably, and counted the strokes, expecting the next one, receiving it just when it was due.

"Eighty-one, eighty-two, eighty-three, eighty-four."

It was like the rolling of drums, mesmerizing and stimulating. Still sniffling feebly, I barely realized my ass was pushing upward in expectation.

Suddenly, without a transition, the sensations changed. The "thuds" became "thwacks." The stings were more focused, yet spread onto a larger area. A flogger had replaced the paddle.

Pain increased. I breathed deeply, as if enjoying a voluptuous massage, and the ache transformed into pleasure. My sex opened, my thighs quivered.

The next whiplash wasn't hard enough. I growled like a frustrated lover, and the flogger responded vigorously. I rode the next wave like an Amazon astride a fierce stallion, with pride and passion.

The rhythm increased. I no longer listened to the numbers, which were way past a hundred, but my muscles followed the whistling tune of the whip. I became frantic. I pulled on the wristcuffs, not to escape, but to find some outlet for the growing tension inside.

And then I came. It was like lightning streaming through my body, or a hurricane blowing me off the ground. A fantastic groan echoed against the brick walls, reverberating all around me. The bed creaked and moved forward. The ceiling came down, and Khyra stopped spinning.

I woke up on the bed, naked, with the usual shackle connecting my ankle to the footboard. All the other accessories and restraints had disappeared, even the cuffs hanging from the ceiling. Which was still firmly in place. I felt pretty confident the planet continued to spin, too.

I smiled as a profound sense of peace spread through me. Then I turned around to look at my bottom. It was nicely pink, with a few red lines crossing the cheeks, but it didn't bleed nor hurt. When I touched it, it felt oily, and it had a pungent perfume smell.

Had Shoan massaged it?

A stab of remorse hit me. It was bad enough to be attracted to another man, but achieving an orgasm under his whipping was probably the worst outrage I could inflict on Khiru. A harsh blow to his self-esteem. Then again, my other half reasoned, Khiru was whipping other girls, and he found it normal, even sane. Perhaps it was only fair. An eye for an eye, and all that.

Except I didn't want to take revenge on Khiru. Despite my fears for the future, despite his unintentional cheating and my inappropriate mistrust, I still loved him, and my feelings for Shoan were terribly confusing.

I stretched on the bed, closed my eyes and inhaled deeply. The whipping had summoned my submissive nature out of its closet and temporarily wiped out my will to escape or live on my own. It was easy to justify resignation with the fact that any new attempt to leave the house was likely to be nipped in the bud, but deep inside, I couldn't deny I was sorely tempted to have another taste of the whip.

Maori interrupted my reverie to bring me lunch. I had apparently missed breakfast. With a wave, I asked her to leave the tray on the bed. I pointed at my ass and grimaced. She nodded and left, careful to lock the door on her way out.

While I took my sweet and lazy time to eat, the door opened again, and Shoan walked in. His hair was pulled in a short ponytail, clearing his face and his bewitching smile.

"How are you doing?" he asked as he sat on the bed next to me.

I instantly warmed up, but remembered my guilt trip and made sure to treat him as the enemy he still was. Vigilantly, I kept my eyes focused on the meat.

"I'm fine."

"How's your bottom?"

"Okay."

He picked up a piece of vegetable that had fallen on the tray and ate it.

"I hadn't played with a Southie for years," he continued. "I'm glad I haven't lost the touch."

His confidence was irritating.

"You forget you weren't playing," I said.

"Megan, if I had wanted to punish you, I would have had you clean the whole house with a toothbrush," he laughed. "Or do you like that, too?"

I shrugged and took another bite, which I chewed forever.

"Anyway," Shoan said, "don't try to escape again. If you want another whipping session, that can be arranged without prior drama."

When he stood up, I asked whether he'd talked to Vogh yet. He replied that he'd sent a message, but because he needed several intermediaries and relay stations to communicate with the class-2 criminal, he hadn't received any answer so far.

I wasn't surprised.

"Can I trust you for the afternoon?" he asked with the obvious intention to cheer me up. "Would you like to go in the garden?"

I looked up. "Sure."

Walking around the bed, he unlocked the shackle with his finger. Then he wrapped leather cuffs around my wrists, and chained them together.

"For extra safety," he said, "you'll stay naked. Although I suppose there's no real deterrent for you to walk in public."

Reining back my growing irritation, I ate another spoonful, doing my best to stay dignified despite the way my hands got in the way of each other.

"Feel free to go when you're done eating," Shoan said as he got up.

"Free is a relative term," I hissed.

"Indeed, it is."

With his mouth twisted in a grin, he walked to the door and turned around.

"It was fun playing with you, you know."

I threw my pillow at him, and his laughter covered the sound of the bolts fitting into their sockets.

I expected to find Maori waiting for me in the garden, but she wasn't. Was Shoan really trusting me? No, the cuffs indicated he didn't. Unless he was still playing.

More confusion.

I leaned on the wooden fence, facing the trees, but staring up at the mountain peaks. The sky was olive green, with patches of whites. It was hot and damp, and soon my skin pearled with sweat.

Shoan was flirting with me, I resolved. I was playing hard to get, but I enjoyed the attention. Maybe this was what people on Earth called the Stockholm Syndrome. I was falling for my kidnapper because I needed affection in times of great despair. But Shoan was no regular criminal. He had worthy, noble goals, and he wasn't evil. He was also very handsome, good-humored, and could handle a whip like a true Master.

I couldn't fall down that hole. Even though Khiru had cheated on me, my heart belonged to him. Besides, things would be easier now. He wouldn't need to quench his needs on another girl. I would take his whippings. I would enjoy them, too.

I put my foot on the fence as if to climb over it. I was in a dangerous place, for more reasons than one, and my instincts urged me to leave.

I missed Khiru. I needed his quiet strength, his unfailing patience, his unconditional love.

My eyes began to prickle.

I was sobbing when I heard hurried footsteps behind me, and then Leeham's voice.

"Megan, are you okay?" he said, audibly concerned.

He put his arm around my shoulders and forced me to lean into his arms.

"Please don't cry. Tell me what's wrong."

My whole life's a mess, I thought to myself. For the first time in two Khyrian years, I missed Earth and the boring, not quite satisfying, but reassuring life I lived. Everything was so complicated here. I was always walking on eggshells, trying to understand new customs, doing my best to fit in. And at the same time, I never did because I was the alien, the precious DNA source, the lab rabbit and now the imprisoned hostage.

On Earth, I never met a man who could satisfy my needs, emotional and sexual. On Khyra, I'd already met two. It was too much.

"I'm fine," I sighed to Leeham. "It's just that I'd like to be home."

Whatever home meant.

"Oh, for a moment, I thought Shoan had really hurt you. He told me about last night. But you enjoyed it, right?"

The word was strong. I had found pleasure at the end of the whipping, but my recollection of the whole scene was not exactly enjoyable. Besides, it was time Leeham learned about Shoan's duality. The boy was full of admiration for his boss and tended to forget he was the accomplice of a criminal.

When I told him the truth in all its perplexing details, Leeham was aghast.

"You mean, he was truly torturing you?"

"At first, yes. Then something happened, and I enjoyed it against my will."

"But you're supposed to like it. You're what they call a Southie, aren't you?"

Poor boy. It was hard enough for me to understand how I could derive pleasure from something I didn't like, but under the conflicting circumstances, where I was a real captive but under the charm of my jailor, how could I explain what was right and wrong? What I liked and didn't like? I wasn't even sure I knew.

Still, because Leeham was young and required proper education, I tried.

"The bottom line," I summed up after a lengthy speech about dominance and submission, "is that when you're playing N/S games, they must be consensual. Obviously here, they aren't."

Leeham had absorbed my words religiously. As he drew his own conclusions, his face morphed into a horrible frown.

"When I spanked you the other day," he said, finally understanding, "you didn't like it, did you?"

"No, I didn't, but it wasn't painful, either."

"Oh, by Mhô, what have I done?" he whimpered, holding his head in his hands. "Megan, I'm so sorry. I had no idea. I thought you liked that kind of games. Kalhan said you did, and—"

Time stopped. Leeham's lips were still moving, but I couldn't hear his words. The air was suddenly oppressively hot, and my head was painfully heavy.

"How did you call him?"

My voice sounded possessed.

"What? Who did I call what?" Leeham seemed genuinely embarrassed. He stuttered, trying to change the subject.

"I said, what name did you use?" I insisted.

"By all Gods, I'm doing everything wrong today. I didn't mean to use his name. I shouldn't have. Please forget it."

I sneered. "Forget it? You must be joking. Tell me, he's Khiru's ex-friend, isn't he? *That* Kalhan?"

"I don't know any Khiru, but yes, his name is Kalhan. You were not supposed to know, and I'm not sure why he made such a big stink out of it." Leeham sighed. "You're an alien. Why would you care about his name, right?"

"Oh, it's all very clear to me, Leeham," I said while the boy was mumbling fearful conjectures such as "he's going to kill me" to himself.

And so everything made sense. The reason he had kidnapped me, why he was trying to seduce me, why he was a whipping expert. What a fucking liar he was!

"Lead me to him, Leeham. Now."

"I'm not sure—"

"I said now."

Not wishing to estrange me, Leeham led me out of the garden, past the coded door into the living room, then up the stairs to Shoan's, or rather Kalhan's, bedroom.

Not bothering to knock, I pushed the door open.

CHAPTER 12

▼

His face was hidden by a collection of 3-D pages. He instantly closed them and looked at me in disbelief.

"What are you doing here? Leeham?"

"Don't blame the boy," I said. "Leeham, leave us alone. You don't want to hear what's coming up."

Kalhan had stood up and was walking toward me. I waited until Leeham had closed the door, then yelled.

"What a pathetic, lying hypocrite you are! And don't you dare lay your hand on me, Kalhan."

The name stopped him in his move.

"So you know."

"Yes."

His self-control was a drastic contrast to my anger.

"Judging from your reaction, Khiru must have spoken poorly of me."

"And he was right, too. You're a traitor." I almost spat at him.

Casually, he dropped on the bed, with his back against the wall, one leg bent, a hand resting on his knee. With a straw between his teeth, the pose would have been perfect. He stared at me with daring nonchalance.

"And how have I been a traitor to you, Megan? I kidnapped you, and yes, I can see why this would upset you. But after that, I was always fair and treated you with respect. I even ruined my reputation for your safety."

"I should be grateful, I suppose."

"A little bit, yes. I could have let Smit take you and washed my hands of it."

"We both know why you didn't do that."

"Because I'm trying to protect you."

"Liar," I said, "You want to fuck me just to get back at Khiru. One girlfriend wasn't enough, was it?"

Kalhan banged his fist into the wall.

"By Mhô, I never abused Suri. She was drunk and kept propositioning me," he started quickly, as if compensating for the years he'd waited to give his version of the story. "She wanted me to top her. I refused, but she insisted. In the end, I took her home and gave her a light whipping. Then I sent her back to her house, and she was pissed because I wouldn't fuck her. The next thing I knew, Khiru charged me with rape."

His sudden rage pleased me. I had finally managed to upset him.

"Why didn't you testify then? You could have proved your innocence, couldn't you?"

"Maybe, maybe not. People had seen me bring Suri home. And she had bruises all over her body, bruises that had nothing to do with me, I assure you. And Khiru believed I'd done it. It would have been hard to contradict the accusation of a Rhysh Master."

"You are a Rhysh Master, too." I checked his wrists where all traces of a bracelet had disappeared behind a long scar. "The court would have listened to you."

"I suppose. But I panicked, okay? I didn't want to be put on a stand. I didn't want to confront him."

"You were best friends!"

"By accusing me, he betrayed me. I didn't want to have anything to do with him again."

I started pacing back and forth across the room.

"You were so proud, the two of you. And so stupid. Khiru was in love for the first time; he was jealous and possessive. You could understand that, couldn't you? And running away, you acted like you were guilty. What possessed you?"

"Could you stand still for a minute? You're making me dizzy."

I went to sit on the chair by his desk where I tried to calm down.

"Does he still think I did it?" Kalhan asked after a minute of thoughtful silence.

He looked more hurt than outraged, a reaction I didn't expect. I told him that Khiru never talked about the past, and I had learned their story from Naari.

Kalhan stared ahead, as if he saw something I couldn't see.

"Naari. He was a good friend. A brave man. Is he a friend of yours?"

"One of my best friends, yes. He's the first Khyrian who talked to me in the cave on Earth."

For a few seconds, we were both lost in our memories. Kalhan snapped out of it first.

"The chance meeting in the cave," he said with his usual irony. "What were you doing there anyway?"

"None of your business." The pathetic sex scene I had plotted in my old child-hood hide-out seemed like a million years away, which was not altogether wrong, considering the distance that now separated me from Earth.

"And don't you change the subject," I continued. "Whatever you did to Suri doesn't alter the fact that you're guilty as far as I'm concerned."

"I never tried to abuse you," he said strongly. "You know the whipping was as much for your benefit as mine. Your body was practically shaking with desire out there in the woods."

I blushed, but didn't give in. I was tired of men who thought they could read me like an open book.

"You're wrong about the whipping. It didn't work the way you think it did. You know an awful lot about me, but one fact obviously escaped your radar."

I told him about my scene with Lodel on the ship, an embarrassing event that the *Noncha* crew and Khyra's Council had kept secret. I told him about my sub-sequent paranoia toward pain.

Kalhan listened attentively, his face becoming darker and darker.

"I didn't know, and I apologize," he said when I was finished. "As Khiru's girl-friend, I figured you were used to much more. In fact, I was afraid I'd disappoint you by going too easy."

Then his features changed from remorse to suspicion.

"Now, wait. I'm no fool. You did enjoy the whipping, and you came. You couldn't have faked that one."

"No, I didn't fake it." I explained the feelings I'd gone through, first the fear, the panic, then a strange form of surrender, and finally, pleasure.

"I don't know why it worked, Kalhan. I'm still confused about it all. But in a strange way, I'm grateful for what you did. You broke an important barrier, and my life should be easier from now on."

He nodded absent-mindedly, not quite understanding what I implied.

"You realize you have to let me go, don't you?" I said. "You made your point. You got back at your ex-best friend, but now, that's it. I won't play a part in your hideous scheme anymore."

"For the last time, Megan," he said, pushing himself forward on the edge of the bed, "I didn't kidnap you because you were Khiru's girlfriend."

I sniggered.

"All right," he admitted, "that was the icing on the cake, but not the main reason."

He stood up and held his hand out.

"Come with me."

Curious, I took his hand. When he held my fingers tight, my temper gave way to an odd surrender.

He led me downstairs and outside the house.

"Kalhan, where are we going?" I asked, worried. "I'm naked."

"Too bad. Your dress is dirty."

He pulled me forward to the road leading down the mountain. The hot gravel dug into my bare feet, and I ran most of the way on tiptoe, cursing from the pain.

After fifty steps, we took a right turn through the trees, toward a tall wooden shack. Muffled animal grunting and stomping emanated from inside.

"What's in there?" I asked.

"An argali."

I had never stood close to an argali before. I had seen a few grazing in distant meadows and many on mediaframes and movies, but they were generally kept away from people and were banned in cities like Mhôakarta. Roughly, they were the Khyrian equivalent of horses. They could be ridden for long distances, pull heavy weight and, with ultimate care and patience, be taught to parade in front of an audience. They also had the shape of a horse, four hoofed legs and a long tail. Beyond that, they were nothing like horses.

Argalis were as tall and impressive as elephants. They had lustrous hides of a consistent sand color, and no manes. Compared to their massive bodies, their bare heads were small and elongated, giving them an eerie reptilian look. And their eyes, like those of a whale, radiated intelligence.

"You don't tame an argali," Khiru had once told me. "You create a partnership and you're grateful for whatever he's willing to do for you." Khiru was an argali rider, a skill he had learned, like so many others, at the Rhysh Academy, but he had never owned one (he would say "accommodate" one). They required too much attention and commitment. Once you left them to their own devices, they became wild again ("they broke the partnership") and refused to serve the person who'd been too careless with them. Argalis were not forgiving.

But if you treated them like four-legged equals, they were very loyal creatures.

Argali movies were extremely popular on Khyra; there was even an on-line network dedicated to them.

The shack where Kalhan was leading me appeared deceptively rugged. Inside, the walls were reinforced with solid dark wood, polished in every corner. It was a very fancy stable, partitioned in three rooms. The door opened onto a storage area with tools and riding equipment. At the back, a narrow hay-carpeted room was used for feeding and cleaning.

"So his proper chamber stays neat," Kalhan explained.

The argali's stall was next, occupying two thirds of the cabin. It opened onto a fenced backyard, but in the heat of the afternoon, the animal preferred to stay indoors.

I remained on the threshold, paralyzed with fear and respect.

Kalhan's argali was huge, at least twice my height. I could have walked under his belly without bending over. Much calmer than I was, the animal looked down on me with interest.

While I remained close to the passage leading to the cleaning room, Kalhan caressed the creature's neck affectionately.

"Hi there, Pagis. I know it's hot outside, but I need you for a ride. Hope it's okay?"

The argali bowed his head twice, prompting me to step further back, and Kalhan grabbed the leather bridle around his neck to lead him out of the stall.

"And by the way, this is Megan, a friend. Say hi, Megan."

I wasn't sure if he was joking, so I said "hi," just in case. I didn't want to be rude to a beast that could knock me down with a kick.

In the next chamber, Pagis stopped to drink water from a large trough. Kalhan and I waited until he was ready to continue to the front area. There, Kalhan climbed on a ladder to saddle him, and came back down to fix the straps around his body.

"Use the ladder to climb on him," Kalhan advised. "Don't worry, he won't move."

Easier said then done. The argali was so large, I had to let go off the ladder before I could straddle him. Pushing myself off, I dropped brutally, and the animal whined.

"Sorry, Pagis," I said, my heart beating.

Kalhan approved my appropriately polite behavior. Then he motioned the mount out of the stable. Pagis' pace was slow, yet my hands gripped the reins fiercely. I felt seasick.

Once we were out, Kalhan closed the wooden door behind us. I was wondering whether he was going to walk alongside us when he tapped Pagis' rump. The animal folded its left hind leg backward. Kalhan placed one foot on the shin and lifted himself up in the saddle behind me.

He took the reins in one hand, wrapped his other arm around my waist and clenched his legs.

Pagis strolled toward the road, adjusting to our double weight, although I doubted he noticed much difference. When the argali's hoofs touched the gravel, Kalhan yelled a sharp order, and the sudden acceleration pushed me back against his chest. I held my breath until Pagis reached a fast gallop, which he maintained without any sign of fatigue.

The fast breeze, whirling around my legs, cooled my naked body and teased my breasts. Between those fresh spots, a suffusion of warmth radiated from Kalhan's arm, starting with my waist and veering dangerously close to my crotch. Combined with the argali's movements, the heat made me weak, and my fingers found their way where they were most needed.

"Don't."

Kalhan grabbed my hands and locked them in his.

"I'll take care of that later," he added, generating a hidden spasm in my loins and a muted groan in my throat.

Around the next bend, the forest cleared up, and a few scattered houses appeared, announcing the village. Pagis slowed down and trotted along the middle road.

The Sweendi village redefined the word "anachronism." A hundred stone houses spread on both sides of the road, all a warm ochre color that absorbed the sunlight like the panels of an oven. They were two-story structures, with most of the roofs turned into lush gardens, green leaves and purple flowers escaping down the facades. There was no space for landing shuttles. A web of dirt paths extended across the village, with gravel used only on the main street. On our right, the houses formed four irregular terraces up the mountain; on our left, they were built on a gentle slope that led down to a river. There were a few isolated buildings higher up, red spots amidst the rocks and bushes.

At first sight, the village was as antique as any third-world stone community on Earth. On closer inspection, it enjoyed most of the modern technologies of the G-Zone.

Round windows were made of versatile glass, the kind that could turn transparent or opaque. The doors, cut from sensitive metal, slid open automatically when someone came near. Looking at the walls, I spotted a few transmitting devices that suggested mediapins and global communications.

It was the end of the afternoon, and there were few people outdoors. We passed two men who greeted Kalhan and stared at me in bedazzlement, and an older woman who frowned when she saw us and hurried up a path between two walls.

"I don't think they approve of my nudity," I said, uncomfortable.

"It's not how you look, it's who you are. You're a source of trouble."

"Like it's my fault?" I protested violently.

Kalhan directed the argali onto a path to our left, and we descended toward the river. Above us, a few villagers looked down from their roofs. I heard a child scream.

"I really wish I wasn't naked," I repeated.

Kalhan's only response was a tighter grip around my hands as we proceeded down the path. Just as I perceived the murmur of the nearby river, he asked Pagis to stop. He dismounted first, then helped me jump off the giant animal.

Grasping my upper arm, Kalhan led me into the house in front of us. We entered the main room, where natural light flooded the whole ceiling, as it would in most Global housings. One large window in the back was clear (I could see a silver line of rippling water beyond a backyard), but the other two in the front were opaque. I searched for a dial pad and found it behind me, by the door. In contrast to the electronics, the furniture was simple and rustic. A low table rested between a coach draped in a velvet fabric and a dark wood cabinet. A lively woven carpet covered the floor from wall to wall. It wasn't as remarkable as Kalhan's, but nonetheless of excellent quality.

On the side, an opening led into the kitchen, from which a slender, beautiful, but sad-looking woman stepped out. Like Leeham and Maori, she had a peculiarly flat nose, definitely a regional trait.

"How's he doing, Fylia?" Kalhan asked in Global language, undoubtedly for my benefit.

"Not well, Shoan," she replied with a sigh. "The implant didn't work. Why don't you go see him? You'll make his day."

"Can Megan come, too? I'd like her to meet him."

Fylia hesitated. "Perhaps your friend would prefer to wear something, then?"

I grinned at Kalhan, who had no choice but to give up.

Fylia retrieved a short, dark-blue dress; it was much too tight around my hips and breasts, but a big improvement over my previous condition. Casting a victorious look at Kalhan, I followed him up the squeaky wooden stairs.

In the faintly-lit bedroom lay a dark-haired boy, perhaps eight, no more than ten. He was pale and thin, but his face lit up when he saw Kalhan.

"Shoan!" he exclaimed before they hugged tight.

While they chatted in Sweendi, I remained on the threshold and observed the room. My attention was caught by an original, very non-Khyrian display. In an alcove carved inside the wall lay a clay bowl full of oil. Like a miniature sea, the liquid gently undulated and dissipated a strong, flowery fragrance through a white, almost invisible smoke. Behind the bowl, an elaborate drawing, reminding me of a treble clef, filled the wall.

Next to the alcove was a more familiar mediaframe with a family portrait. Three other frames hung in the room, one of them with a funny cartoon figure. A control panel was screwed to the wall by the bed, within the boy's reach.

Again, technology cohabitated with old-fashioned items such as the heavy cabinet, the coarse bed linen, and, of course, the archaic shrine. It was like a holiday cabin filled with the latest groovy equipment.

I took a step back to peek into the bathroom: a stone bathtub, a sink, a carpet on the floor. And a versatile glass window.

"Megan," Kalhan called out to me. "Come say hi to Mhowli."

The boy couldn't speak the only Khyrian language I knew, but his hug and vibrant expression were all the welcome I needed. With Kalhan acting as interpreter, the boy asked me about Earth, the space travel, and how I liked Khyra. His curiosity was insatiable, and he made me promise to come visit him again. When we left, he collapsed on his bed and appeared to fall asleep instantly.

"He's exhausted," Kalhan told Fylia on our way down. "I'm afraid it was too much for him."

"No, don't worry. You brought him joy, and he will talk about you for days. It's probably as effective as another implant!"

Outside Fylia's house, Kalhan took Pagis' reins in his hand, and we walked around the building, to the river. Fylia had let me keep the dress, but I was still barefoot, and my feet quickly turned an exotic shade of red on the dry dirt path.

When we reached the narrow waterway that rushed wildly through small trees and rocks, we found a large, flat stone for sitting while the argali dipped his head in the fresh water.

"Okay," I started, "why did you want me to see this boy? Because he's sick?"

"He's not only sick," Kalhan said. "He's dying."

"Oh." I suddenly wished I hadn't left him so quickly. "What does he have?"

"Bad cell division in his intestines. They've implanted new ones, but it didn't stop the lethal process."

Some sort of cancer, I figured. "Can't you cure it?"

"The Globals can. We can't."

"But surely, they will treat the boy if he goes there, won't they? Is it a question of money, I mean, quota? I have unlimited quota, I can—"

"No, it's not about quota. It's about losing the war, and paying the consequences."

"The Gene War was hundreds of years ago!"

"You think the effects of war don't last that long? Like the other Free Territories, Sweendi refused to submit to the Global Zone. Its population didn't want to lose its culture by merging with the masses. But its independence had a price: Sweendi's freemen were able to organize trade for consuming goods such as mediaframes in exchange for natural resources, but they lost access to the latest medical achievements, among other things."

"But aren't they allowed to go in the Global Zone to get treatment?"

"It would be too easy, wouldn't it?" Kalhan sneered. "The Globals hate freemen. They're a slap in their face. They want to assimilate them, or annihilate them, as the case may be. If freemen want medical treatment, they have to play by the rules and submit. Trust me, they won't."

"So they die."

"Everybody dies," he shrugged.

"Don't be ridiculous." I got up and started walking along the river. "Can't they develop their own techniques? Freemen have hospitals, don't they?"

"Yes, very good ones, too. But they don't have resources for research. Their labs are aging, and smuggling medical equipment from the G-Zone is practically impossible."

"You smuggled me in, though."

"Exactly. For you, we took risks, and a few men died. But that's because you're more useful than any cell divider. With you as a bargaining chip, we will obtain treatments as well as the new genome."

I threw a couple of stones in the river, then resumed my pacing.

"Aren't you overly optimistic? I'm not sure I'm worth all that much. They already have many samples to work on, you know."

"Not enough. Hardly enough. I've thought this through," Kalhan went on. "They can't afford losing you, and they will yield to our requests."

"Have you sent them a message yet?" I asked, still walking.

"No. That was going to be Vogh's job, but I'm afraid I might have to improvise if I don't hear from him. By the way, you're making me dizzy again. Sit down, will you?"

"No, you walk with me. I'm too nervous to sit."

Kalhan got up. "You're right. Besides, I promised you something."

He led Pagis to a tree where he tied the reins loosely to a branch. The argali was still able to drink from the river and walk around.

Returning to where I stood waiting, Kalhan grabbed my arm—this was becoming a habit—and led me back into the village.

"Will you stop pulling me like I'm a child?" I grunted, trying to follow his fast steps.

In reply, his fingers dug deeper into my skin, and my walk turned into a brisk trot.

CHAPTER 13

▼

"Kalhan, there's someone downstairs!" I whispered nervously.

I tried to lift myself off the bed, but Kalhan held down my hands above my head. He had already removed my dress, and his tongue and teeth were paying their respects to my nipples.

"Not to worry," he said between one bite left, one bite right. "No one will bother us."

"Are you sure we can be here?"

We had entered a (then empty) house, similar in size and equipment to Fylia's, and taken possession of a tiny bedroom on the first floor, or more precisely, its only piece of furniture, a single bed. Kalhan didn't even shut the door before assaulting my, I confess, very willing body.

"Megan," he said with mock exasperation, "you're the very reason why we invented gags. Too bad I didn't bring any toys with me.

"But come to think of it," he added as he removed his pants and straddled me, "I have what it takes."

While I sucked his long and hard erection, he lowered one hand to my breasts (his other clasping my wrists all the more forcefully). Despite his tweezing, flicking and rubbing, I resisted the urge to bite back at him. But it was all I could do to stop my legs from jerking around and bouncing on the sheet. A vicious pinch led to a violent kick from my knee to his back.

"By Mhô, you need serious training, Earth girl. I'll teach you to hit me."

And with that, he brought my hands to my sides and used his pants to tie them to my waist. Then he turned around, readjusted himself inside my mouth, and pushed my legs wide open, as if preparing me to give birth. When he dove headfirst between them, an electroshock almost knocked me down. Before I could breathe again, he was licking my sex with the gusto of a dog relishing a bone, searching for meat and exploring every detour until it was perfectly clean. In my case, the source of nutrients was unquenchable; the more Kalhan took, the more he received. And he was starving.

With his ass forcing my head down, his body weighing on mine, and his arms entwined around my legs, I was trapped inside an infernal machine that gathered speed and power with every passing minute. My temperature rose sharply, particularly in one spot, which now received Kalhan's special attention.

He sucked my clit as if drinking from a straw. In my bewitched brain, I saw the tiny bud grow, like a living snake emerging from my loins, a monster engorged on my desire and burning my flesh as it slithered out.

Kalhan, please stop, I begged silently, my tongue still pressing on his penis. I'm going to die.

While Kalhan's teeth teased the agonizing creature, his hands grabbed my feet and grazed my soles. I started sobbing from contained pressure and pain. Or pleasure. I couldn't tell the difference.

Kalhan let go of my clit to lick me clean once again, like a never-tiring Sisyphus. The snake would have loved to escape, retreat to its safe, dark den, but it was out in the open, vulnerable and helpless. Its flesh was barren, sensitive to air itself. Any touch would cause it to burst into flames.

Kalhan moved away, allowing me to swallow a mouthful of fresh air, but before I could regain the use of my legs, he shifted position, held them up, and thrust himself inside me.

His tanned face above mine was surprisingly fresh and clear. His dark eyes were victorious and cheerful. His mouth was smiling, almost happy. There was no mischief hidden in a grin, no challenge in a squint. Kalhan was as openly pleased as a teenager on his first successful date.

Quite unexpectedly, I felt my heart melt at the sight of this man who revealed his feelings without the usual excess of pride. Staring at his warm, wet lips, I parted mine in a sign of welcome.

I watched him hesitate, but when he bent down over me, he kissed my earlobe before tracing a line down my skin to my neck.

Kissing a mouth was a stronger statement than vaginal penetration for Khyrians. It implied emotional commitment. Obviously, Kalhan wasn't in that space.

Before I could mull over the issue, Kalhan sent his fingers to tickle my clitorian snake. The fiery prolongation of my body revved up in a hiss, furious to be awoken, but now claiming victory and repose. Unable to escape the torment of more brushing and chafing, it seemed to spit angry flames of fire backward inside me.

In retaliation, I tried to bite Kalhan's shoulder, but a nasty twist of my left nipple took my breath and spite away. I fell down, defeated, and at the same time triumphant. I came violently, thrashingly, passionately. Squeezed of his substance, Kalhan groaned as he blasted inside me. We both closed our eyes at the same time.

After a few minutes, his weight shifted from my torso to my left side, and his hand came to rest on the opposite breast. My head found natural shelter near his neck, and there, warm and safe, I fell asleep.

"Why does everyone call you Shoan?" I asked when I woke up.

Night had fallen. The pale moonlight, hardly perceptible through the opaque window, added faint shadows to the darkness. I could see the open door in front of the bed, a black mediaframe on one wall, the shape of an alcove on another, and Kalhan's long silhouette next to me.

He must have been awake for a while because he was gently playing with my nipple, which was already hard as stone. If my hands had been free, I would have stopped him.

"It means 'boss' in Sweendi," he explained. "Leeham nicknamed me as a joke, not realizing it would stick. I didn't try to stop the trend as it served my purpose well. Now only he and a few trusted friends know my real name."

"Don't you miss being Kalhan?"

He propped himself up on his elbow and peered through the dark to stare at my face.

"You mean, do I miss the Global Zone?"

I nodded.

"I miss my parents and some friends. I also miss playing with cute Southies."

He smiled, and I smiled back.

"Freemen don't believe in erotic games, do they?" I asked, remembering how the villagers had frowned upon my nudity or how confused Leeham was about sexual dominance.

"I can't speak for other territories, but here in Sweendi, they have a very different approach to sex. They disapprove of our casual attitude—another reason why they resist integration—and believe that orgasms are divine manifestations that should be respected as such."

I noted with interest that Kalhan increasingly referred to freemen as "they," as if his mind had already brought him back amongst the Globals.

"But divine or not," he continued, "their sexual adventures are every bit as daring as ours. You'll stay here long enough to witness an offering. I, for one, prefer a good whipping session."

"When you say 'divine,' do you mean they believe in a god?"

I thought the two moons, Mhô and Plya, were the only deities left on Khyra, relics of older superstitious times which amused people like zodiac signs on Earth. I had never considered that religions might have survived in Free Territories.

"Gods," Kalhan corrected. "They have plenty of them, for every chunk of gravel and every leaf on the trees. It's charming, but a bit goofy."

"They did a poor job of converting you!"

"Not for lack of trying, trust me. But Leeham's burning oil for me every night, so I'm in good shape," he laughed.

Following my own thread of thoughts, I reverted to Kalhan's life before his forced exile: "So you miss your good old S/N games. What else?"

"Not much, actually. Freedom, I suppose. Oh, and flying."

His eyes had lit up.

"Right, you're an engineer and a pilot, too, aren't you?"

As I hinted at Khiru, a black veil darkened his face. He just nodded in reply.

"They don't allow shuttles here?" I asked quickly to distract his mind from the unwanted subject.

"They have public shuttles and emergency vehicles. You will see the landing platform at the other end of the village. But individual transports are practically non-existent."

"You have your argali," I pointed out.

"Don't insult Pagis," he said, faking indignation. "He's a friend, not a means of transportation."

"I apologize for my blatant lack of respect," I continued, with excessive seriousness.

"And so you should. Especially when you're in such a helpless condition."

He moved his hand between my legs, which I promptly closed.

"Tsk, tsk. That's not appropriate behavior."

"Oh, you Rhysh Masters, you never take a break!" I laughed, not realizing quickly enough that I was again comparing him to Khiru.

"Megan, can you stop thinking of him for a minute?" Humor was now absent from his words. "I no longer have anything in common with him. I'm not even a Rhysh Master anymore."

He showed me the scar on his arm.

"Did you cut the bracelet yourself?" I asked.

"On my first day here. I was so mad, the blade slipped. But the blood felt good at the time. It was like purifying myself from my previous life. Anyway…"

The charm was gone. Kalhan untied his pants around my waist and arms, and put them on.

"I have to get going. We'll continue our talk later."

I stood up next to him and tried to find my own garment in the dark.

"Light on," I said out loud, spontaneously.

Kalhan pressed a dial near the bed. "No voice control here."

Light spurted across the ceiling, and I blinked. Suddenly standing naked next to Kalhan made me very self-conscious. I fished for the dress, a small blue bundle on the floor.

"Where are we going?" I asked, as I tried to conceal my breasts.

"You're not going anywhere. I'm going back home, and I'll see you tomorrow morning."

My hands froze around my waist for a second, holding the dress just above my pubis.

"What?"

Kalhan explained that his house was no longer a safe place for me. Thanks to my escape, Smit thought I was still roaming around the mountains, but he would probably keep an eye on the house in case one of the villagers found me and brought me back. It was better for me to stay in the village, where no stranger could venture without being spotted first and where the maze of narrow streets would offer enough protection.

"But one of his goons must have seen us ride in," I objected after pulling the dress down.

"No, I've had men surveying the area all day, and I knew the road was clear. But I can't keep those men off their works forever."

It went without saying that I wasn't supposed to leave the house without a proper escort. Even then, I was to wear a farda, a traditional full-body tunic that would hide my face as well as my curvaceous shape. Even under such accoutrement, I was advised to stay away from the main road. In fact, the less I was outside, the better.

"So I'm back in jail," I sighed.

"Fylia lives around the corner. Visit her and Mhowli as often as you like. They'll appreciate it. Also, Leeham will keep you company. He's utterly devastated by what he's done. Can't get over that spanking he gave you," he laughed. "From now on, he'll live to serve you."

An interesting choice of words, I thought, for a boy who was trying to play a Northie.

"By the way," I said, "you should improve your lessons in the art of dominance. Your pupil is not very good at it."

Kalhan grinned. "I know, he sucks. But, between you and me, I'm not surprised. He's a Southie and would be better off at the other end of the whip."

"How can you tell?" I asked, interested that he was so clear-cut about it.

"His whole attitude, his humbleness, the way he apologizes all the time. And the fact that he takes no pleasure whatsoever in dominating someone. He tried very hard with you, but I'm certain he hated every second of it."

I agreed. Leeham had seemed more comfortable once he was allowed to be kind to me.

"I suppose he did it to be more like you?" I suggested, knowing how devoted he was to Kalhan.

"Probably. Also, I did nothing to contradict him. In times of war, better to learn how to act bravely than how to submit. Besides, finding harmony with his sexual desires is a minor detail in poor Leeham's life."

It occurred to me that instead of using the boy as an accomplice, Kalhan would have been a better substitute dad if he'd sent Leeham to college. I told him so.

Kalhan shook his head. "He insisted on staying with me. He has his own reasons to get back at the Globals."

A man and a boy, both bitter and vengeful, misguided by anger. Their lives could use some improvement.

"Does he know I'm here?" I asked.

"It's his house. He lives here with his mother and, by now, they're probably waiting for you to join them for dinner. Let's go."

Downstairs, Leeham was indeed expecting us. Kalhan introduced me to the boy's mother, a heavyweight, middle-aged woman whose face expressed the burden of her whole life. She barely looked at me, but I saw her frown at the sight of my dirty red feet. After wishing me a shy welcome in her house, she turned to her pot on the table and started serving a hot stew on ceramic plates. When Kalhan stopped her from filling the fourth one, they argued in Sweendi until Leeham interfered in favor of his "boss."

When some quiet was restored, Kalhan bade us goodnight. I followed him to the door.

"Kalhan, please," I begged, "take me with you. I'll feel safer. How can you leave these people in charge of my protection?"

"They'll do better than you think. They know what you're worth. They may resent the whole procedure and the danger they run, but they know you're their last chance for survival. They'll take care of you. Don't worry."

"But—"

"That's it, Megan. I'll see you tomorrow. In the meantime, ask Leeham about his father. If I haven't convinced you yet, maybe he will."

And he walked off with long strides.

"You were wrong," I shouted at his back. "You're every last bit like Khiru, dominant and arrogant to the core!"

CHAPTER 14

▼

My new life in the Sweendi village, the name of which I would never learn to better guarantee its safety, fell into a dull routine. Leeham's taciturn mother was boring me to death, and I preferred spending time with Mhowli, Fylia and, when he wasn't working, her partner, Suok. I talked more about Earth than they did about Sweendi, but we found many subjects of common interest, including religion. They were thrilled to hear my stories of the antique Egyptian, Greek and Aztec gods and to find similarities with their own cult. They showed a particularly morbid interest in blood sacrifices.

"Our ancestors used to offer human lives to the Gods," Suok said. "But we know better now."

It was reassuring. In more ways than one, Sweendi's old-fashioned customs sent unpleasant reminders of Earth's most cruel traditions. Take the farda, for instance.

To reach Fylia's house, merely two minutes away from Leeham's, I had to wear the hideous local outfit. It was merely a long tube that opened around the feet, encasing me from head to toe. Thanks to a tight mesh of fabric in front of my eyes, I could see ahead of me. Leeham explained that it was used for punishment, when the offender, man or woman, had deprived the gods of their dues. After ten days, I hadn't see anyone wearing it and I concluded that the villagers were very respectful of their gods.

"People see me in the farda every day. They must think I'm a terrible sinner," I once complained to Fylia.

Laughing, she said that my disguise was only meant to fool foreigners. Most villagers knew about me, and even if they didn't, they would easily figure it out.

Leeham refused to give me additional explanations. Unlike erotic games in the Global Zone, this was a serious, religious matter. Nothing to laugh about. They were equally mysterious about the "offering," a weekly ceremony held in a compound on the west side of the river, where the whole village congregated until long past midnight. They had already celebrated it twice, but hadn't invited me to join the celebration. Leeham had stayed home with me both nights, although I could see he hated to miss the event.

Kalhan had temporarily disappeared. Breaking his promise, he hadn't visited me the day after our argali ride. According to Leeham, he was trying to keep Vogh away by pretending to search for me further and further from the village. It was thoughtful of him, but I missed his company. He had completely moved me to his cause now, especially after I heard the story of Leeham's father.

The man, Leeham told me one evening, fell seriously ill in the prime of his adult years. He had received the best treatments in Sweendi hospitals, had even traveled to other Free Territories, but the viral infection was spreading. When Kalhan found refuge in the village, he heard about the young man dying and checked on him. As it was, he knew about the virus; one of his relatives had caught it in the past. He also knew there was a cure available in Mhôakarta and most Global cities.

Hacking on a communication platform with a false identity, Kalhan searched for practical information. For weeks, he tried to obtain either the drugs or the visit of a doctor, but there was no exception to the ban of medical treatment in NGAs, even when a twelve-year-old boy was about to lose his father to a perfectly curable disease. Kalhan fought to obtain the right for the man to be brought to a Global hospital, but the condition was the full integration of Sweendi in the G-Zone. A few villagers considered it, but Leeham's father refused.

"I will not let our culture be assimilated by these godless sinners," he said two days before dying.

The village mourned for a month. Leeham's mother became withdrawn, and the boy turned to Kalhan for comfort. Leeham called him "boss," but what he needed was a new father.

From my alien perspective, the dispute between the Global Zone and the peaceful Free Territories was based on sterile principles on both sides, principles that became absurd when they cost innocent lives. I decided to help Kalhan and lobby the Council to bring a solution to this nonsense.

I had no doubt, back then, that my kidnapping adventure was coming to a close. Kalhan had convinced me of his righteousness. While I still disapproved of his initial decision to be a part of Vogh's criminal plot, I couldn't deny he had handled his part of the scheme well and safely. My escape hadn't been such a fail-ure since Smit had lost track of me and would soon report my disappearance to his leader. How Vogh would react was anyone's guess, but now that Kalhan and I were on the same side, nothing seemed too difficult for us. We would see this through.

In hindsight, my days as his captive hadn't been such a terrible price to pay for a better life for freemen. Together, we would obtain if not a political decision, at least practical aid like treatments and medical equipment in exchange for my release. (We would have to draw up a list of what was needed. Perhaps he had one ready?) Once the goods were delivered, I would return to Mhôakarta. And per-suade Kalhan to come with me.

I wasn't quite sure of my last objective, but I liked toying with the idea. I couldn't stand the thought of leaving Kalhan here, living as a recluse in his gloomy cabin, when he had so much to give in the Global Zone. But would he come? And should he? What could he expect if he abandoned the relative safety of Sweendi?

Kalhan missed freedom; he was unlikely to get it back if he returned to the Global Zone. Khyrian justice had little mercy for those who defied stability and peace. It took less than a criminal offense to get a sentence, as I had had the opportunity to observe.

Within the first weeks of my landing on the green planet, I was a significant witness to a trial in front of an N/S court, a legal body that passed judgments on incidents that occurred within a Northie/Southie relationship, and I saw a man I considered to be innocent condemned to two years of communal servicing. Lodel, my whipping partner on the *Noncha*, was charged with involuntary physi-cal damage and, more seriously, hazardous carelessness in preparing and enacting an N/S scene. I refused to press charges against him and convinced Khiru to stay out of it. As far as I was concerned, Lodel had been an object in my incapable hands. The way I saw it, I should have been put on trial for my lack of judgment leading to the public humiliation of a Northie.

But damaging a Southie was a serious offense on Khyra, where the whole sex-ual system relied on safety and trust. A breach in the equilibrium could lead to many abuses and errors. Southies had an obvious advantage from a legal stand-point. As a principle, they were always considered innocent because once a scene started and the Southie was helpless, the Northie was in charge and should act responsibly. As Khiru pointed out, what a Southie asked before a scene was irrel-evant.

The Court declared Lodel guilty with mitigating circumstances. Had he played with a Khyrian woman, he would have got away with six months of servicing. Because Lodel had made the mistake of indulging an Earthling—an inexperienced and clueless submissive who was, to make matters worse, the nation's most precious persona—he was sentenced to two years, perhaps as a warning to anyone who might think of abusing my naïveté.

Communal servicing was an ordinary sentence for such cases involving careless but well-meaning Northies. It didn't imply any imprisonment or, for that matter, any major change in a person's life. In fact, all an N/S convict had to do was to report to a designated unit every day, sometimes just in the afternoon, after work. A special committee selected the required labor according to the Northie's gender, age and skills, but also in keeping with the local calendar and social needs. Activities ranged from agricultural to manufacturing duties, as well as taking care of children or the elderly, or even helping with administrative work. It was varied and useful, an efficient way to deal with time-absorbing tasks in the interest of all.

For his first two months, Lodel was sent on all-day harvesting campaigns. I paid him a few visits to make sure he was all right and show him I cared. As it was, he had a good time. After four years on a spacecraft, he enjoyed the outdoor activity, and his service companions were good-humored chaps who loved to hear his colorful tales of the mission and, in particular, the sexy episodes that led to his punishment. Lodel's only complaint concerned the boring coveralls he had to wear at all times, a major contrast to the flamboyant costumes in which he often paraded.

I was satisfied that Lodel would make it through his sentence with humility and grace. While he had no shortage of the second, he could certainly use a crash course in the first. The Court had judged well.

But what would happen to Kalhan if he stood trial? Even if he proved his innocence in Suri's affair, despite her lies and Khiru's accusations, having run away would aggravate his circumstances. And now he had to respond to a real kidnapping and association with heavy criminals. I would speak in his favor, but the Court would undoubtedly sentence him severely. Communal servicing would hardly be enough. He faced partial or full jail detention. If blessed with partial detention, he would enjoy restricted freedom, but a location chip would be implanted in his neck to allow surveillance across the planet. And that was in case things went well.

The prospects of a trial were dreadful enough. There was no need for me to address another issue, more personal, equally challenging, with unfathomable consequences: could I love two men? On Khyra, it was more than an option; it was a recommendation. But two enemies?

As I was sounding out my heart, and occasionally my brain, on the side of the river, a hand touched my shoulder through the farda. I turned around to see Suok.

"Come back to the house, Megan," he said. "Two strangers have been spotted walking down the main road. You'll be safer inside."

I followed him, and spent the rest of the day with Fylia and Mhowli. The boy was a brave little soldier; he helped me forget my own concerns, almost irrelevant compared to his.

In the evening, I was confined to Leeham's house. One of the sentries Kalhan had hired to keep watch around his house came to stay with us. To kill time, we watched Sweendi's mediabox programs, but even the 3-D movies and shows couldn't distract me from my more dramatic reality. I became nervous, and lost my newfound optimism. If Smit's troops decided to attack, my guard would be feeble. I wished Kalhan would show up.

The next day was equally nerve-wracking, with Leeham going out for news while I was commanded to stay in the room upstairs. Men stayed with us in shifts, one downstairs, one in the street. They used their mediapins incessantly to communicate with scouts spread over the village and its surroundings. Sometimes news was good ("they're gone"), sometimes it wasn't ("we found footprints on the west bank").

I hardly ate and I slept poorly, even though Leeham insisted on spending the night on the carpet by the bed.

I woke up to the sound of several footsteps.

As I squinted through the feeble light of dawn, Leeham was leaving the room, grumbling and massaging his neck, while Kalhan walked toward me, smiling and removing his clothes.

"Morning, pretty girl," he said as he lifted the sheets to lie at my side.

"It's awfully early for a wake-up call," I yawned, concealing my joy.

"Nobody said you had to get up."

His cold hands stole the heat off my body, and I struggled to keep them away.

"Warm them up first."

"As you wish."

I choked when he inserted his fingers inside my unyielding sex. The tearing pain felt like losing another hymen.

"By Plya, you can't force me like this," I grunted.

"Actually, yes, I can, and I will. Because it's the way I like it. And this time, dear disobedient slave of mine, I have rope."

He withdrew his fingers, and produced a coil from the floor. In a succession of quick, expert moves, he tied my wrists together and secured them to the bed base underneath the mattress. Next, he spread my legs and connected each ankle to a post, then each knee and thigh to the sides of the bed. Finally, he looped various sections of rope above and under my breasts, and around my hips.

He gave my bondage a final, and undoubtedly useful, touch by condemning my mouth shut with four layers of sticky tape.

"Now, where were we?"

In the interlude, my sex had opened and dampened; Kalhan's fingers slipped inside with relative ease. I stretched within my bonds like a cat enjoying a caress.

"Time for number four," Kalhan announced ominously.

My vagina reluctantly gave way to his palm. All feelings of comfort had gone; I was on my guard, worried at the turn Kalhan's unexpected visit was taking. I wasn't ready for strenuous efforts without prior warning and warm-up.

Khiru would be more cautious, I reflected like a spoiled child, immediately regretting the untimely comparison.

Oblivious of my inner struggle, Kalhan was cajoling me, breaking down my defenses with every twist of his fingers. When he found my G-spot, he tested its reactions for long minutes. I was breathless when he paused.

A spontaneous sigh escaped my chest when his hand slipped out, but relief was never so deceiving.

"And five," Kalhan simply said.

It took him some coaxing and pushing, but he made it. His whole fist was inside me. My brain immediately sent signals of distress: danger! He could rip me apart, tear me to blood. A wave of panic turned my body rigid, afraid of the slightest move.

Kalhan noticed and kept still, his head bent over mine, his eyes beckoning me to give in and depend on him.

My face relaxed first. Drawing comfort from his quiet assurance, I loosened my muscles one by one, transforming myself into a compliant doll. Kalhan didn't flinch, but his fingers expressed his contentment. Their touch was gentle, hardly perceptible, as if they were plucking the fragile petals of a rare flower. They had very little room to maneuver; yet they probed around, always deeper, exciting every nerve they met on the way. I was taking slow breaths, pushing down pleasure, making it last, not burst. A time bomb was ticking inside my loins, and as its deadline drew nearer, my mind filled with gory, blood-stained images.

Could I really trust this man?

Suddenly my pelvis contracted to get rid of the invading hand, and I growled and jerked from the violent pain.

Under control, Kalhan placed his other hand on my belly, flat and unthreatening.

"Calm down," he whispered. "You can take it."

I shook my head, wincing under the gag. I couldn't stop the contractions, and with each one, Kalhan's fist resisted the squeeze, chafing my flesh, pressing against my uterus, my kidneys, whatever was down there that hurt so much.

"Megan!" he almost yelled. "Let go now."

I confronted his stare, not so much angry as resolute. One of us had to yield, and he didn't look like he would be the one.

My eyes got wet; his features became blurry, like a painting under rain. Then he kissed my cheeks, my forehead, my nose, even, very quickly, the tape covering my mouth. His lips moved down to my breasts and licked around my nipples. Then, they returned to my face and covered it with more gentle kisses before traveling down again.

Inside me, his hand was waiting for me to accept it. Eventually, when the tears dried out, I did.

His fingers took possession of me while his mouth continued its progression south, stopping at my navel before reaching its final goal. Teasing my clitoris on both ends, pressing and sucking, grazing and biting, Kalhan brought me to a pinnacle of desire and abandon. When I came, it was as much for him as for me, gratitude and reward merging into profound bliss.

"This is my first happy morning in days," I said after a long sleep-in.

Kalhan had dialed for the window to clear, and bright rays of sunlight hit our bodies in the middle of the bed. I was hungry and thirsty, but reveled in the pleasure of lying next to him. I was afraid to get up only to watch him leave me again.

"I know," he said, as he pulled me on top of him and caressed my back. "These days are stressful, but all this will be over soon, I promise."

"Smit has left?"

"I think he has. Their boat is gone, and the mountains are quiet. They must be searching further inland."

His fingers softly slid up and down in the crevice between my cheeks, then move up to my waist.

"I like that curve," he whispered as his hand rested between my rib bones and my hips. "I'm claiming this spot as mine."

I purred and kissed his chest.

"Still no news from Vogh?" I asked after a few minutes.

"No, although I'm sure he got my message and had time to reply. His position is clear. So is ours. From now on, we're going alone."

"Your ex-partner won't like it," I pointed out.

"I'm not concerned," Kalhan replied. "He can't provoke a major assault here without drawing unwanted attention. His only chance is to find and take you to Gahra. But I won't let that happen, trust me."

His arm tightened around me.

"Tomorrow," he continued, "I will fly to another class-1 territory. From there, I can contact the Council without leaving a trace that will send them directly here."

Kalhan had every confidence that the Globals would react promptly and positively. After a week, the secret of my disappearance had come out, and online networks were saturated with forums related to my captivity. Based on the light evidence they had, the Council forces rightly deducted that freemen had abducted me. Because of the recent incident at Gahra's border, they searched Vogh's realm extensively, then the other class-2 territories. They started more formal enquiries inside class-1 NGAs, but were at a loss for what to do next.

The Khyrian population increasingly blamed the Council for its inappropriate handling of the situation, and had started to use the case as a platform to question a number of Global policies that needed "serious readjustment." Those in favor of a non-discriminatory treatment of NGAs were gaining ground with their demands. Some said it was only a matter of time before class-1 territories were granted the same rights as the G-Zone.

And Kalhan hadn't even sent his claim yet.

I rolled off him and, propped on my arms, I studied his face.

"What will you do once you've obtained what you wanted?" I asked.

"I will order life-size statues of me to be placed in every capital of the territories."

He grinned like a mischievous child and, again, my heart missed a beat. I could see how he'd been Khiru's best friend for so long. They had a shared interest for adventure and science, superior intellects, evident physical charms, and unfailing dedication to S/N arts. Beyond their resemblance, they supplemented each other with opposing personality traits. Both men were equally dominant and demanding of others, but where Khiru used his tact and manners as convincing means, Kalhan preferred humor and derision. With his composed and thoughtful personality, Khiru could reign in Kalhan's boisterousness. Conversely,

Kalhan would push Khiru beyond his reasonable limits. As friends, they could probably achieve any goal to which they set their minds. As enemies, they would fight until the bitter end.

It was frightening to realize I had come to stand between them.

"Statues are a very noble aspiration, Kalhan," I mocked. "And beyond that?"

"Beyond that?" Pushing my shoulders, he forced me to roll on my back and held me still. "Keep away from judges and jails. Not to mention Vogh's predictable revenge."

That gave me the opening I needed.

"You'd be safer in the G-Zone than here."

"I don't care about being safe, Megan. I want to be free. You know as well as I do that freedom won't be an option for me if I set foot in the G-Zone."

"Not necessarily. I will speak on your behalf, explain how you rescued me."

"And how I kidnapped you," Kalhan sighed. "Don't overestimate your influence, Earth girl. The Council won't absolve a criminal for beautiful eyes or delicious nipples."

He slipped down the bed to find my breasts, and ended our discussion.

Sadness overcame me. I closed my eyes and enjoyed his licking as if it was the last time, as if I was never to see him again after this day.

CHAPTER 15

▼

Kalhan spent the whole day with me, mostly in bed, and left the village before sunset. He was nervous about staying too long near me, even though Smit's party hadn't been seen nor heard from in two days. Before his departure, we visited Fylia's family. There, Kalhan surprised me by asking Suok to take me to the offering ceremony the next night. Fylia's partner first refused, but Kalhan insisted. He argued that I would be safer with the whole community inside the sacred temple than alone with a man or two in the house. Of course, I would wear the farda.

"I've already left instructions for Leeham," Kalhan said to us all. Then to me, he added, "I want you to do exactly as he tells you. No argument, no fight, or you're not going. Is that clear?"

Dumbfounded but secretly excited, I nodded.

"I'll be curious to hear how you enjoyed it," he teased. "Or not."

Despite Kalhan's absence, the next day found me in a cheerful mood, and I almost counted the minutes until Leeham summoned me to my bedroom. The farda lay on the bed, next to an assemblage of resina and metal. I had no problem making out the shape of a chastity belt, although the term was probably not apt considering the two prods sticking out of the central strap.

I frowned.

"I see we're going to have fun."

"Kalhan said not to make any comment," Leeham quickly replied, like a lesson well learned.

I realized he was more nervous and worried than me. He was probably torn between his desire to follow in Kalhan's dominant footsteps and his fear of hurting me again. Poor boy, not quite the Rhysh Master yet. I decided to help him and lowered my head in the best mock submissive attitude I could come up with.

"Sorry. Do what you need to do."

Leeham straightened up and proceeded to undress me. I refrained from grunting or asking why. After all, I knew, and any question would unsettle him.

Once I was naked, the boy toiled with the complicated ornament, which he eventually locked tightly around my crotch, all systems functional and ready to go. He tested the dildos with a remote and, satisfied by my wobbling, covered my whole body with the farda.

"Now you're going to understand why you didn't look like a real sinner to the villagers. Your walk was too smooth. But it won't be today."

I shot him a startled look.

"Don't worry," he added reassuringly. "I will try to make you enjoy it."

I smiled leniently. "I'm sure you will, Leeham. And, by the way, a good Northie doesn't reveal his true intentions. What you want is to scare me."

That concerned look again.

"I'm sorry," he said.

"Don't apologize!" I laughed. "Come on, let's go. I don't want to miss the beginning. And no, Leeham, you don't help me down the stairs. You let me go first and enjoy my struggling with an evil grin on your face."

By the time we had walked, or in my case hopped, down the maze of streets and across the river, Leeham had gained assurance, and I had lost my breath. As we gathered in front of the massive double doors with the incoming crowd, I begged him to let me rest until we'd found our seats, and he did. This time, I didn't tease him about his lack of resilience.

From the outside, the ceremonial hall looked like a large ochre-colored warehouse, deprived of windows or ornaments. Inside, however, it was a stunning piece of work.

Splitting the difference between medieval catacombs and a fancy sports hall, the House of the Gods, as it was officially named, was organized around a central stage. From all four sides, rows of benches went up in terraces, the last row leaning against the wall. At regular intervals, heavy columns supported the ceiling, each of them linked to the next one by a delicately sculpted arch. White drawings and treble-clef symbols decorated the walls and columns, which, a long time ago, must have been red, but were now a dark, old brown. Impressive chandeliers hung all over the room, diffusing a dim, shaky light, brighter in the center, hardly perceptible on the sides. Inside each column, an alcove contained an earthenware bowl with burning scented oil.

The pungent fragrance made me feel dizzy, and I was grateful to sit, even on the cold stone of the coarse bench. Leeham had led us to the middle of one of the longer sides, three rows up. We had a perfect view on the stage, or "altar," as Leeham corrected.

On the right, filling most of the low platform, were fifteen wooden boards, set up in staggered rows and oriented in different directions. Tilted at a 45-degree angle and supported by a beam in their backs, they were wide enough to accommodate a person lying in a spreadeagle. Not that my guess was particularly smart: a series of opened straps hung from the board, forming the rough shape of an X. I could even spot foot supports at the bottom.

On the left of the altar stood a big table covered with a long, white cloth, and flanked by two trunks on each side. A bowl of sacred oil burned in the middle of the table, its frail smoke spiraling in the light produced by a wide chandelier. Behind the table was a high chair of stone, some sort of throne draped in purple and gold fabric. It had pride of place in the middle of a stupendous carpet, its rich and colorful embroidering reaching down the sides of the platform.

The House was practically full, but nonetheless quiet and respectful. Some people in the back whispered, but most sat in silent contemplation, perhaps praying, definitely meditating.

I had a hundred questions for Leeham, but the boy was staring at the boards, transfixed by the show they promised to offer. He had even forgotten about the remote.

Soon, I felt, more than I heard, the low tempo of drums, like the heavy steps of a giant coming closer. I followed everyone's stare to the left and distinguished shapes in the semi-darkness. Preceded by drummers banging on instruments bigger than their chests, a parade of important persons marched toward the altar.

Two by two, the musicians reached the platform and, after walking up three small steps, split into groups on each side of the stairs. Two celebrants followed, both dressed in flowing orange robes. They went to stand behind the table, leaving room for one more person between them. Four women were now climbing up the stairs before making their way on each side of the table, behind the trunks. Their hair was tied in high elaborate buns; their bodies adorned by strange bikinis made of golden metal.

The religious head of the village, the Grand Ordonant, followed the golden girls onto the altar. He was wearing an ample burgundy robe, lavishly threaded with gold motives. He went to stand between his two acolytes, his two hands resting on the table as if he was taking possession of its soul.

More drummers closed the procession and joined those who had arrived first. On cue, they stopped playing and sat down on the carpet around the celebrants.

The congregation waited in silence.

Then the Grand Ordonant spoke. His words were lost on me, but his magisterial tone and grand gestures were good indications of the essence of the speech.

"He's summoning the Gods," Leeham whispered in my ear. "Asking them to forgive our weaknesses and protect us."

Same story everywhere, I reflected, somewhat amused.

But what came next was not religious by any Earth standard.

The drums started again, and were echoed by a similar beat on the other side of the House. Turning around, I watched another procession reach the platform. A group of musicians gave way to four orange-clad assistants, then fifteen villagers. Completely naked. Five more assistants followed, and more drummers.

While the musicians sat around the stage, the assistants and the sexy priestesses directed each villager to a board.

The audience was not so calm anymore. There were murmurs and low exclamations as everyone recognized the victims and commented on the selection.

"Leeham," I said, making the most of the first opportunity to talk, "have these people done something wrong?"

"No," he replied, his tone slightly shocked. "They're the honored ones, those who will give the offering."

I dreaded to think of what the offering consisted of.

"Have you already been selected?" I asked quickly before silence returned.

"Of course, everyone is, in turn. It would be awful if we weren't."

"How—"

Leeham motioned for me to keep quiet. The woman in front of me had already turned around twice with an irritated look on her face.

On the altar, the preparations had progressed. All the villagers, the honored ones, were properly tied up. I counted eleven men for four women, the Khyrian genetic disorder knowing no border. They were of all ages between twenty and maybe sixty. Freemen looked older than the rest of the Khyrian population where you could still pass for a young adult at the age of fifty, young enough for people who easily lived to be 130. In Free Territories, where diseases and hard labor took their tolls, the lifespan was shorter, and old age kicked in earlier.

The Grand Ordonant gave another summons, at the end of which the audience chanted. Then he sat on his chair, his arms crossed on his lap, and nodded for the ceremony to continue.

The congregation exhaled one deep common sigh as the musicians resumed their drumming, and the acolytes went to work.

The golden girls opened the trunks and revealed a wealth of torture instruments, the scope of which I had never dreamed to see, even in Khiru's dungeon. I held my breath as I finally realized the import of the "offering." What had Kalhan said? "Their sexual adventures are every bit as daring as ours."

I was going to watch a live, erotic version of the Inquisition. I hoped it wouldn't end in flames.

Retrieving tools from the trunks, the celebrants went to work on the fifteen martyrs, provoking a sigh here, a groan there, and much fidgeting on the benches around the stage. At least the holy torture had a definite sexual overtone as it was mostly directed onto breasts and genital parts. I recognized penis cages, clamps and pins, and an outstanding variety of whips and floggers.

While the sacrificial villagers strived to maintain a noble attitude, belied by their grimaces and squirming, the Grand Ordonant appeared to have fallen asleep on his chair, oblivious to what I considered to be Khyra's carnal orgy of the year. But I remembered the ceremony was held every week, that's every five days. Perhaps the old man was entitled to be bored.

The congregation, on the other hand, was absorbed in the proceedings. The fact that each one of them had been, or would soon be, a victim lent an ultimate thrill to the show.

"Do you know when your turn will come again?" I breathed in Leeham's ear.

Keeping his eyes on the scene in front of him, he lifted three fingers.

At the time, I thought fifteen days must have seemed like an awfully short reprieve, but I was wrong. Leeham, like the rest of the village, was looking forward to being tied up on a sacred board. It was, I learned much later, the only moment when they were allowed to climax.

"An orgasm is a gift from the Gods," he would explain to me days later, at a time when he and I had nothing to do but talk. "It's only fair to keep them all and offer them as a sacrifice."

Trying to do the math to see how much time each villager had to wait for relief and finding it impossibly long, I asked, "what happens if you, well, have an accident?"

"The Gods will find a way to punish you."

"That's all?"

Leeham disapproved of my impious remark.

"And if anyone finds out," he added, "you must wear the farda, with full accessories, for a determined number of days. The chastisement is physical, moral and social."

Had I known, I would have watched the live ordeals with more detachment. The villagers on stage were the luckiest in the House, definitely honored. But this was hard to reconcile when you witnessed their physical exhaustion and growing sexual frustration.

In front of me, a fifty-year-old man had whip stripes all over his chest, and the tip of his penis, wrapped in a series of golden rings, had turned purple. His fists were sealed in tight balls; his toes gripped their wooden support, trying to find strength where there was none. With his eyes closed, he was whimpering weakly.

Next to him was a younger woman. Her breasts had disappeared under a colorful collection of pins. Kneeling in front of her, a celebrant was pushing a dildo inside her vagina, his arm making wide up-and-down movements. Tied to the end of the probe, a rope went under the board. It ended in a knot around the woman's hair, which had been raised and twisted in a tail pulled behind the wood. Each time the man shoved the vibrator in, her face expressed a perfect mix of pain and pleasure. If she hadn't been gagged, I'm sure her screams would have competed with her neighbors.

The noise had become unbearable. Or perhaps it was the heat. The tension. I wished Leeham would lose his trance and focus on the remote he'd now completely erased from his mind.

I was about to grab it from his hand when I perceived a change on my left. The Grand Ordonant had risen.

Once again he talked to the gods, the musicians drummed, the audience chanted—rather impatiently, I thought—and the head of ceremony raised his arms in a general embrace. We held our breaths. As the order was given, the celebrants inflicted a last torment on their respective victims: a twist of the wrist here, a good shove there, a last crucial pin here, a tightening there. The uproar that followed blew through the audience like the detonation of a bomb. For the first time, I wondered whether being on stage wasn't better than sitting around it. At least, the participants would leave the hall with a certain degree of satisfaction.

Which was hardly the case for Leeham and I, or as far as I could judge, most of the villagers. I figured they would all go have sex now—something I was seriously considering, too—but their ultimate reliefs would have to wait another week, or ten.

I tried to tease Leeham into a happier mood, to talk him into finding a young girl for the night, but he pretended not to hear me, and we made our way up the village in silence. He was still holding the remote.

The crowd around us had dispersed as everyone took different paths back to their homes. We found ourselves alone in a narrow street that led to Leeham's house. On the dirt, our footsteps were light, hardly more noticeable than the distant murmur of the river. There was a chilly breeze coming down from the mountains, and each breath felt cold in my chest.

Because there were few lamps in the streets, the darkness was almost complete, making the sky a glittering screen. Hundreds of stars, Earth's sun maybe amongst them, cast their tiny dots of light. In their center hung the moons, in their most humble appearance: two indistinct commas, one first crescent, one last, too pale to make a difference in the darkest of night. I was staring at them, trying to guess which one was Mhô, which Plya, when Leeham swore. A large shadow came between us, and I received a violent blow on the head.

It's not fair, I thought incongruously before blacking out, I've been kidnapped once, and lightning doesn't strike twice. Or maybe it does on Khyra. After all, the planet has two moons.

CHAPTER 16

▼

I woke up sick and frightened, with a terrible headache. The ground heaved up and down as if my balance was temporarily out of order. But my brain was not playing tricks on me. The salty taste in the air confirmed that I was on a boat, pitching somewhere at sea.

I opened my eyes and was immediately relieved to see Leeham sitting next to me, not in his best shape and mood either. We were hunched on the floor of a closed cabin, or a storage room if I could judge from the paraphernalia scattered around us: nets, ropes, life jackets (a good thing, that), drums full of an undetermined liquid. There was no porthole.

Leeham was curled up in a ball, his head bent forward, his eyes absent.

"Are you all right?" I whispered, my voice not as reassuring as I would have liked.

He barely nodded. I noticed an open wound on his right temple, and instinctively touched the bump on top of my head. My fingers didn't reveal any trace of blood.

"Does your head hurt?" I asked.

He shrugged. "Doesn't matter. I feel so terrible, I might as well be dead."

"Don't say that. I'm glad to have you around."

"If it wasn't for me, you'd still be safe in Sweendi. I failed you, I failed Kalhan, I failed the village. I ruined everything."

As he hid his head under his arms, I scrambled through the ropes and wrapped his hands in mine.

"Will you stop this?" I admonished gently. "If anyone should be blamed, it's Kalhan. He shouldn't have left you in charge. Or told us to attend the ceremony.

More importantly, he shouldn't have struck a deal with those bastards, let alone kidnapped me. He used you, Leeham, and you're too young and kind to feel guilty about any of this."

He raised his eyes, almost persuaded.

"Besides," I added, "now you can be my hero and help us escape."

Which wasn't the right thing to say as he slumped back down and sighed deeply.

"I'm useless," he said, "how can I fight an army of armed bandits?"

"Who said anything about fighting? You and I are smarter than the whole stinking lot of Gahra. We'll find a way, trust me."

I hoped I sounded more convinced than I felt. To be honest, things were looking bad. And the only heroes I was counting on were the men who disputed my heart. I had no doubt that Khiru was still looking for me, probably enraged by the Council's inefficiency as well as his own helplessness. The Globals had lost track of me, but they had increased surveillance over class-1 territories. Entering Gahra would hopefully leave a suspicious trace somewhere in the monitoring system, unless Vogh's scheme worked too well, in which case I was doomed.

But at least Kalhan knew where to find me. Not that I thought he would miss me enough to put his life at risk, but I was a treasure he couldn't afford to lose. Provided he wouldn't be killed in the meantime, a hypothesis I couldn't dismiss, he would retaliate and organize a rescue mission. But how long would it take?

There was little room for Leeham in all this, and I felt sorry for the boy. I cuddled close to him and sat in silence, trying to forget the upheaval in my stomach and the lingering headache. My feet, bare and frozen, diverted my thoughts for a minute or two. As did the punishment belt I still wore under the farda. It occurred to me that it protected me efficiently, if only temporarily.

"Leeham, do you have the key for this?" I asked, pointing in the direction of my navel.

He shook his head. "I left it home, I'm sorry."

"Not a problem." At least nobody could steal it from him. "What about the remote?"

He looked at his empty hand, as if he expected it to appear.

"I must have dropped it when they attacked," he reflected.

Even better. Rape was not going to be part of the cruise entertainment. I hadn't forgotten Smit's failed attempt when I was captive in Kalhan's house. The man was probably eager to take revenge.

The next hour proved me right.

The door opened a first time. The ugliest man I'd ever seen grinned at us. His bald skull and half his face were scorched and scarred as if he'd been dipped into boiling water. His mouth, deprived of lips, was contorted in a permanent scowl. His nose, pink like only new flesh can be, was reduced to one nostril. But his eyes were worse. The left one was a deformed bulge, like a patch of red clay sticking to his face. His right eye, intact, was loaded with hatred and contempt. When he looked at me, I backed off in fear.

"Water" was the only word I made out in the phrase he painfully pronounced. The jar and the basket of stale bread he left on the floor spoke better than he did.

I was still shaking when he closed the door and had lost what little appetite seasickness had left me. I sipped some water and gave my portion of bread to Lee-ham, who devoured it with the energy only the young have. The food somewhat restored his mood, and we began to chat about everything but our current predic-ament. By unspoken agreement, we had decided to ignore what we couldn't resolve.

Then the door opened a second time, and Smit came in. Even with his mass of untidy dark hair and his beard, he was a visual improvement over the scarred sailor, but his sudden appearance caused my heart to fibrillate. Through the tunic, I touched the reassuring metal of the dildo belt.

"Feeling safe, aren't you?" he mocked.

He grabbed my arm in a brutal grip and pulled me up.

"We'll see how long it takes to make you beg for me to hack it open."

Stumbling in the wake of his long, jerky strides, too scared to resist, scream or argue, I reached the deck where a strong gust almost knocked me down.

The boat, of shiny metal, had no sails, but two elongated "wings" protruded from its sides. Engines were throbbing underneath them, competing with the howling of the wind and the crashing of the waves against the keel. Khyra had never sounded so noisy to my ears.

Making his way between half a dozen dirty, smelly seamen, Smit dragged me toward the captain's cabin in the middle of the deck. Extending from the top of the cabin to the prow, a large metallic panel provided an unexpected ceiling. I leaned sideways to observe a similar extension in the second half of the boat. Both panels were shaped to cover the oval surface of the deck exactly. To hide it, I sur-mised. Hide it from radars. The "wings" were built with the same material, reflecting the sunlight and waves of all kinds, even the surveillance waves that could find and save me.

A rusted bar ran around the length of the cabin. Smit forced me to stand with my back to it, just under the main window, facing the prow.

Using coarse ropes that were a far cry from the smooth fibers advocated by careful Northies, Smit lashed my wrists to the bar and my ankles to thick rings on the floor. Then he produced a knife, and I thought my life was going to end in a very dramatic and painful way. I shut my eyes, as much to avoid the wind as the strike of death, and reopened them when a violent slash of air whipped my naked body.

Smit had sliced the farda open and was staring at my breasts. He wasn't the only one. The whole crew seemed to have formed a circle around us.

"Fuck you," I said, my strength returning when I realized I was going to live a while longer.

In retaliation, he pinched my nipples until I moaned.

"No, fuck *you*," he replied. "Let's see how this works."

In front of my eyes, Smit's hand held the remote-control. As he tested the dials, both dildos inside me stirred into action. I gave a little jump.

"You're lucky Vogh has ordered you not to be touched," Smit said, his face close to mine. "If he hadn't, you'd have my dick inside you instead. And probably a few others next."

The fact that Vogh had ensured my protection for the duration of the trip was comforting, and I allowed myself to breathe deeply once Smit had walked away, even when I saw him toss the remote to his scar-faced second.

At first, the sailors kept their distance. They watched in silence, their gaze moving from the remote to my ass. Some of them also studied my ears, which came in sight each time the wind blew into my hair. But mostly they gaped at my breasts, ready to eat them alive.

The vibrators buzzed at a low speed, barely distracting. I held a fierce stance, thinking I would impress them, perhaps even confuse them. After all, I was a quasi-sacred alien woman. It might be enough to keep the bastards off me.

Not for long. Those guys were too stupid to imagine the historical side of the moment and too evil to consider mercy for an innocent outsider.

"Lars, gimme the fucking box if you can't use it," one of them shouted.

At that moment, the anal dildo roared to life, forcing a wince out of my composed face. The crew approved loudly, and it was the beginning of a long ordeal.

Lars, the scarred man with the remote, learned to use his toy. With visible delight, which made him even ghostlier, he activated the vibrators individually or simultaneously, changing the settings as if playing a video game. Quick, slow, grinding, teasing.

Soon I began to pull hard on the ropes, which only served to tighten them around my wrists and ankles. I bent forward, hiding my nascent tears, trying to forget the sneering males around me.

One of them broke the circle, grabbed my shoulders and pulled me back up. He had vicious eyes, filthy hair and even the shadow of a beard; for a Khyrian, it meant he hadn't shaved for weeks. The touch of his slimy hands brought back nausea.

"The girl doesn't like you, Shorty!" someone yelled, while others were laughing.

"Must prefer her primitive Earthmen," said Shorty, who was two heads taller than me.

He held my chin up to force me to look at him.

"Not as primitive as you are," I retorted while the vaginal vibrator was chafing my G-spot relentlessly.

His answer was violently physical. He seized my breasts, taut from the cold and sexual tension, and squeezed them until he could practically close his fists. I screamed and banged my head into his chest. Abandoning one breast for my hair, he yanked me back and whipped my nipples with his hand.

When he walked away, not out of mercy but because his friends were claiming their right of play, I sank into a painful stupor. The next hours left an indistinctive gray fog in my mind. I hear shouts and laughters, I feel burns inside and wounds outside, I smell the sea and the filth of unwashed clothes. I also hear the consoling motto I constantly repeated to myself as a magic formula: "they can't rape me, they can't rape me." But I don't remember the vision of hell that was my day on the ship deck.

The next image I have is Leeham nursing me in the cabin. His face was stained with dry tears, and his hands were shaking as he cleaned my body with a piece of his own shirt soaked in water.

"Oh, Megan," he kept saying, "I'm so sorry."

Too stunned for words, I let him console me and even found sleep in his arms. I dreamed of Khiru and Kalhan. I was kissing one, and hugging the other. Khiru was taking my clothes off, and Kalhan was leading me toward the bed. The next minute, they were fighting and screaming. One of them slapped me when I tried to separate them. I was crying, but they wouldn't listen. In the chaos, the room began to quake. A cabinet fell down on Kalhan, and Khiru dragged me outside. I resisted, struggling to go back inside, but the house tumbled down, and I woke up.

The sea was rough, and the boat swayed precariously. The light in our cabin had been turned off, so I could only presume it was nighttime. Leeham was still holding me tight; on my back, his breathing was slow and regular.

Both of us spent the second navigation day inside the storage room. A sailor visited us twice to give us food, fresh water and a bucket for our needs. He also brought a worn-out but clean shirt for me. Each time the door opened, I shivered, and Leeham moved closer to me. Even when night and darkness returned, I remained in a state of anxiety, making a jump at the slightest noise in the corridor. When the third day dawned, and the same quiet man brought us breakfast, I began to relax. The pitching of the boat had weakened, and so had my nausea.

"Have you ever thought of emigrating to the Global Zone, Leeham?" I asked for the sake of conversation.

"I have, yes. I would like to see what scenemats look like. Is it true that people have sex all the time and everywhere?"

I laughed.

"No, you don't see orgies in the streets, if that's what you mean. There is a very healthy sexual atmosphere. Nobody's shy about it, but no one's forcing it on you either. If I managed to adjust, you will."

Leeham daydreamed for a moment, then lit up.

"You know where I'd *really* like to go?"

"Tell me."

"To the Rhysh Academy."

There was no need to wonder from where he got the idea. But I didn't think our sweet and humble Leeham was Rhysh material, unless he applied as a slave candidate.

"You think you have the strength and dedication it takes, Leeham? There's a lot of hard work behind the glamour, you know."

I shouldn't have been so demeaning. He'd perked up for a few minutes, and now he was sulking again. I should have let the boy dream while he could.

"Forget what I said." I patted his arm. "At your age, nothing is impossible. It's only a matter of motivation, which I'm sure you have. The important thing is to know what is good for you, what will make you happy. You're very different from Kalhan. Perhaps what worked for him wouldn't work for you."

Leeham redressed with his chest lightly stuck out.

"I feel very close to Kalhan. There's a connection between us that I don't have with anyone else, not even my mother."

That doesn't make you a Northie, I thought to myself. Maybe you look up to Kalhan because he is what you need, not what you want to be.

I tested him gently.

"Have you ever considered being at the receiving end? Like me?"

His eyes opened wide.

"You mean being whipped and all that? By Gods, no. It must be awful."

"Not if it's what you need."

"But the pain…I don't know how you can stand it, not to mention enjoy it. I become very uncomfortable when I see a whip."

From where I stood, that was a good sign.

"And do you enjoy using it on someone?"

"I've never tried, but it's something you learn, isn't it? One thing I know is that I don't want to be in pain."

"Being a Southie is not necessarily about pain." I gave him various examples of people I knew, described different scenes, explained the many aspects of submission. But I could see Leeham was afraid of the concept. He was adamant he was a Northie because he thought it was the only way for him to make it through a tough life.

I didn't have the heart to contradict him, at least not in this smelly boat taking us to more trouble.

"There you go," I said cheerfully. "As soon as we get out of Gahra, we'll see how we can make a Rhysh Master out of you."

He smiled, not quite sure whether I was mocking or encouraging him, but the light in his eyes indicated he was more hopeful than ever.

The topic of Rhysh had distracted us from our current situation. When Smit appeared in the doorframe, I was thoroughly shocked.

My legs almost gave way as he led me to his cabin, a sober, functional room at the front of the boat.

After pushing me inside, Smit locked the door behind him. Trapped between his elevated berth, a sink, and a chair in front of a desk, I couldn't take more than one step away from him.

"Remove the shirt," he ordered behind me.

When I failed to immediately obey, he insisted. "If you don't, I'll rip it apart like the other one, and you'll spend the rest of the journey naked."

That implied I would put the shirt back on at some point, and that somehow comforted me. With my back to him, I undressed, left the shirt on the bed, and stood still with my chastity belt daring Smit.

With an audible sigh, he pulled my hands behind me and tied them together with rope. Next, he gripped my waist and forced me to turn around.

"Kneel."

I knew what was coming, and received his dick in my mouth placidly, as if bored by his lack of imagination. It infuriated him. He yanked at my hair while ramming violently inside me, as deep as my throat would allow. But his outburst was short-lived, and he pushed me away as soon as he was done.

Physical relief didn't improve his mood. I thought he would unleash his anger unto me for the duration of the day, but instead, he called a sailor and ordered him to take me back to steerage.

"Give her the shirt once she's in the room," Smit commanded as he tossed the white garment to the man. He didn't look at me once.

With my hands still bound and my chest naked, I left the cabin, relieved to be done with Smit, but apprehensive to meet his boss. A man who, with a single order, could reduce Smit to that degree of frustration was an awe-inspiring character.

Leeham was overjoyed to see me return so quickly and apparently unharmed. He untied the rope as soon as the sailor left, and we tried to resume a normal conversation without dwelling on Smit's behavior longer than necessary.

However, we soon fell silent, neither of us quite capable of ignoring our fates. We cuddled to fight the chill in the room and the fear in our hearts, and let the day pass.

We were getting close to our destination.

If Smit maneuvered according to Vogh's plan, he would wait a safe distance from Gahra's maritime border until he received clearance. When the signal came, he would navigate toward land while, on the other side of the territory, a group of Gahra's men attempted to cross the surveillance field. Their diversion—and presumably their deaths—would allow us to sail past the border within the limited time during which the fatal field would be turned off.

For a long time, I waited for something to happen. A shock, an electric wave, a sudden backward maneuver, something to indicate they'd failed. When the engines stopped, and the boat stabilized, I knew they hadn't.

Welcome to Gahra, home of the most dangerous criminals on Khyra.

CHAPTER 17

▼

Vogh's dominion, Gahra, was a cold and windy island built on chalk cliffs, where pasture was rare and natural resources mainly consisted of wood and rocks. Most of its criminal inhabitants lived in precarious shacks assembled in two settlements down the only valley the island offered: two filth-infested towns where thefts and crimes were commonplace, and where hundreds of revenge plots against the Global Zone took shape every day. One settlement was located at the river mouth, where fishing boats moored; the other was further upstream, closer to the local lord's residence.

New convicts were dispatched to Gahra in air shuttles that landed on a platform overhanging the harbor and flew back into the green sky as soon as they had delivered their troublesome cargo. Once on Gahra, there was technically no way out. A magnetized belt surrounded the island, leaving just enough room on the sea to allow fishing. In addition to the belt, surveillance radars covered most of the island, with a higher concentration along the river and in both settlements.

Recent history, however, proved that those precautions were not enough. If you didn't mind sacrificing a few lives to the belt, and Vogh certainly didn't, it was possible to escape the island and return, as Smit had done. Not something to do too often, but twice in a few weeks had been enough to organize my kidnapping. Hopefully the second breach had caught the Globals' attention.

Our boat anchored at the foot of a cliff, underneath a hole that turned out to be a tunnel carved in the chalk. Four armed men were waiting for us at the entrance to hoist us up with harnesses. First me, then Leeham, then Smit.

As dawn cast tongues of fire on the ocean, we stepped into the cold and dark passage and made our way through the rock, following the flickering light of two lamps. Behind me, Leeham, who was wearing only a shirt, was shivering. I was luckier since Smit had concealed my identity under several layers of clothes, including a hooded coat that wrapped me from head to ankles. Only my feet were bare, as the cutting rocks kept reminding me.

When we stumbled out of the tunnel, the morning air felt brisk in comparison to the dampness inside. We had reached a forest of tall trees, and I could only spot patches of pale green sky between the upper foliage.

Nervous and impatient, Smit prompted me to keep walking. I grumbled about the lack of hospitality on the island, but knew better than to resist five men. The escort formed a circle around Leeham and me, forcing us to keep in stride with their long footsteps. The dildos squirmed inside me like the restless fingers of a nervous giant. I was exhausted and panting when fewer trees indicated the edge of the forest.

We came onto a dirt road that ran alongside a river. On our left, downstream, were the outskirts of the inland settlement. On our right, halfway up a cliff that forced the river to take a sharp bend, lay the core of Gahra's resistance.

Partly built, partly carved, Vogh's palace took up the whole depth and length of a natural promontory that dominated the valley. The mid-morning sun reflected on its white façade, and I had to shield my eyes to observe it. A porch, supported by six columns, stood out as the main entrance to a three-story building completely encased between the mountain rocks. The first two floors were discernible thanks to rows of narrow slits for the first one, and larger square openings for the second. The third landing was not as wide as it shrunk under the curved ceiling of the cave, but it boasted two balconies with sumptuous arches, a very Gothic design.

Its sheltered location protected the palace from the winds that battered the upper plateaus and the sea breeze that blew up the river. More prosaically, it also allowed Vogh's guards to spot visitors from a generous distance.

Passing between armed guards, I realized they must have announced our arrival long before we reached the porch.

We followed our escort inside a paved hall. The floor felt smooth under my feet, and the air was much warmer than outside. Leeham relaxed his shoulders under the pleasant sensation, while I removed my hood.

Once accustomed to a dimmer light, I noticed six more guards in front of us. One of them asked Smit to follow him through a side door. Two others led Leeham and me up a flight of stairs. On the first landing, Leeham and I were separated. The boy was pushed into a feebly-lit corridor that disappeared further into the cave, and I was brought to the third floor, where two new guards took over from their colleague.

The men led me through a succession of chambers, each one lower than the previous one as we moved closer to the cave wall. I vaguely guessed a storage room, a lounge and a bathroom, the latter appearing to be our destination.

The room, small and low, was brightly lit thanks to a unique oval-shaped window.

As we entered, an old man with long gray hair, but a well-toned chest that showed even under his loose shirt, was filling a stone tub with water steaming out of a pipe in the wall. Vapor rose and disappeared through a row of holes pierced in the ceiling.

When the man saw us, he frowned.

"By Mhô, look at the state you're in," he said, walking toward us. He touched my tangled hair, then looked down at my red, swollen feet. "Guys, leave us alone. I have some serious scraping to do."

"We'll be waiting outside," one of the guards said before closing the door.

"My, my, what are you wearing here?"

The old man had removed my clothes, exposing my bruised chest, and was looking at the chastity belt.

"Do you have the key, cutie?"

As he spoke, I saw two front teeth missing in his mouth. Yet he had a fresh, clean smell, contrasting his decrepit look. I shook my head.

"I thought so," he grinned, revealing a hundred wrinkles on his face. "Then, we'll have to cut it, won't we?"

He called out to a guard and asked for pliers. Ten minutes later, I was relieved of the dildos, but none too thrilled about it. Who knew what new pain would replace the old one?

Obeying an order, I stepped into the tub, slowly adjusting to the heat that helped my body relax.

The old man stepped behind me and proceeded to wash my hair with more soap than necessary for all the hair in Gahra. He took special care of my ears, commenting on how odd and alien-looking they were.

While he rinsed, then washed and rinsed again, I tried to make out the coarse frescos that ran around the white chalk walls, and decided they were the worst pornographic drawings I'd ever seen. I looked away and absent-mindedly stared at the collection of flasks arranged on a shelf.

After drying my hair with a hot towel, Olan moved to the rest of my body.

"I can do that myself," I feebly protested when he brought his sponge in contact with my shoulder.

"No, you can't. It's my job."

He pushed my hand off and began to brush.

I was clearly not the first woman he was treating to a bath, as his practiced moves testified. As my appreciation of his grooming talents grew, I wondered whether I could draw information from him, if not help or advice.

"Do you have a name?" I asked in an effort to be docile and friendly.

He looked up from the leg he was rubbing up and down. "Olan."

What could I ask him next? Whether he was born here? In all likelihood, Olan was a criminal who'd been confronted by Khyrian justice a long time ago. And to be sentenced as an outcast on Gahra, you had to do a lot more than inflict an involuntary wound on a Southie.

"How long have you been here?" I asked instead.

"Forty years and some. Must be one of the oldest. Men die young in these parts."

With a sure hand, he brushed my toes one after the other. I repressed a giggle.

"Have you always done this?" I inquired.

"Nah. Used to be a guard." He paused before starting on the next foot. "Got too old for the job. So Vogh put me in charge of the ladies. A nice gesture, that was."

He was nodding his head in respect for his master.

Olan asked me to get up so he could wrap me in a towel. When I was dry, he indicated a long wooden bench by the opposite wall.

"Lie down."

Who would have thought such old hands could be so soft? Olan applied oil on my whole body, back and front, and his skilled massage made me forget the questions I needed to ask. I was thoroughly refreshed when he was done.

He continued his work by dressing me in a micro-skirt and a sleeveless blouse that opened in the middle and hardly hid anything but my shoulders and my back. Both clothes were cut in a delicate black fabric that the slightest draft would blow away. I was wearing no underwear. I might as well have been naked.

"Olan," I asked while he was combing my hair, "are there many ladies in the house?"

"I'm not supposed to reply to that sort of question. You'll find out soon enough."

I would, indeed. Although the number of women in Vogh's palace varied from one season to the next, four concubines currently shared the quarters reserved for the female contingent. Considering the scarcity of Khyrian women in general, and on Gahra in particular, it was an outstanding number, a definitive sign of power and wealth.

In addition to his official harem, Vogh also entertained any new convict who set foot on the island, although fresh female blood was a rare treat. Convicted women had the right to choose, and usually preferred full-time detention in the G-Zone rather than exile in NGAs.

As to native women, they were more precious than water in the desert. The depraved population of Gahra coupled off more often than not, but the odds of procreating without technological assistance were low. Even then, four out of five newborns were boys.

Vogh must have been impatient to meet me, not only for his personal amusement, but also for the hopes I brought him to create new generations of warriors and concubines.

One might argue, as Khiru often did, that criminals should be left without the possibility of having descendants. But on Khyra, children were sacred, and no birth was unwelcome. Therefore, Gahra was allowed to flourish, provided it found a way to do so. This was a leniency the Global Council might have to reconsider if my DNA suddenly increased the fertility of their worst opponents.

Olan checked me one last time and, satisfied I was presentable, opened the door to let me out. The sentries immediately surrounded me and led me back the way I came, through the lounge and the storage room. We didn't stop at the flight of stairs, but proceeded further until we reached a heavy door protected by two men.

Behind the door was a blinding display of megalomania: a profusion of marble, gold, crystal, velvet, or their Khyrian equivalents. With fancy armchairs and delicate tables in all corners, lush carpets, and glittering chandeliers, the hall looked like an extravagant waiting room, a place where you bade your time as gracefully as possible until the lord conceded to meet you. A place that conveyed enough power to provoke fear, if not respect.

I heard the wooden panel close loudly behind me and realized I was alone. There was another door across the room, smaller, but richly decorated with gold motives. Interlacing signs reminded me of the "Rh" initial. As I stepped closer, the door opened.

"Welcome to my humble abode, my dear."

CHAPTER 18

▼

Vogh was the archetypal villain who won't settle for anything less than world domination. He was Dr. No to James Bond, Lex Luthor to Superman. He was smart, patient and Machiavellian; he enjoyed luxury and grandeur; and he loved to seduce women.

When he appeared in the doorframe, I involuntarily took a step back. For weeks now, the name "Vogh" had represented pure evil, and I had prepared myself to come face to face with an ugly, repulsive creature, somebody worse than Smit and Shorty combined. A man so vicious that one glimpse would make you sick with disgust and terror.

Instead, the lord of Gahra was a tall and distinguished man. With black hair combed back elegantly, fine facial features and well-manicured hands, he had a confident bearing and undeniable charm. He might have been handsome, had his eyes not betrayed a darker soul. Even when he smiled, he appeared cruel and malicious, untrustworthy and dangerous.

I had expected a monster; I was staring at the devil.

Beyond the pose and the deceiving smile, what disturbed me most was his costume. It was a long robe with ample sleeves, its front panels joining in the middle and maintained with a belt knotted around the waist, like kimonos on Earth. Its woven texture looked heavy and rigid, but was actually comfortable and supple. On the side of the heart was the same imitation of the "Rh" initial I had observed on the door; not quite the correct symbol, but close enough.

The hint was obvious to anyone who knew what it referred to, and I did. Khiru had a similar robe: it was the official Rhysh costume, which he had received upon graduation and wore on special occasions. He had once put it on to indulge me, and I had warmed nicely at the sight of such a prestigious, power-conveying look. He had kept the robe during the bondage scene that followed, proving that it was convenient and practical, even during the most physically intense moments.

Khiru's Rhysh robe was a dark purple, matching his bracelet. Vogh's was a sinister red, the color of blood.

Vogh wasn't a Rhysh Master, but that was his deepest regret in life, probably the source of his wrath and desire of revenge. In the next days, I was to learn from the friendliest concubine, Eeno, that thirty years ago, Vogh had been a student at the famous Academy. He was a natural dominant, with a strong taste for discipline, pain and humiliation. For his uncompromising nature, the first year was a nightmare. Like his fellow students, Southies or Northies alike, he was forced to curb his assertiveness—in his case, one could say "aggressiveness"—and learn to submit before he could learn to dominate. During fifteen Khyrian months, he underwent strenuous physical training and mental exercises that put his psyche to the test, a program that most students compared to military service or forced labor.

When he passed into the second year, where Southies and Northies followed different curricula more in line with their sexual inclinations, he thought the worse part was over. However, the second year proved almost as challenging as he had to absorb extensive health and safety lessons, study the art of dominance through history and geography, and understand the psychological aspects of sexual games. Worse, he had to draw the mental portraits of different Southies, analyze them and explain how he would stimulate their conflicting desires while protecting their well-being at all times. All he wanted to do was whip them without a look back. Still, he patiently studied every line in his books and went on to the third year.

That was when training started in earnest. He would learn the knots, practice with whips, improve his inborn skill at inflicting pain. However, teachers soon noted his negative attitude, how he didn't seem to care for pleasure or respect. He received several warnings, each one prompting him to modify his behavior for a few weeks. Southie students were scared to partner with him and complained frequently.

Despite his obvious shortcomings, Vogh managed to fool the examination board. He passed into the fourth and final year, where Northies and Southies worked on their preferred fields of expertise. Vogh majored in "Extreme Pain" and "Whipping Arts." He chose "Psychological Dominance" as a side subject.

Thanks to his natural dispositions, he was a talented student. Now older and slightly wiser, he no longer challenged teachers by acting too rough with a Southie. He practiced flicking his wrist until it hurt so much he could no longer write, but he hit the bull's eye each time he fired. During lessons, he took care to administer proper whippings, arousing pleasure in his victims. However, he also knew how to provoke opposite reactions; only he chose not to advertise his skills in that department.

Vogh's class was two months away from final graduation when an incident happened during one of the parties frequently organized by the fourth-year students. Vogh, like most of his friends, had drunk too much. When that happened, Rhysh rules were strict: no pain-inducing games were allowed. Vogh usually respected the ban; at this stage, he couldn't allow himself to fail. But that night, probably because he was too far gone, possibly because the girl had mocked and challenged him, he decided to whip a Southie, intoxicated like the rest of the students. They went outside the party hall, and he tied her naked to a trunk, gagging her when she whined the rope was cutting too deeply, slapping her when she fidgeted too much.

The thorough whipping he gave her was a natural outcome of his four years of frustration. Every urge he'd had to resist, he was now unleashing onto her. His facade of gentleman behavior crumbled down; only the beast in him remained.

Fortunately, a group of students caught Vogh in his insane act. Despite their inebriated states, they were brave enough to bring him straight to the board, with the martyred girl unconscious in their arms.

Vogh was expelled instantly. He never received the customized Rhysh robe he had already ordered in his favorite color. But he left the Academy with potentially explosive baggage: life-threatening skills and hatred.

After that, it didn't take him long to become an enraged player and to commit his first criminal assault on a Rhysh slave he'd met in a bar. With his good looks and stylish manners, he had no problem attracting willing victims. He went from town to town, changing names, never looking back. He never killed the girls; he preferred to maim them for life, branding their thighs, burning their clits, slicing off their breasts.

Vogh was eventually caught, sentenced to life imprisonment and sent to Gahra, where he created his evil version of Rhysh.

I moved my eyes from the false initial on the robe to Vogh's equally fake smile. He had thin lips, but I felt certain his bite was ferocious. As I confronted his eyes, he stepped forward and extended his hand, palm down.

"Please come with me," he said. "This outrageous waiting room doesn't befit you. Unlike most of my visitors who, let me assure you, need to be constantly flushed with magnificence, you are a person of taste. Let me show you my private quarters."

Ignoring his hand, I preceded him through the door.

The new lounge had a sober and elegant appeal. White walls, parsimoniously painted with ochre drawings, reflected the light that flooded through a large arcade. The floor-to-ceiling window opened onto one of the balconies I'd seen from outside.

On the other side of the room were two low couches, draped in crimson velvet, with small tables conveniently positioned on each end. Huge stone vases with tall, freshly cut flowers filled the corners. These alone indicated power. Who would spend time harvesting flowers on inhospitable Gahra if it weren't to please the local lord?

"I will make sure you have some in your room," Vogh said to my back. "Flowers," he added as I turned to direct an inquisitive stare at him. "I see you like them."

Without gratifying him with a grin, I followed him into the next room, his office. Its furniture included a large varnished desk and a chair set by the window, and three more chairs leaning against the opposite wall. More evidence of wealth: four mediaframes hung behind the desk, and in the middle of the latter was a black cube, the source of 3-D screens. How did Vogh manage to bring such products here, behind the surveillance belt? Of course, he was the man who had enough harilium to hide a boat from G-radars. You would expect him to find ways to buy a computer.

"You must have a very efficient trading network," I said, unable to control my curiosity.

He smiled as if he'd won the first set in a game of many.

"I do. It's only a matter of finding the right freeman with enough spite against the Globals, and he'll get me what I want."

I could see how friendly class-2 territories would be the obvious link between the G-Zone, with which they traded, and class-1 areas, with which they shared eviction, but that didn't explain how they smuggled forbidden goods through the belt that surrounded Gahra.

"We sink them," Vogh proudly explained. "Freemen bring their inconspicuous boats close to the border. There, through a trapdoor cut in the keel under sea level, they unload the material previously packed in special boxes. The boxes sink to the bottom of the sea, on platforms that we can pull back and forth with pulleys."

"Underneath the belt," I said.

"That's right. I wish we could do the same with pretty girls, but I've been told they wouldn't survive the water pressure. Too bad."

"And the Globals never notice the movements of boats near the border?" I asked.

"Free Territories represent a large area to scan and observe, with lots of boats coming and going. We use various sinking areas, and deliveries only happen two or three times a year. Surveillance is a vain concept, Megan. It takes more than a few satellites to outwit the spirit of one man."

He pointed at a door.

"You'll visit the last room later," he said. "It's getting late, and I'm sure your morning hike made you hungry. Let's go back to the lounge."

He placed his hand against my back and pressed me forward. Walking back the way we came, I observed rings screwed randomly around the floor, both in the office and the lounge. There were a number of them on the walls, too. Disturbing images popped up in my mind.

During lunch, Vogh questioned me about Earth. He showed interest in politics and war stories, but was more curious about social customs, particularly the relationships between men and women. He seemed delighted to hear about man's supremacy in general, his enthusiasm reaching unbearable proportions when he forced me to admit horrid details such as the ablation of the clitoris or stoning for adultery.

"Your planet is very much to my liking. It would be fun to organize another type of mission there, something closer to an invasion than this sediment-digging joke of a trip! If I'd been in charge, I would have brought back hundreds of you, willing or not, preferably not!" He laughed out loud, then turned serious.

"But of course, now I have you," he said in a quiet voice, "and I don't care if I'm the only one who benefits from your genes. In fact, I quite fancy the idea."

My face turned white at this brutal reminder of his plans concerning me.

"Do you intend to experiment on my DNA?" I asked weakly.

His smile sent shivers down my spine.

"I certainly intend to experiment, my dear. In more ways than one."

I stopped eating. "You do know that five laboratories have been trying to incorporate my DNA to the Khyrian genome and haven't succeeded yet. Do you expect to do better here?"

"Those laboratories are obsessed with safe, clinical procedures. My approach will be, let's say, more pragmatic. And quite honestly, I don't care about the Khyrian genome. As long as the best of us survive.

"Now, if you'll excuse me," he added quickly, "I have a few work meetings to attend. Let me show you to your apartment."

Vogh led me back to the waiting room, then the main corridor. Abandoning the front aisle, the only one with windows looking onto the valley, we strode to the right, in the direction Leeham had taken, deeper into the cave.

We reached another heavy door, guarded by two men, that led to the women's quarters: six rooms built around a common area with the traditional couches and low tables.

Artificial light was the only way to defeat darkness in these parts. As Vogh described how they regulated it according to the time of day, I experienced a flashback to my first day aboard the *Noncha* starship when Naari had given me similar explanations. In space, I'd lived under artificial light for a year, but it had never seemed as depressing as this. Perhaps it was the stone walls, the low ceiling, or the dampness that permeated my body; perhaps it was the uncanny feeling that I would never leave this place, that I would never see the light of day again. Despair fell on me like lead.

I felt my eyes water.

"Don't worry," Vogh said. "You won't spend much time in here. You have more useful occupations to perform."

He opened the third door on the left. There was a bed, and empty shelves. Even a prison cell would be better than this.

"Your room," he announced. "Sparsely furnished, but if you please me, I will reward you generously. If you visit the other rooms, you will see that you can make yourself quite comfortable."

I didn't enter the room. Instead, I looked back to the common space. Why was it empty? Where were the four concubines?

"There is a small bathroom over there," Vogh said, pointing at a small passage between the last cell and the wall. "When you need special care, Olan will take you to the main bathroom, which you've already visited."

He turned to the main corridor and hesitated.

"I don't like leaving you alone on your first day. Let me call Olan."

He pulled what looked like an old walkie-talkie out of a pocket.

"I know," he said, catching my frown, "not the state of the art, is it? I must admit, there are a few loopholes in our delivery service. But rest assured that the freeman who was responsible for this absurdity didn't live to tell the tale."

The archaic device emitted a few cracks, and Vogh spoke to Olan. A few seconds later, the old man was hurrying down the hall to meet us.

"Ah, there you are," Vogh said as if he'd waited an hour. "I believe the ladies are exercising at the moment. Do bring our new friend down to the gym, but tell Fharsk to take it easy on her. We want her fit and healthy, very healthy."

The gym was located on the ground floor, at the back of the cave. As Olan led me there, I pouted at the thought of working out. It had never been one of my hobbies, and I was grateful Khiru didn't care much for that sport either. We stayed fit in our much more entertaining way.

I shouldn't have worried. The gym was a euphemism. Although the contraptions I found in the hall did imply physical activities, they were a far cry from steps and weights. Filling most of the room, complicated assemblages of wooden boards were bent, stretched or flattened to accommodate bodies in a variety of positions. Four of them were occupied.

One, in the loose shape of a "Z," supported a woman kneeling backward. Her breasts were clamped and chained. The metal links went up through a ring in the ceiling, then down to a double plug in her ass. Another contraption, a "Y" in reverse, held a second woman standing with her legs wide open. The third concubine hung from a bar like a monkey swinging down the branch of a tree. A collar around her neck held her head up, and a cascade of long black hair floated behind her. The fourth contraption was an "L" on which the last woman lay with her legs stretched above her.

They were all naked, save for a few accessories, and their bodies showed many marks, old and new.

Four trainers were entertaining them with floggers, pins and vibrators. All the women were severely gagged, and the only sounds in the hall came from the toys or the men. One of them, a blond-haired giant, dropped the whip he was using to lash the bottom of the kneeling woman and joined us.

Olan repeated Vogh's instructions to take it easy and handed me over. Like a frightened child, I felt like clinging to his shirt and begging him to take me home. The other trainers had interrupted their sessions and were watching me. So did the concubines, with a combination of apprehension, disdain and interest in their eyes.

Fharsk eyed me up and down appreciatively.

"Gotta do something with those breasts," he muttered to himself before ordering me to strip.

I had little time to observe the T-shaped contraption to which Fharsk was leading me. He pushed me down on my knees, and forced me to lie with my chest on the horizontal board where my breasts squeezed inside two holes. Fharsk pulled my arms behind my back and cuffed my wrists. Next, he secured my ankles and knees to the floor, and my thighs to the vertical slat. He completed his binding work with a belt wrapped around my arms, my waist and the wooden support.

Compared to what I had previously observed in the hall, my position wasn't the most strenuous, but Fharsk compensated his leniency in bondage with ferocity in the pain department. After pinching my nipples between metallic clamps, he loaded my breasts with a series of weights that he added one by one.

When I yelped, he interrupted his careful assemblage to gag me with a gruesome resina penis, and resumed his work. My breasts probably extended to the floor by the time he stood up. Because I moaned too hard, he punished me with a fat anal plut. After that, I was as quiet as a ghost.

CHAPTER 19

▼

The ladies' quarters were nicknamed after an antique Khyrian concept where women used to live in separate areas of the house, not unlike the ancient Greeks on Earth. When we returned to Gahra's gynoecium, the four ladies introduced themselves while Olan took us one at a time for a bath and massage. It would be my second session that day, but I wouldn't complain.

Two concubines were freegirls who'd been kidnapped twelve and five years ago. Lohrie was a shy thirty-something brunette, burned out from long years of captivity. She hardly spoke, never resisted, and seemed petrified each time the master asked for her. The other freegirl, Santra, was ten years younger and still had some of her enthusiasm for life. She was Vogh's current favorite, and she hoped he would soon make her his unique lifepartner, with awards and honors. She talked about her future reign with a careless assurance that didn't make her popular among the other women. Santra had magnificent blond hair, bright blue eyes, and a cute curly nose. Her fairy-tale beauty had probably been the rationale for her abduction.

The other two concubines were convicts who'd opted for Gahra instead of a women's confinement unit in the G-Zone. Irhma was a serial killer who'd slaughtered enough male Southies in her prime to deserve Vogh's cruel treatment. The whip lashes and various torments she had received over the years had disciplined her violent temperament, but hadn't quenched her anger. Next to her, I felt like I was walking on the slope of a sleeping volcano. I avoided her whenever I could.

Eeno, on the other hand, became a much-needed ally. A few years older than me, she was the dark-haired woman I'd seen hanging from a pole at the gym. Eeno was a passionate Northie who had accidentally killed a play partner during a poorly executed scene. She sincerely regretted her act and accepted the sentence of full-time detention with resignation. But she nursed a deep hatred of Vogh and had resolved to escape, or at least die trying. She had already attempted to bribe Olan and had once jumped out of a front window. Her pathetic results—a four-day exclusive session in the gym for the first attempt, one broken leg for the second—had not deterred her spirit in the slightest.

"Eeno, why did you come to Gahra?" I asked her when we were alone in the common area. Irhma and Lohrie, cleaned and oiled, had retreated to their rooms, and Santra had taken her turn in the bathroom with Olan. "Your life would have been easier in the G-Zone."

"At the time, I couldn't bear the thought of losing my freedom," she replied. "But I've regretted my decision ever since I set foot on this cursed island. It didn't take Vogh longer than a day to hear about me and claim me as his third concubine after Irhma and Lohrie. I was so enraged, he kept me in bondage for two whole months to obtain my submission, if only a costume version."

"He will never have mine," I declared fiercely. "And I don't care if he locks me in a cage for a year.

For a second, I thought Eeno was going to mock my foolish bravery, but she didn't. I suspected she could use every spark of energy she could find and every soldier she could enlist in her war.

As for me, I was relieved to meet a strong and intelligent woman. Eeno was assertive and clueful and knew all about Vogh's palace, its inhabitants and its staff. As a Northie, she could use tools and toys effectively, which was always an asset. She reminded me of my friend Myhre, in a taller and heavier format. I could certainly use her on my side.

Eeno had similar thoughts about me. I was a new piece on the chessboard, much more than just an anonymous pawn. The whole planet was looking for me, with one man actually knowing where to search.

When I told her my story, Eeno was visibly interested.

"You think your Kalhan will attack Vogh?" she asked, her hopes rising high.

I thought of the villagers Kalhan had at his disposal, the magnetized belt surrounding Gahra, and the risk of exposing his identity to surveillance G-radars.

"I don't expect an invasion of the island," I said cautiously, "but he's a man of resources. I'm sure he'll figure out something."

Eeno's face dropped slightly.

"Well, we're not going to wait for outsiders to rescue us," she said. "We have to find a way out by ourselves. I don't know how your presence is going to affect our lives, but any change in the routine is good. All we need is a flaw in the system, one guard missing, one open door. So far I've had no luck; Vogh controls everything too efficiently. But lay one more block on a pile, and the edifice collapses."

I mentioned Vogh's plans to experiment with my genome and asked Eeno if she knew about a laboratory in the cave.

She thought for a minute.

"There are many rooms we're not allowed to enter on the first floor," she said. "And also a door in his bedroom that is permanently locked. I've heard people working in there recently. But building a lab would be an exceptional achievement on Gahra. I can't see how he would get the required equipment or qualified personnel."

With the limited information we had and no evidence to the contrary, we assumed that Vogh intended to sample my DNA one way or another. This gave me an unusual status compared to the other concubines.

"Evidently," Eeno reflected, "he wants to treat you well and keep you fit. We can use that in our favor."

Eeno was convinced that if I charmed Vogh and behaved as he expected, he would grant me some freedom inside the house.

"Santra," she explained, "may walk around as she pleases. She's even allowed to stay in his room in the morning after he's gone. If you could achieve that, it would definitely help."

I objected as long as I could. I didn't fancy yielding to Vogh's desires, even with an ulterior purpose. But Eeno convinced me that the master of Gahra would have his way with me whether I submitted or not.

"And having you locked up for weeks will do us no good," she concluded.

I promised not to oppose the master unnecessarily. Meanwhile, Eeno would collect food and any material that could help us escape.

"Find enough food for three," I said. "I came with a friend."

Eeno was thrilled to hear about another potential rebel, even though I warned her that Leeham might be a greater source of concern than assistance.

"He must be in a cell downstairs," she said. "If he's not looking for trouble, they'll use him as a servant, which may always be useful."

"Only if we can communicate with him," I pointed out.

"That's why we need you to walk around, Megan. Oh, by Plya's light, if there are three of us, maybe we can make it."

Eeno's faith was contagious, and I saw us running away to freedom in a couple of days.

We decided to keep our connivance secret from the other concubines. Eeno didn't trust them, and I saw no reason to argue.

The next day put my resolutions to a test, but in a most unexpected way.

After a healthy breakfast in the common room of the gynoecium, Eeno and the other women were led downstairs for another painful workout while I was summoned to Vogh's apartments.

Wearing his fake Rhysh robe, the Lord of Gahra welcomed me with open arms and clutched my shoulders possessively.

"Megan," he said cheerfully, like the manager of a fancy hotel, "I hope you had a restful night. Were you satisfied with breakfast?"

Not waiting for an answer, he led me to his office where we walked behind the chairs facing his desk and stopped by a wall ominously decorated with rings. A profusion of shiny resina ornaments rested on the chairs, a vision that caused a drastic rise in my body temperature.

"It is incredibly hot today, isn't it?" Vogh said after observing my reddened cheeks. "Here. Why don't we remove that quite superfluous outfit?"

He pulled my skimpy top over my head, then dragged the matching skirt down to my feet.

Naked, I stood calmly in front of him, waiting for the inevitable, remembering Eeno's advice, and the guards behind the door.

"Please place your back against the wall," Vogh requested.

One by one, he stretched my limbs out and secured them with large resina straps that attached to the wall thanks to velcro-like edges. I tested their adherence and found they were impossible to unfasten.

Vogh used two for each arm and three for each leg. He wrapped the remaining two around my waist and shoulders. When I was effectively restrained, he forced a gag inside my mouth and finger-locked the strap tightly. I hadn't said a single word since I'd entered his private chambers, and I regretted not using the opportunity while I could.

"I would like you to get to know me better," Vogh continued his monologue. "And there's no better way than watching me at work."

Turning around, he walked to his desk.

"Of course, I realize that politics may be tedious."

He was rummaging in a drawer.

"And I would hate to see you bored."

After removing a cardboard box, he came back to me.

"A new arrival," he grinned, indicating the parcel, which he tore open like a birthday present.

My expert eyes recognized a bag of powered clips, a fancy vibrator with a clitoral extension, a remote control, and a small resina harness.

Vogh fitted the dildo inside me, provoking a few muffled grunts, and fixed it with the straps of the harness that he looped around my thighs and waist.

"Now the clips," Vogh said. "I've been told these are the latest treat in Rhysh. Took me months to obtain a handful. Let's try them, shall we?"

He pinched one on the flesh of my inner thigh, and a mild electric shock spread down to my knee and up to my navel. The second one, applied to the side of a breast, created a miniature tornado that blew through my nipple and vanished into the air.

Vogh used all the clips, a dozen in total, and concentrated them on my chest and around my sex.

"I wish I had more," he sighed. "I would have loved to cover your whole body. Hopefully, these few will have the local effects we're looking for."

They did. As Vogh walked back to his desk, I ground my teeth and grimaced. Constantly turned on and off, and sending vibrations in all directions, the clips had already transformed my breasts and my pubic area into searing foyers. I wouldn't have been surprised to see smoke rising out of them.

Apparently losing interest in me, Vogh sat down and called a couple of 3-D screens out of his computer cube. Occasionally frowning or mumbling a curse, he remained absorbed by his reading. As my body continued to combust, I observed how his face transformed from anger to disdain, exasperation to hatred. Was this man capable of any positive feeling?

The heat was more tantalizing than painful, but severely challenged my impatience. When Vogh activated the vibrator without a glance at me, I was grateful. For a while, the rhythmic stirring took care of my needs. Then it made them worse. Glued to the wall, with the resina straps sticking to my wet skin like duct tape, I wished for a more fulfilling treatment. Yet I was wary of revealing my desires to Vogh. Not quite the torturer, but not an attentive lover either, his behavior bedazzled me. I had no idea what to expect from him, and decided that this moderate teasing was only the opening to a more grandiose show. It even occurred to me that a warm-up was a prerequisite to sampling my reproductive cells. His probing might involve vaginal penetration, for which a very wet passage would be needed.

While I conjectured about my fate, present and future, Vogh was making mediacalls to various subalterns, apparently unconcerned that I could hear him. He ruled the execution of two men, sent Smit to quench a minor fight in the harbor town, and ordered the delivery of flowers.

Between the second and third calls, he activated the tongue of the vibrator that was directly applied to my clit. I would have jumped if I could move. Instead, I bit harder into the gag and clenched my fists and toes until they hurt. Vogh turned the power off before I could achieve any substantial outcome.

"I don't care if the whole island is barren," he was groaning to the screen. "Search better."

After a last call to the kitchen and ordering "a light lunch for two," he smiled at me.

"I'd say you've had enough administrative work for the day, haven't you?"

Leaving the remote on his desk, Vogh approached me. Although he looked as threatening as a snake curling up before biting, something in me stirred nicely when he stood close in front of me, with a hand carelessly hanging in proximity of my sex.

When he snatched the first powered clip free, I growled in anger as much as in pain. I looked up to study his face, still frozen into a duplicitous smile, unperturbed by my reaction. Staring at me, he removed another clip from my labia. This time, I had anticipated his move and didn't flinch despite the ferocious burn. In the strange game we were playing, Vogh scored the next point by snapping a clip off my nipple with his other hand. I couldn't repress a long moan and closed my eyes to avert any light of victory in his. He waited until I re-opened them to strike again, on the side of the other breast. Then, in rapid succession, he removed a series of clips with both hands, and my whole body burst in flames.

I was drenched in sweat, panting and increasingly aroused.

Vogh's smile widened, and I admitted defeat. There were a few clips left, one on a nipple, at least two on my labia, and I could never continue fighting until those were gone.

Surprisingly, Vogh moderated his final moves. For each new burn, he lowered his head, first to my breast, then to my sex, and sucked the blood back into the limp flesh. When all the clips were removed, his tongue lingered on my clit as if to test its compliance. Satisfied, Vogh stood up.

"Time to reward you," he said softly, throwing me off balance again.

A reward was not something I expected.

Vogh peeled the resina bounds off the wall and my body, and carried me into the room behind his office.

A colossal poster bed lay in the center, occupying most of the space. It was made of fake-wood kauchu, with a sober design that contrasted with the four ornate purple drapes that floated from a central point in the canopy down to the floor in each corner. The phony Rhysh initial was embroidered in golden thread all over the fabric. The color and design of the bed cover matched the drapes, albeit in a lighter lilk texture. This was a royal bed for a forged monarch.

The only other piece of furniture in the room was a tall wooden cabinet. I wondered whether Vogh had a collection of Rhysh robes in it.

An opening next to the cabinet led to a bathroom. Another door in the room, in line with the first one, led toward the back of the cave. On the wall next to it, a digit pad controlled its opening.

After bringing me down on the floor, Vogh uncovered the bed—a concern that amused me—and asked me to lie down.

Locking my wrists into heavy cuffs attached to the headboard was more in line with the program I had in mind, and being restrained paradoxically restored my confidence. The last thing I needed was for Vogh to get sentimental on me. Mentally, I would deal better with duress than unwanted feelings.

But Vogh was incapable of any romantic emotion beyond lust. After cuffing my ankles to opposite posts, he removed his pants, straddled me and took possession of me without further ado. He held on for a few minutes, enough to ignite my sexual desire, then came and withdrew.

"I'll come back later with lunch," he said as put his pants back on and made for the door.

And there I was, spread and tied to the bed, with an itch to be seriously scratched, and a furious need to laugh or cry. And he called *that* a reward? Everything that man did or said was deceitful. A lesson I would never forget.

Vogh did come back for lunch, and unlocked the gag to feed me. He tried to initiate a social chat, but I refused to answer. Beyond his manners, Vogh was the most treacherous man I'd ever met. I feared anything I gave him, even a word or a smile, would be used against me. From then on, I vowed to limit my contribution to simple obedience.

When we were done eating, Vogh replaced the gag and fucked me again. He forced a few groans and twists out of me by grabbing and flicking at my breasts, but he completely ignored my still-insatiate needs.

I spent the whole afternoon bound to the bed, trying to figure out Vogh's intentions. In the end, I decided he wasn't ready yet for the sampling and was killing time by playing with his new toy.

"You say he fucked you three times?" Eeno exclaimed when I summed up my day with Vogh once I was allowed back in the gynoecium and found refuge in my friend's bedroom.

Before sending me off, Vogh had used me once more, although that time he'd had to indulge in a minimum of foreplay as I had decidedly cooled down during my long wait. He had, however, not taken care of finishing the job any better than the two previous times.

"Yes," I answered, still angry, "like I was some masturbation device."

"Vogh is the worst sadist you'll ever know, so using you is no surprise, but fucking you is quite exceptional. And only in your vagina? Not your mouth, your ass?"

"Nope. Just fucked me pure and simple."

Eeno was genuinely confused.

"Must be your Earth charm or something. Do you have a very tight vagina?"

I'd never had to discuss the size of my vagina with a friend, but I was beyond being shocked.

"Never been told that I had," I said. "I know my anus is very narrow, though," I added with a smirk.

"Perhaps you squeeze stronger," Eeno was saying to herself, still looking for reasons why Vogh would honor me in such an obvious way.

"Or perhaps he has this alien-girl fantasy," I suggested. "The man is weird."

"You must be right. And this was your first day. Things will probably go back to normal tomorrow."

They didn't. Again, as Eeno and the rest of the female posse followed Olan down the stairs to the dreaded gym, I was escorted to the front aisle where Vogh waited for me. This time, he tied me to a chair in front of his desk, and used metallic chains instead of resina straps. He swapped the clips for a heating ointment, which he generously applied on my sexual parts with the same objective in mind. Then, like the day before, Vogh went to work. A few more men lost their lives while I was slowly forced to arousal. As the morning was drawing to its end, Vogh brought my shaking body to his bed. Once I was secured in a wide spread-eagle, he fucked me.

The week passed, and each day was a repeat of the day before, only worse. There was something increasingly mechanical in Vogh's maneuvers, as if he applied a doctor's prescription. He no longer seemed excited or charmed. Because I reacted poorly, if at all, to his seducing attempts, he dropped his gentleman's mask. He practically stopped talking to me; his conversation was limited to cynical comments while he worked on the restraints or when I inadvertently emitted a sigh or a groan.

I expected him to tire of the game. Each morning, I hoped to accompany the other women down to the gym, even though my plight would not improve significantly. Still, basic physical torment seemed preferable to another day spent with a cold psychopath deprived of most human feelings. The only expression I was able to read in his eyes was relentless determination.

Nothing seemed to deter him from his mysterious scheme. When I pleaded not to be tied up to the bed all afternoon, his only justification was that he didn't want me to move. To prove his point, after locking the usual cuffs around my ankles and wrists, he added ropes around my knees, my thighs and my waist, all connected to the sides of the bed.

I also tested him about the sampling procedure. Eeno and I remained convinced that it was his ultimate goal, although he never referred to any such plan.

"Are you waiting for the lab to be finished?" I asked before he had a chance to gag me. He laughed, but didn't answer. However, my question kept him in a happy mood all day. I believe he enjoyed keeping me on edge more than he enjoyed fucking me.

Meanwhile, Eeno was making progress with our escape strategy. She had found Leeham, who worked in the kitchen on the first floor, not far from the gym. Eeno had made eye contact with him a few times, and the boy was smart enough to linger in the passage between the staircase coming down from the women's quarters and the gym. They had started to exchange secret notes, and Leeham had promised to hide dried food.

It was a first step in the right direction.

CHAPTER 20

▼

For far too many days, my life revolved around sexual torment with Vogh, prolonged bathroom sessions with Olan, and evening chats with Eeno. I briefly met the other concubines during breakfast and dinner, but the five of us rarely sat together in the common area. Santra loved to use her privileged freedom to leave the gynoecium as often as possible, and Irhma and Lohrie preferred to nurture their pains, physical and mental, in the privacy of their bedrooms.

There were, however, occasional reunions where Santra regaled us with Gahra's latest gossip, or where we strolled down memory lanes and learned about each other's pasts. I became a favorite evening storyteller with dozens of Earth-related anecdotes. Even Irhma ventured a smile when I explained high school or wedding traditions.

One evening, our quiet party turned into a tragedy when Santra provoked Irhma. The blond girl and the old serial killer fiercely hated each other, but managed their hostility by ignoring each other. That night, Santra crossed the line. Because of Vogh's infatuation with me, and despite the fact that he was still asking for her at night, the blond girl had become worried about her preferential status. Too scared to strike directly at me because I could complain to the master, she launched her spite against her old adversary.

Irhma was usually wise and turned a deaf ear to Santra's provocations. That day, she probably had a bad session at the gym and needed some form of retaliation. She rose to the bait.

After a short exchange of insults and threats, the two women fell upon each other with fever in their eyes. Their clash was violent. Santra was younger and in better physical condition, but Irhma had years of assaulting experience at her disposal. Both of them shrieked as fingers poked eyes, feet kicked ankles, hands pulled at hair. Santra slapped Irhma, who retaliated with her fist into the girl's side. Then they gripped each other's shoulders, trying to force the other one down.

Despite her young blood, Santra was losing ground. Her kicks and blows were fast, but she aimed poorly. Irhma was more systematic. She knew where to hit and how to inflict effective pain. Soon, Santra was yelling. When Irhma launched a naughty blow on her chest, the girl lost her balance and fell on the low table, her head almost over the edge. Irhma jumped on her and closed her hands around her throat, squeezing.

Lohrie, Eeno and I stared in silence, no one daring to interrupt the fight. But Santra's groans became feeble, and her eyes pleaded for mercy. Irhma, on the other hand, was prepared for the kill. Her mouth was already grinning with anticipation.

"Irhma, stop," Eeno said softly. "If you kill her, Vogh will get back at you."

Irhma didn't seem to hear. Her thumbs pressed further into Santra's flesh.

While Lohrie ran to her bedroom, I cautiously placed a hand on Irhma's shoulder.

"Let go, woman," I told her. "You made your point. She'll be quiet now."

At that moment, Olan and two guards broke into the gynoecium. A whip landed on Irhma's back, but instead of stopping her, the lash, one too many in her life on Gahra, caused her to tighten her hold around Santra's throat.

The guards yanked Irhma backward, but the girl underneath her didn't move. With her eyes open wide, her face purple, she had just bid farewell to her dreams of greatness or, as I would rather phrase it, a whole life of slavery.

Olan took away the dead body while the guards dragged a very calm Irhma downstairs. I never saw her again.

Although the fatal fight had reduced his harem almost by half, Vogh didn't react as badly as we all feared. The next day, he sent the remaining three of us for a long punitive session at the gym—an arduous, yet welcome distraction for me—but, after that, life continued as if Santra's death and Irhma's disappearance had been minor setbacks.

"The man's losing his spite," Eeno said, as she casually massaged her legs which had hung above her for four hours. "Years ago, he would have had us whipped to blood."

"He must have other things on his mind," I ventured, thinking how Vogh's eagerness to play with me would increase now that his favorite sex slave was gone. My worse concern was that he would keep me for the nights as well.

Vogh, however, didn't prolong my infamous routine. Deprived of Santra, he momentarily set his cap on poor Lohrie to replace her. Eeno was thankful he was sparing her.

"I bet he's afraid of me now," she laughed. "The last night he used me, I sucked his dick a little too ferociously. It got me a few hours in the wall, but it was worth it."

"The wall" was a punishment Vogh reserved for a lack of obedience in his bedroom. All concubines had experienced it to various extents. It was said to be particularly effective, as I would learn only a few days later.

Despite his obstinacy to follow the same daily drills, Vogh eventually had to adjust to a new situation. Shocked by the endless ordeal, my body turned cold to all the toys and gadgets. One morning, Vogh found that, despite the vibrating clamps on my nipples and the dildo he'd left on for two hours, my vagina was as dry as the desert. It seemed to upset him.

In his bedroom, he tied me to the bed face down. Then he spanked me. He finally achieved his goal: a moist passage to get through. Those were days when I hated the way my body betrayed me.

As time went on, I learned to improve my resistance, but that only served to enrage the master.

"That's it," he said angrily as he withdrew a dry finger from my unyielding sex. "If you don't cooperate, I'm going to show you the alternative."

Ten minutes later, Vogh was dragging me down one flight of stairs, with two guards scurrying at our sides. We walked further into the cave through the servants' quarters, and, despite my apprehension, I paid attention to all the details I had time to observe like doors, passages, and the number of servants, which was impressive. I didn't see Leeham, but several men stared at me, all expressing empathy or horror.

We reached a door, heavily locked and guarded, and Vogh pulled me into his private prison.

Damn, I thought to myself, I hadn't done better than Eeno. I was going to spend the next weeks in jail. I didn't find the idea too appalling, considering I would be rid of Vogh for a while, but I resented the impossibility to communicate with my friend.

We passed four wooden doors with tiny grid windows in the center, then reached the end of the corridor. I thought Vogh had lost his way inside his own palace when he activated a handle on the wall, and a panel of stone opened in front of us. Behind it was a narrow space, tall and wide enough for a person to stand in.

My brain refused to comprehend what this was for until Vogh ordered me to enter the horrifying hole.

When I instantly froze, he pushed me in. In a few clicks, he locked my wrists and ankles to aptly located shackles. Still gagged, I was unable to scream the rage that rose in my throat.

"Make sure your body is more compliant when you leave this cell," Vogh threatened before closing the wall.

I don't think I stayed "in the wall" more than a few hours. Even then, I was thoroughly chastised when I came out. Olan revived me with a full bath and massage treatment, at the end of which he led me back to my room. It was another cell, but a palace compared to where I came from. I stayed by myself until dinnertime. I cried a little, daydreamed a lot, and wondered how, by Plya, I would ever escape Vogh's clutches.

"What happened to you?" Eeno asked after she'd joined me with a bowl of stew and fresh water. "Lohrie heard you'd been in the wall?"

"Not for long, but that was enough. I don't ever want to go back in there."

"Can't blame you. But what did you do to deserve it?" Eeno asked, curious.

"I didn't get wet."

"And that's all?" Eeno was as disappointed as intrigued. "Power's messing with his mind. He hardly shrugged when Santra died, but puts you in the wall when you don't get aroused. We need to get out of here before we go crazy, too."

"Any news from Leeham?" I asked her.

"Oh, I almost forgot! Your protégé is audacious. He came in the gym this afternoon."

My admiration for the young boy grew. Although Fharsk and his assistants regularly left the gym, safe in the knowledge that all the women were properly restrained and silenced, no one in the palace dared enter the forbidden hall. The concubines were Vogh's sacred property. Unless he offered them as a reward for a job well done, he didn't allow anyone but the gym team and Olan to touch them. Entering the gynoecium or the gym without an authorized escort was strictly forbidden. For Leeham to challenge this rule was a very brave move.

"It's easier now that Santra's gone," Eeno explained. "The bitch would have denounced him. Now, it's just Lorhie and me, and she won't say a word. I had written a message to Leeham asking him to try, but I didn't think he would."

"So did you talk to him?"

"Let's say he talked to me, once he recovered his speech ability. You should have seen how shocked and embarrassed he was when he found me naked and in bondage. He was so cute. Definitely aroused the Northie in me," she said dreamily.

"And what did he say?"

After spending the first weeks locked in a prison cell after his work was done, Leeham was now allowed in the servants' quarters at all times. He shared a room with five other men, but most importantly, he could spend time in the common room where a 3-D mediabox was the main source of entertainment.

Programs were limited to class-2 broadcasts and a few Global networks that Vogh's technicians had managed to hack. They didn't offer the customized options that most Khyrians enjoyed in the G-Zone, but they provided a sufficient quota of movies, shows and news.

A few days before, Leeham had caught a special newsflash on medical rights in the Free Territories broadcast on a Sweendi channel. It only lasted ten minutes, and looked more like rushed propaganda for improved rights than a serious analysis of the situation. What caught Leeham's attention was the sudden appearance of a Rhysh Master on the screen. His name was Khiru.

"By Plya," I exclaimed, "my Khiru?"

"Leeham didn't know," Eeno replied, "but what the man on the m-box said was confusing. He mentioned something about the need to establish fair medical treatment in class-2 territories and that everything would be done to secure it. Leeham forgot his exact words, but he said they sounded like a secret code, a hidden message that only the right person would decipher."

"Did Leeham tell you what the man looked like?"

"He only remembers short black hair and dark eyes. And a purple Rhysh robe."

There were too many coincidences. A Sweendi broadcast, Kalhan's major goal for the territories, and a purple Rhysh robe. Was it a message for me?

"Leeham added that the newsflash had been broadcast again two hours later, but he didn't see Khiru because the men zapped to another program."

"And no sign of Kalhan, I suppose?"

"No, but the boy wasn't very attentive at the beginning of the flash, and he's afraid he might have missed an important clue."

"Still, he was lucky to catch it in the first place. Eeno," I asked, "what if it was Khiru telling me he found my trace in Sweendi?"

Neither of us wanted to believe in the possibility that Khiru might be on my trail, but we could certainly dream it. For the first time in weeks, I felt hopeful.

The next day was well within its usual frame. I thought a lot of Khiru, and it helped me satisfy Vogh in the moisture department. After a warm-up session on the floor of his office, I found myself bound to the bed with my legs stretched upward and chained to the canopy. Angered by the uncomfortable position, I spent most of the day musing about a sudden Global invasion of Gahra, and also came up with a frightening, yet plausible theory about Vogh's intentions with me. I needed to confirm it with Eeno.

"Get you pregnant?" she repeated when I told her the results of my brain session.

"Yes, it makes sense," I said. "I told you how Vogh looked particularly evil when he climaxed inside me. As if he had injected poison or performed black magic. I can't believe I didn't think about this before, but I'm pretty sure now. Vogh has no intention of sampling my DNA; he only wants to secure his own lineage, so he's using me as a baby machine."

"And of course, this is why you need to get wet," Eeno concluded. "It's a requirement for pregnancy, isn't it?

I smiled at her. Like most Khyrians, Eeno didn't know anything about intra-body pregnancy. For them, babies were born in test tubes and artificial wombs. Getting pregnant was nothing short of a miracle, with all the superstitions that implied. But she was right: Vogh was probably using all the tricks he thought would improve his chances to procreate. This was also why he kept me strapped to the bed in an effort to keep his sperm inside. And why he never used violence on me. He was too afraid of damaging my womb. Eeno confirmed my reasoning; Vogh's objective was suddenly crystal clear.

"So you could get pregnant?" she asked, with a mute admiration that didn't quite befit my mood.

In fact, I wasn't sure of the answer. On Earth, I used an intra-dermal patch as a contraceptive means. Hidden on the inside of my arm where it diffused hormones continuously, it gave me the foolproof protection I needed, and, as a cherry on the cake, it suppressed my monthly periods. A patch lasted five Earth years. Converting Khyrian time, I estimated that the one I was wearing had been implanted about five and a half Earth years ago, give or take a month or two. But my natural cycle hadn't resumed yet, and there was a chance the patch would continue to protect me for a few weeks. I could hardly hope for more.

"You wouldn't know of any herbs, do you?" I asked Eeno quite unnecessarily since she didn't understand the theory of contraception. Having a child was a gift no Khyrian would ever refuse, even if it was the result of a rape. I was certain Eeno or any other woman would bear Vogh's child with pride and joy if they could. Not me. But I didn't see how I could avoid it if he continued inseminating me with such regularity and precision.

When Eeno finally understood that I wasn't particularly thrilled with Vogh's family plans, she came up with a brilliant idea.

"Now that we know what he wants, we can play with him," she said.

"You mean, blackmail him?"

"Not really, but you could pretend you're pregnant and obtain special privileges."

"I could tell him I need rest and quiet," I said, understanding how my life could change if Vogh thought I was carrying his baby. "Yes, he would probably fall in the trap, at least for a while."

"All we need is a few weeks."

"I could even tell him that I need fresh air, daily walks," I continued, my excitement rising as more ideas occurred to me. "And of course, no more bondage, nor sex. That would put the baby's life at risk."

"And you'd need food, a lot of good food," Eeno played along.

"And warm clothes, to keep the baby comfortable."

Vogh wanted a child; he was going to have one. Tomorrow morning.

CHAPTER 21

▼

My fake pregnancy started, as planned, the next day. During breakfast, I pretended to feel nauseous in front of Lohrie and made a big show of throwing up in the bathroom. Eeno added a few spicy details when she reported my poor condition to the guards who were to escort me to the front aisle. By the time Vogh heard the story, he thought I'd been poisoned.

I didn't try to contradict him. I was waiting for him to jump to the conclusion for which he was hoping, even if it took an extra day or two.

Cautious, Vogh sent me back to my room for the whole day, with Olan attending to my needs. In the evening, the master of Gahra honored me with a personal visit. With my hand nonchalantly resting on my belly, I told him the nausea had subsided, but I felt oddly tired. I yawned a few times and closed my eyes before he walked out the door.

The next day found me sick again. Lohrie called the guards before breakfast was over and told them, under Eeno's bemused stare, that I had surely caught a terrible virus. Vogh entered the gynoecium a few minutes later. He was wearing a long dark robe made of lilk, with a short tail brushing against the stone floor.

"Do you feel any pain?" he asked when I came out of the bathroom, my hand ostensibly holding my stomach.

"No," I replied. "I only feel like throwing up, even though I've hardly eaten at all."

"Hmm. Come into your room, will you?"

He closed the door behind me and waited until I'd settled comfortably on the bed to sit next to me.

"Have you ever felt that way before?" he questioned.

"I've had indigestions and cramps, but this is new. It's not just my stomach either. Last night, it was as if somebody had cast a sleeping spell on me. I was so tired."

"Does it look like any Earth disease you know?"

Vogh didn't look concerned at all. His eyes glittered with hope, and his breathing was deeper than usual.

"No, but..."

He leaned forward. "But what?"

I shook my head. "Nothing. It's probably just a minor virus. If you let me rest for another day, I'm sure I'll be fine tomorrow."

Vogh hesitated. He would have liked confirmation of his wishful thinking, but was afraid of claiming victory too soon.

"Guards!" he called, and the door immediately opened. "Carry Megan to my room and stay posted until I return."

Eeno and I had anticipated this decision, as well as the physical examination that followed when Vogh joined me in his bedroom, accompanied by a tall gray-haired man carrying a briefcase. Eeno was confident that, if I played the part well, no doctor would dismiss a pregnancy unless he clearly saw an empty uterus on a scan screen. We both hoped Vogh hadn't smuggled such fancy medical equipment onto the island. I was more worried about the higher probability of a blood test. The results would instantly seal our doom.

"Not necessarily," Eeno had argued. "Intra-uterus pregnancy is rare, and there is no established blood test for it. Finding a convict on Gahra who can interpret the right symptoms would be bad luck!"

For a change, the stars were benevolently watching over me. Vogh's doctor palpated my belly, aiming for my bladder rather than my uterus; he asked me a few irrelevant questions, then cautiously inserted a finger inside my vagina. Vogh, who was watching the examination with the care of a mother for her sick child, was literally holding his breath.

I had never been pregnant, but had had my share of ob-gyn exams on Earth. This doctor had no idea of what he was doing or looking for. Incidentally or not, he pressed my G-spot, and I gave a little start.

"Don't hurt her!" Vogh grunted severely.

The doctor withdrew his hand, and wiped his forehead with the other. He looked like he'd just climbed one of Gahra's cliffs.

"This is an early stage," he mumbled. "It's too hard to tell."

"Check her blood," Vogh commanded.

Obediently, the doctor strapped a blood analyzer around my arm. He opened a reading device and spent a few minutes observing the flow of data that appeared on the small screen.

Did he know what would indicate pregnancy? Fear had a bitter taste in my mouth.

"So?"

Vogh was as impatient as I was.

"I can't be sure," the doctor said. "Her blood cells are different from ours. The data don't corroborate with our standards."

He was lying. My blood showed no more variations than those that differentiated an O-type from an A-type on Earth. Scientists in the Global Zone had even found that I was fully compatible with one of the rare blood types on Khyra.

Vogh drew a long inhalation, preparing himself to launch into a reprimand, when the doctor had a sudden inspiration.

"Have you been bleeding lately, Megan?" he asked me.

I stared at him and drew a deep breath in a sign of abrupt comprehension.

"Actually, I've lost track of weeks recently," I said nervously. "But now that you're asking, no, I haven't lost vaginal blood for a long time."

The doctor looked triumphant, but Vogh hadn't understood yet.

"Before the Gene War, women used to bleed every month," the doctor explained. "When they didn't, it meant they were pregnant. I believe the same principle applies to Earth women, doesn't it?"

I nodded, making sure I looked worried and undignified at the same time.

"I haven't seen her bleed since she came here," Vogh concurred, his face now beaming with pride. He flashed a victorious smile at me. "You're carrying my baby, Megan. It worked!"

Oh, did it ever work. After listening to the doctor's advice, Vogh ordered him to visit me every afternoon and sent him off. Once we were alone, he sat on the bed and put his hand on my belly. He had become a gentleman again. But his courteousness would transform into cold rage if he discovered my deceit. From now on, I would walk on thin ice.

"You have pleased me beyond measure," Vogh said calmly. "The doctor said you needed rest and comfort, and I'll make sure you get them in abundance. Anything you want, ask, and I'll see how we can satisfy you."

I had a list ready, but I figured I would remain shocked by the news for at least the rest of the day.

"I would like to be alone," I said coldly.

"Quite understandable."

Vogh got up and pointed at the code-protected door I had never seen open. "Let me show you your new room."

The secret room was a nursery. It contained a wooden poster bed, draped in crimson and gold, and next to it, a crib with matching colors and textures. They were small and miniature versions of Vogh's master bed, only without the false "Rh" initial. The similarities made me cringe; I would never be his queen.

"Please look around," Vogh said, "and tell me what is missing. You probably have better ideas than my advisers."

He left without locking the door, but posted two guards in his office, thus allowing me to move freely between his bedroom and the nursery. This wasn't the freedom I needed, but it was a good start for someone who'd been kept in restraints for weeks.

In addition to the beds, the nursery contained a full-length cabinet and a smaller one. In the drawers, I found baby items such as textile diapers and lotions, as well as minuscule shirts and pajamas. I held one between my hands and felt overly emotional. Perhaps one day I would give a baby to Khiru.

So strange he'd never noticed my lack of periods, I thought. Neither had anyone else: Myhre, doctors, Kalhan. As if they didn't know, or were afraid to ask. Natural pregnancy was possibly the last and only Khyrian taboo. I suppose they would all have been shocked if I'd told them about the patch, especially Khiru. Once my periods resumed, I would have a few uncomfortable explanations to give, but the prospect of being a father would hopefully mollify Khiru's indignation.

I replaced the tiny garment in the drawer with a long sigh. Why was I concerned about explaining the basics of contraception to Khiru when I might not see him again? I'd better get with the program and see if there was a way to escape from here.

The nursery was located inside the cave, with four walls and no window, but it offered an interesting peculiarity. A square hole opened in one corner of the ceiling to ventilate the room. As I peeked from underneath, I saw a square emerald patch at the top. It seemed enticingly closed, but even though the shaft was big enough for me to slither in, I would never have the strength to climb.

Leeham, however, might be able to. The boy was both slender and athletic. If I managed to bring him here, it would be worth trying.

That evening, I discussed the possibility with Eeno. She agreed it was feasible.

"As a kitchen boy, Leeham may find a way to bring you food in the nursery. Once he's climbed through the vent, he can throw a rope down and help you out."

"Help *us* out," I corrected.

"Megan, getting me and Leeham in the nursery at the same time will arouse too much attention. I'll be more useful creating a diversion to keep the guards off your back. What matters is for you to get in the open. Once the surveillance radar has caught you, the Globals will rescue us in no time."

"Eeno," I objected, "I won't leave you here."

"Yes, you will," said the Northie in her. "Besides, I'm probably too big for the hole."

Eeno was the sturdiest of us, and I had to admit she was right. But I hated to lose her help. Without her, I feared Leeham and I would not make it.

"All you'll need to do," Eeno added when she saw me frown, "is hide for a day, hopefully less. If you escape early in the morning, Vogh won't find out until lunchtime. That gives you a few hours to find shelter."

With all of Gahra's troops searching for us, the plan was feeble.

"Let's not rush this," I said. "Tomorrow, I will ask Vogh's permission to get out of the cave. If I can explore the surroundings, I may come up with a better idea."

Eeno agreed half-heartedly. She had already waited too long for an opportunity like this.

"But if you don't find another way out by the end of this week," she decided, "we go for the air shaft."

I had to make a conscious effort to look sick and weak the next day. During breakfast, Lohrie commented that I looked much healthier, and I rushed to the bathroom to prove her wrong.

Vogh welcomed me in his office with open arms, and I tried to be amenable to him. Although it cost me, it was important to appease the beast before the strike.

"Do you think you'll be able to find a few toys?" I asked him. As his mouth twisted in a smirk, I specified "for the baby."

"Oh, of course," he said. "I will send an order immediately. Anything else?"

"A pram. He or she will need fresh air, you know."

He didn't seem to relish the idea, but couldn't possibly oppose it either. He would get me a baby carriage. Because he was in a good mood, I tried my luck and asked whether he would allow me to get some air, too. It would be excellent for the fetus, I mentioned. But I pushed too far too soon.

"We'll see about that later," Vogh said. "Right now, you need peace and quiet, and there's no better place than your bedroom for such requirements."

To alleviate his refusal, he handed me a reading tablet with more than five hundred books in its memory.

"*The enslavement of Sylia*," I read out loud from the table of contents once Vogh had gone. "This is not going to help me much."

Again, I stared at the air vent. If we pushed the small cabinet underneath, we would have no difficulty accessing it. But the passage appeared narrower than I remembered it. Was it foolish to even try?

Three days went by. I spent them all in the nursery, biting my nails, unable to read more than four pages of each novel I pulled up on the tablet. The doctor visited me every day after lunch, always in Vogh's presence, and maintained a prudent stance, neither confirming nor refuting the pregnancy. When I asked him whether outdoor exercise would benefit me, he first glanced at Vogh, then cautiously denied my request.

"Your room is properly ventilated," Vogh taunted, eager to show that he didn't trust me.

Eeno was becoming impatient.

"You won't get anything more from him in the short term," she said. "And the longer we wait, the higher the risks. What if your bleeding resumes?"

Leeham was ready for action, too. Eeno had passed the message that he needed to find a way into the now much-discussed nursery. He should bring a rope and food.

"What are we waiting for, Megan?" Eeno insisted. "We might never get a better chance."

"Have you thought of your diversion?" I asked.

"Yes, I'm going to whip Fharsk's ass!" she laughed.

Eeno was plotting to wreak havoc in the gym when Leeham was supposed to bring me the pastries I would order. Once she had defeated Fharsk and his assistant, she planned to run up the stairs to the front aisle and step out on the balcony in Vogh's waiting room. This should distract the guards for a moment, long enough for us to escape.

"I will steal a whip and keep them nicely entertained," she promised.

It all seemed a bit adventurous, if not outwardly crazy.

"Are you sure you can pull that off?"

"Absolutely. The only reason why I haven't done this for years is that it would have gotten me no further than jail. But now I'm only trying to buy you time. And jail will only be a short prelude to freedom. Right?"

"Right."

Neither of us mentioned that Vogh would undoubtedly direct his wrath onto her once he discovered I had run away. When you go to war, you can't dodge every bullet.

The big escape was set for the day after. I spent most of the night revising our plan, finding it more foolhardy each time. I woke up feeling like the first Earth astronaut about to be hustled into space on top of a war missile.

CHAPTER 22

▼

"Megan, I need you to push me," Leeham's voice echoed inside the air vent. Half his body had disappeared, but his legs dangled below him.

When he joined me in the nursery, halfway through morning, I had already dragged the cabinet under the chimney. Because our success depended on how fast we acted, I had no time to hug him or ask how he'd managed to be in charge of my food tray. I only noted how thin and tired he looked, a physical depravation that served him now. He fit easily inside the shaft.

I climbed on the desk and offered my shoulders for support. His feet gave a strong push, and he burst upward. Pressing on the walls with his arms and knees, he heaved himself up toward the surface.

While my eyes tracked Leeham's progression in the vent, my ears remained tuned to the noises coming from the other rooms. A woman's mad scream had just resonated, followed by the shouts of two men and the thuds of furniture falling down. Only one of the two guards stationed at the office door walked off to the parlor, but I hoped the one who stayed was sufficiently distracted by the general uproar to forget about Leeham and me.

"Megan, catch the rope." Leeham's voice reverberated in the shaft.

I grabbed the coarse, dirty strand the boy dropped and wrapped the end securely around my waist. I was wearing the black veil outfit I'd been given on my first day, and the flimsy fabric offered no protection against the abrasive fibers. I debated using a towel as an extra layer around me, but the clock was ticking. Abandoning all idea of comfort, I gripped the rope that had become my lifeline.

Now came the moment I dreaded most. Would Leeham be strong enough to pull me up?

"Ready?" I heard him ask quietly.

I looked up and saw his spread legs forming a conic ceiling above me. Between them, his hands firmly held the rope.

"Yes," I whispered, "all set."

The rope went taunt, and the loop around me tightened. Holding the length to alleviate the pressure around my waist, I tried to jump and reach for the vent. I fell back down.

From the parlor, I heard screams and orders, and the unmistakable whistle of a whip.

"Don't hold the rope," Leeham advised. "Try to cling to the chimney walls with your arms."

I did as he said and placed my hands inside the chute, preparing to push on both sides once Leeham pulled.

The rope tightened again, chafing my flesh. I focused all my strength into my arms, willing them to haul me up, and after a few seconds that lasted forever, my feet rose off the cabinet. Once my elbows were inside the vent, I managed to hold on to the walls. Leeham pulled harder, and I crawled high enough for my knees to reach the shaft and support part of my weight.

My ascension was slow and difficult, but the chimney was only the height of an extra floor. It didn't take me more than a few minutes to reach the top where Leeham grabbed me under the shoulders. Dropping on his back, he dragged me up, and I landed on his chest.

"Leeham, we made it!" I exclaimed before kissing him on the cheek.

A genuine smile spread across his face.

"Yes, but we'd better find a place to hide before they start looking for us."

My shy little boy was turning into a man of decision.

I got off him and looked around while I removed the rope that had left an ugly purple ring around my waist.

We were on top of a rocky plateau, bathed in timid sunshine. In front of us, the cliff that hosted the cave and Vogh's palace dropped abruptly to the river. Behind us to our left, stones and bushes extended as far as the eye could see, a flat ground with no possibility for hiding. The forest on our right was the only salvation, and without a word, we both turned to the trees.

"Wait." I caught Leeham's arm before he began to run. "This open plain is where the Globals can see us best with their radars. Shouldn't we stay here a while?"

"We can't. If the guards realize we're gone, they'll come looking for us here."

Leeham started to take long strides toward the forest.

"But if the Globals miss us, our efforts are useless."

Leeham considered it. "No, we've been here long enough. Gahra must be their focal point. If they haven't spotted us now, they never will."

He caught my hand.

"Come on, let's run."

Not quite convinced, but unable to resist Leeham's pressure nor my instincts, I darted with him toward the relative safety of the woods.

We ran until my body threatened to mutiny. My chest was on fire, my feet were bleeding, and my legs sent painful warnings to my brain.

"Leeham, stop!" I shouted to the boy who was well ahead of me. I sat down on a rock, holding my side and trying to catch my breath. The ridiculous top I was wearing was completely torn apart, resembling an old kitchen rag. It no longer covered anything, and I took it off, hoping that the matching skirt would be more resistant.

We had reached a dense part of the forest where the light was dim, and the air smelled heavily of trees and mucus. Around us, twigs cracked, and leaves rustled. Birds were singing in the higher branches. Nature was peaceful, and I breathed deeply to savor the moment.

"Are you okay?" Leeham had walked back to me. His eyes lingered on my breasts, then lowered to his own shirt. Although its stronger cotton-like texture had survived the climbing better, it was in a pitiful stained and worn-out condition.

"I would give it to you," he offered, "but—"

I shrugged. "Never mind. I'm warm enough."

I knew that as a Sweendi man, Leeham wasn't used to nudity. Challenging him made me feel playful.

"Come here." I patted the stone next to me. "I need to rest."

The boy scanned the woods around us. Satisfied, he sat down next to me, far enough to avoid body contact.

"I suppose we can. Would you like to drink?"

For the first time, I noticed the small backpack Leeham was carrying. He removed a flask and handed it to me. I saw how his palms had been badly chafed by the rope.

"Drink all you want," Leeham said. "We'll find a spring to refill it."

"What else do you have in there?" I asked after quenching my thirst and giving him back the flask.

He took a sip before he answered.

"Food, more rope, and a torchlight. It's all I could lay my hands on," he said apologetically. "Actually, my greatest find was the bag itself."

"You've done great, Leeham. None of this would have been possible without you."

The boy blushed, then suddenly frowned. "Can you hear?"

I listened attentively in the direction he indicated, exactly where we were headed. After a few seconds, I heard the distant sound of men's voices. My heart vacillated. Was it the end already?

"We need to move," Leeham ordered unnecessarily. I was already up and searching for the best route to take. Around us, the trees all looked the same, but the ground seemed to rise on one side, between the strangers coming up our way and what we felt was the direction to Vogh's palace.

"Leeham, can it be we walked back on our tracks?" I asked. "Are you sure the cave is behind us?"

Leeham searched for the sun amidst the treetops. "Absolutely," he said. "The cave is west. The men we hear are coming from the east. But it doesn't mean anything. Vogh may have sent troops all around the island."

I had a vision of columns of men surrounding us, with Vogh walking toward me, a cruel smile crossing his lips. I shivered, then regained control of myself.

"Let's go up," I said. "We'll have a clearer view of who's coming and can better defend ourselves."

Leeham agreed and walked off hurriedly. Despite the various aches and burns in my body, I followed his fast gait with apparent ease. The dread of being caught and taken back to the cave lent me wings.

The gentle ascent became steeper. Trees were more scattered, replaced by tall rocks announcing a mountain. Leeham had to help me climb them, and only fear made me forget my bleeding soles. When we emerged out of the forest, a façade of boulders stood in front of us. Khyra's noon sun dotted the peak of the mountain; under the light, the rocks shone like precious metal.

Searching for the easier path, we veered slightly to the east, where the slope was smoother. We crossed a chilly mountain spring, and Leeham filled the flask with fresh water.

Rock after rock, we made our way up the mountain until we stumbled onto a grassy spot hidden between the stones.

"Let's rest for a while," Leeham suggested.

My throat was burning too much to answer. I dropped on the ground where I lay still and closed my eyes. I wouldn't be able to continue at this speed for much longer.

"I don't see or hear anyone," Leeham said. "The mountain's clear."

I squinted to see him peering over a rock, his hand barring his forehead, a perfect army scout searching for the enemy.

"We should climb as high as possible," I said with difficulty, my body not quite agreeing with my proposal.

Leeham turned around. "You need to eat first."

While he kept his surveillance position behind the rock, I ate some of the dried food he'd brought along and drank more water. My strength and resolve returned.

Beyond the clearing, a dirt path ascended the mountain. However, we decided to avoid a route that was too obvious and where the risks of meeting someone would be higher.

We resumed our climbing amongst the rocks, albeit more slowly. From our vantage point, we would see anyone walk out of the forest. The only way to catch us by surprise was to descend from the mountaintop, but the higher we climbed, the safer we were.

My feet had stopped bleeding, but a searing pain flashed through my legs with each step. Leeham offered to carry me, but I refused to slow down our progress.

"It's already way past noon, Leeham," I said as I walked past him, taking the lead. "By now, Vogh is definitely on our tracks. We don't have a single minute to lose. Besides, we're almost there."

Ahead of us lay a raised ground made of dirt and dry grass. Only a few more rocks to pass.

"Leeham, look!" I exclaimed.

"A hunter's shack!"

Wedged between two boulders was a wooden cabin, camouflaged with branches and dried mud. We had walked underneath it for a long time, but hadn't noticed it. It was only accessible from the plain side at the top.

Leeham pulled the slightly distorted door open and revealed a grim room that had clearly not been inhabited for years. Two boards protruding from the sides served as benches or beds. A thick layer of dust coated them.

In the middle of the wall opposite the door, at eye level, was a long slit that offered a magnificent view on the mountain slopes and, further below, the forest.

Leeham removed his shirt and gave it to me.

"Can you make this a bit more hospitable? I'm going to explore our surroundings a bit."

I nodded, slightly taken aback by his new assurance. Clearly, Kalhan's training was paying off. Perhaps we should revise our judgment about the boy's submissive traits.

When Leeham returned, the boards were perfectly clean, and his shirt a black bundle on the ground.

"I have good news," he said. "The other side of the mountain opens onto a ravine. Nobody can climb up that way."

Our new home suddenly became a very safe place where we could wait until the Globals found us. Leeham decided he would mount guard inside the hut while I remained outdoors, like a visible beacon for any shuttle flying our way. Unfortunately, the air at the top of the mountain was chilly, and once the heat of our climbing efforts subsided, my nudity became an obvious discomfort. I solved the problem by gathering rocks and writing my name on the ground in big letters, hopefully detectable from above.

The day was drawing to its end, with the sun setting behind the trees on our left. I was watching through the slit, grateful for the shelter we had found, when a bright reflection on the edge of the forest caught my eyes.

I called Leeham who was sitting on a bench, trying to wipe his shirt clean.

"Is that the sun reflecting on rocks?" I asked him, afraid to hear his answer.

'No, it's a night lamp. People."

If my sense of orientation was correct, they had set a camp near the spring we'd crossed earlier.

"If those are the men we heard this morning, they didn't go far," I pointed out.

"I know, and it worries me. Who would waste a whole afternoon in the same spot?"

"Maybe they're not the same men, then."

We stared at each other, not knowing how to react.

Leeham made up his mind first. "Look, we're safe here. They are at least three hours away from us, and they won't climb the mountain in the dark."

The sun had practically disappeared, and nature was losing its colors and shapes. Darkness would be complete in a few minutes, with only one scary source of light darting through.

"I'll keep an eye on them all night," Leeham said bravely. "You may sleep in peace."

I fought for the right to keep watch in shifts, but Leeham forced me to sleep first, and he never woke me up. Although my mind was troubled, physical exercise had done me in, and I only opened my eyes when the faintest rays of dawn were slipping through the slit of the cabin.

I was alone.

Squatting on the bed, I stretched my neck to look through the narrow hole. No one. I jumped on the floor, groaning under the sudden pain in my wounded feet, and went for the door on the other side.

Before I could reach it, the wooden panel opened wide. Two large shadows were outlined against the dimly lit background. I stepped back in terror and collided with the wall behind me. One of the men moved forward. Unable to scream, too conscious of my breasts and the rippled tissue that barely hid my sex, I closed my eyes and prayed that Vogh had forbidden his guards to touch me.

I heard another step. Then two strong hands encircled my waist.

"Megan!"

CHAPTER 23

▼

After a prolonged kiss that filled my body with desire, he grabbed me under the arms and lifted me up on the wooden board. With one hand pressing my back against his chest, his mouth explored my neck fervently, and teased my ear until I tried to break away. Tightening his hold, he lowered his other hand to my thigh, rubbing it slowly as if to summon the genie inside. As he moved between my legs, an old fire surged back to life.

Overwhelmed by the suddenness of it all, I hid my face against his shoulder and shed a few tears. I hadn't said a word; all I could do was submit to him, let him recapture my body and soul.

His fingers reached for my chin. Gently forcing me to look up, he lowered his head and licked my wet cheeks with the tip of his tongue.

Moving slightly away, he reached for the miserable rag around my hips and ripped it apart. Then he opened my legs wide and, after lowering his pants, took possession of me.

Pinning my hands down to the bench, he re-claimed me, thrust after thrust. His passion fueled the flames in me, causing an inferno that spread throughout my body. Heat glowed from us like an aura.

I was panting, crying, stuttering words without meaning.

When he let go off my hands, I seized his shoulders and brought him closer, as if to lose myself in him. I held on desperately, my face awash with tears, calling to him to take me.

His fingers slipped down between my legs and carefully brushed my clitoris.

Bringing his mouth close to my ear, he whispered: "You're mine."

Once our bodies were sedated, we were able to marvel at the miracle of being together again.

I was still sitting on the board, my back leaning against the wall, my legs wrapping his hips. He had readjusted his pants and was holding my hands, staring at me, trying to read the story behind my tired face.

"Khiru," I asked, breaking a long and emotional silence, "how did you find me here?"

He smiled and gave me a long once-over as if he couldn't believe I was a real woman, not a ghost.

"I found this."

He fished for a black bundle in his pocket: the useless top I'd abandoned in the forest. Realizing what a silly move that had been, I was relieved it had fallen into the right hands.

"And you immediately knew it was mine?" I teased him.

He brought the dirty fabric to his nose. "Yes, it smelled like you."

I squinted and grinned. "Not true."

Khiru laughed, and my heart gave a jolt. I had missed him so much.

"Alright," he admitted, "I didn't know it was yours, but before I found it, I'd heard a woman's voice and, whether I recognized you unconsciously or not, I had a hunch about this rag and I kept it."

Khiru was the man I'd heard in the woods. At least one of them. I distinctively remembered two voices, and two silhouettes in front of the cabin. I looked to the door, almost expecting the other person to walk in.

"A few hours later," Khiru went on, "we stumbled onto a group of men with weapons. We hid behind trees and listened to them trying to decide which way to take. One of them mentioned "the Earth girl," and I understood you'd run away. We decided to walk back to the place where we'd heard you. From there, it wasn't hard to guess you'd taken cover in the mountain."

"Was it your night lamp we saw last night, near the river?"

He shook his head. "We were higher up by then, and not foolish enough to turn on a light. The people you saw were Vogh's guards."

A ripple of concern crossed my heart.

"Then we're in danger. They must be climbing up the mountain as we speak."

I tried to get up, but Khiru held me back.

"Dawn is only rising," he said. "If they leave now, we still have two peaceful hours ahead of us. And you found a perfect place to wait."

Dropping my hands, he turned away to peek out of the window slit. I went to stand next to him. Under the newborn sunrays of early morning, the mountain was deceptively quiet. Somewhere below us, a group of armed men was on its way to catch us.

Khiru put one arm around my waist. "Don't worry," he said, still looking ahead, "We have a weapon to defend ourselves if we get to that point."

The thought was as frightening as it was reassuring. I trusted Khiru knew better than to confront Gahra's men on his own. Which brought me back to the stranger who was traveling with him.

"Did you come with the Global militia? Has it invaded the island?"

He was still looking out, but his eyes didn't move. His thoughts were elsewhere.

"No," he answered, "although I suspect it will arrive soon."

He didn't seem overly thrilled with the idea.

"Then, who's with you?" I finally asked, realizing he wasn't going to volunteer the information until I urged him to.

Khiru turned to face me. His face was serious, and I wondered what tragic news he was going to deliver.

"Do you still love me, Megan?"

The question startled me. Vogh's men were heading toward us, and Khiru was worried about my feelings?

I placed my hands behind his neck and fixed his eyes. "Yes, I love you." Then I remembered the last days we'd spent together before I was kidnapped. "Are you worried I left because of our fight?"

"No, I know what happened and I never doubted you'd been kidnapped. Not like the damned Council," he groaned. "They wasted precious moments when we could have stopped your assailants, just because some stupid officials thought you'd run away."

"Then why do you have doubts?"

He silenced me with a finger on my lips.

"I don't, but I needed to ask you because, well…" He led me toward the door. "There's someone who's equally impatient to see you."

He was going to push the panel when he seemed to notice I was naked.

"Here." He removed his black t-shirt. "It's a bit early in the day to be parading your luscious body."

Once I'd donned the garment, enveloping myself in Khiru's masculine smell, he opened the door and stepped aside.

I walked into the daylight and stopped. In front of me, sitting side by side next to the stones that formed my name, were two men facing away. They both had unruly hair. One was blond; the other was brown. Gesturing wildly, Leeham was sharing an animated story with his "boss," Kalhan.

For more reasons than one, I hardly dared interrupt their conversation, but Kalhan sensed my presence and turned around. His eyes traveled between me and Khiru.

"Glad to see you're safe and sound, Earth girl," he said with a smile of relief that belied his lackadaisical tone.

"Glad to see they didn't kill you," I retorted, copying him.

I moved forward, oblivious to the gravel under my feet. With Khiru observing the scene behind me, I felt like prey caught between two predators. Each step was a victory against my growing nervousness. Although my chest didn't seem big enough to contain my heartbeats, I froze my face into a friendly, composed grin. Then I noticed a big purplish lump on Kalhan's temple.

"What happened to you?" I exclaimed, pointing at the wound.

Kalhan frowned comically. "I had a bad encounter with a torchlight."

He looked at Leeham, who was bending his head sheepishly.

The bubble of pressure surrounding us deflated at once. I burst out laughing, followed by Kalhan and, a few seconds later, Leeham. As I sat down in front of them, still giggling, I saw that even Khiru had given in to our hilarity. A remnant of a smile enlightened his face.

"What have you guys been doing while I was sleeping?" I asked to no one in particular. "And you, mister," I pretended to scowl at Leeham, "how come you left me alone in the hut?"

"I saw them coming," he said defensively. "When I realized there were only two of them, I figured I could defeat them by surprise. So I went outside and took position behind a rock."

"Two men against you, Leeham?" I frowned. "That was foolish. You should have woken me up."

"You were so tired."

"Megan's right," Kalhan interrupted sternly. "You could have got killed, kid. And Megan would have been caught."

Leeham instantly reverted to the shy boy he once was.

"Sorry," he mumbled, drawing a smile from both Kalhan and me. "But, hey, if I hadn't seen your face at the last minute, I would have kicked harder."

At that moment, Kalhan noticed my swollen soles. "By Mhô, what happened to your feet? You have a serious infection there."

Khiru, who had surreptitiously sat down between Leeham and me, bent forward and caught my left leg. His brow furrowed as if he shared my pain.

"We need to clean this," he said. "Kal, you have the med box in there?"

Kalhan was already rummaging inside a big backpack from which he removed a white container. After handing what I knew to be a wound-fixing laser to Khiru, he began to unwrap a bag containing bandages.

While they both attended to my feet with similar care and cluefulness, I tried to make sense of their behavior. They talked and acted with the fluency that old friends have, but I perceived uneasiness beneath their amenable manners. This restrained embarrassment, however, was nothing compared to the hostility they were supposed to nurture toward each other. Even if Kalhan had convinced Khiru of his innocence in Suri's case, a fact that I'm sure Khiru knew too well, kidnapping me should have placed him in very dire straights. To say nothing of what had happened between him and me, which, I decided, remained unknown to Khiru.

Had they sealed a pact for the duration of their dangerous expedition on Gahra? And why were they here on their own? Where were the Global troops?

As usual with these elusive men, mine was to question why.

"Isn't it time you explained what happened?" I asked them while Kalhan wrapped one foot in smooth layers of bandage, and Khiru healed the other with the laser.

They seemed too absorbed by their tasks to answer me.

"How you two came in contact?" I insisted exasperatedly. "How you got here? Did you swim?"

"Kalhan called me as soon as he heard about Vogh abducting you," Khiru explained without interrupting the healing process. "He told me where you were, and how he planned to rescue you."

"Technically," Kalhan continued, "it was simple. Finding one of Vogh's illegal traders on Sweendi was easy, as was convincing him to take us on his boat. The poor man was terrified we were going to denounce him to the Globals."

"How did you sail through the surveillance belt?" I asked. This wasn't the question I was dying to ask, but I feared I would have to wait to learn more intimate details. For the time being, I was stuck with technicalities in which I had scant interest.

"I knew about Vogh's trick of sinking material under the belt," Kalhan said as he started to bandage my other foot. "We followed the same route and did some deep-sea diving before reaching a deserted shore. I've been on this island before and knew where to find Vogh's cave. We were heading there. That's all."

It seemed like an awfully convoluted way to rescue me when it would have been much easier to tell the Council and wait for the Globals to take control of the island.

"We're very independent men," Kalhan mocked me. "We like to solve problems on our own."

I shook my head to indicate I didn't believe a word he said, but before I could ask more questions, the sound of roaring engines filled the air.

We all looked up and stared at the amazing sight of a six-shuttle squadron whisking over us.

"The Globals!" Leeham yelled.

Khiru and Kalhan eyed each other in silence. Then Khiru got up and returned to the cabin, while Kalhan seemed lost in mystical contemplation.

What was wrong with them? Shouldn't we all wave our arms and sing happy songs? At least Leeham responded to our liberators with appropriate joy.

"You'll soon be free, Megan," he exclaimed.

Kalhan heard and gently winked at me.

Behind him, Khiru was coming out of the shack. "Vogh's guards are speeding off," he announced. "The coast is clear."

"Want to get your shirt back before we set off?" Kalhan asked him, pointing at me.

When Khiru nodded, I swapped his ample shirt for a much tighter one and a pair of slacks they had brought in their bag, in the likely event that I would need comfortable clothes.

Once we were all set, Kalhan sealed his bag and asked Leeham to carry it. Then he knelt down on my right side and waited for Khiru to do likewise on the left. Without a word, both men crossed their arms and, holding each other's hands, offered me a makeshift seat.

"Oh, I think I can walk," I attempted.

"No way."

"Sit."

Contradicting them was not an option. I took position on their joined arms and held on to their shoulders in time to be lifted off.

And thus we made our way down the mountain, this time using the smooth dirt path we had avoided on our way up. Leeham preceded us, hopping happily like a Boy Scout on a Sunday hike.

Behind him, Khiru, Kalhan and I started the descent in a more serious mood. I was very conscious of my presence between them, physically and mentally. Despite the chilly morning air, my temperature was on a constant high, and my breasts had a way of poking through my shirt of which I strongly disapproved. There was also the small matter of regular spasms in my loins. I wondered how long it would take to climax from pure sexual longing.

Neither of the men spoke, so I scanned my brain for a neutral topic of conversation.

"You know, Kalhan," I said, "Leeham has matured a lot during our captivity. You should have seen how brave and resourceful he was when we escaped."

"I noticed," Kalhan answered with pride in his voice. "He's growing up."

"Don't you think you might have been wrong about his tendency? I'm now more inclined to see him as a Northie."

Khiru sneered. "This boy, a Northie? Not in a million years!"

I resented what I perceived as an insult to Leeham's courage. "He's not weak! He's only young, with a lot to learn."

"We're not saying he's weak, Megan," Kalhan explained. "You mustn't mix up sexual inclinations with character traits. Leeham is a strong boy, but, trust me, he can only be happy at the submissive end of an N/S relationship. Same as you. You're not a helpless person by any means, but you need a good spanking once in a while."

I felt my cheeks turn hot red.

"I fully agree," Khiru added. "And Leeham blushes almost as much as you. He hasn't looked directly at me once since we've met."

"Because you're a very dominant Rhysh Master," I hissed.

"Exactly," they said in unison.

I was under the impression I had scored against my own team, but wasn't sure how I'd let that happen. I was still trying to clarify my thoughts when we reached the spring, and the men decided to rest.

While we ate a late breakfast of dried food and water, I observed how Leeham obeyed both Kalhan and Khiru without any sign of annoyance, how his face beamed with satisfaction each time one of them thanked him. The boy was also studying Khiru's Rhysh bracelet with acute interest and frank admiration. But his nervousness reminded me of my own, and I understood why we were on the same Southie side.

"Leeham!" Khiru's sudden call startled both the boy and me. "Why don't you come with me to check if the forest is safe before we venture into it with Megan?"

It wasn't a question, and Leeham immediately stood ready, eager to comply.

When they were gone, and I realized I was alone with Kalhan, I wondered about Khiru's real intentions. We all knew the forest was safe.

I was lying on my elbows on a patch of dry grass, enjoying the warmth of the sun on my face. Kalhan, who'd been sitting by the spring, came closer to me.

"I believe we've been granted a moment of privacy," he said rightly.

I sat up.

"Does Khiru know about us, Kalhan?"

He nodded.

"Everything?"

"Definitely enough."

That would explain Khiru's concerns about my feelings for him, but not why he was so easygoing about it all.

"Does he know about the whipping?"

"Yes."

"And he let you live?" I exclaimed.

Kalhan laughed. "I'm not saying he didn't feel like strangling me when I told him, but we worked it out."

It didn't fit with Khiru's pride and possessiveness.

"Megan," Kalhan went on, "Khiru and I have spent the last five weeks together. We've had time to talk and we put the past behind us. The distant past and the more recent past."

Khiru had first wronged Kalhan by forcing him into exile, and Kalhan had got back at him by kidnapping me.

"You called it even?"

"Something like that, yes."

He threw a stone in the spring and watched it sink. "Khiru and I were best friends since childhood. We always believed we had a future together. Besides…"

Another stone splashed in the water.

"Besides what?"

He stared at me.

"We don't want you to suffer more because of us. We've caused you enough pain."

He took my face in his hands. "I hope you can forgive me for everything I provoked. You went through hell because of me."

A knot formed in my stomach at the evocation of the last weeks, and before I knew it, tears were running down my face. I had been strong; now I could let go and be weak.

Kalhan wrapped his arms around me, and the flow became a torrent, washing away the pain and the fear. I cried a long time, lulled by Kalhan's soothing hands in my back.

"What's going to happen now?" I asked when I finally calmed down.

Kalhan brushed away the hair sticking to my cheeks. "You're going back to a quiet life with Khiru. You're going to heal and rest and be a happy woman again."

It was a tempting idea, but it wasn't going to work. I couldn't forget what had happened in Sweendi. I couldn't forget him.

"What about you, Kalhan? Where are you going from here?"

He gave me a brave smile. "Where the Court will send me."

"No!" I cried out. "You're not going to stand trial, are you? Don't let them catch you. Run away!"

He picked up another stone. "No, I'm not running away this time. Ten years ago, I was innocent and betrayed by my best friend. It's different now. I deserve whatever's coming."

I tried to imagine him in jail, or worse, as a convict of Gahra. I was going to cry again.

"Don't worry," he comforted me. "Khiru will testify in my favor in front of the Court; hopefully, the fact that I helped rescue you will benefit me. Perhaps I will only get a servicing sentence."

I had a better idea. "I won't say that you kidnapped me. I'll tell them it had always been Vogh."

He shook his head. "No, Megan, don't lie to the Court. They will figure out the truth, and any lie will only make things worse. But you can always tell them I treated you well and that my cause was just. Not that it justified anything," he sighed, throwing the stone as far as he could.

I gave him another one. "Is this why you and Khiru came here alone, without alerting the militia?"

"Khiru took risks," he nodded, "but he knew I wanted to see you before giving myself in."

"You could have stayed on Sweendi while he led the Globals here."

The next stone landed beyond the water.

"And give up on you?" Kalhan objected. "No such luck."

Instead of choosing another pebble, Kalhan brought me against him. "I may have to wait a few years before I can take you in my arms again, but, by Mhô, I will."

As his face bent over mine, I closed my eyes and received, with wonder, the softest kiss on the lips.

CHAPTER 24

▼

As the shuttle began its descent, the watery mint sky around us gradually intensified to a darker emerald green. We had flown a long way south, and I still hadn't picked up any clue as to our final destination. I only knew it would be our new home for the next three years, a decision that Khiru had made without consulting me.

A long time ago, I would have complained about such authoritarian manners. But these days, I didn't have the heart to discuss anything of importance, nor anything trivial, for that matter.

Six months had passed since my return to the G-Zone, and I was still trying to cope with the emotional impact of my captivity.

At first, there was much good news to rejoice. Obviously, flying back to Mhôakarta with Khiru, reuniting with my friends and rediscovering the sweet taste of freedom boosted my energy.

I had worried Khiru would react poorly to what Earth social rules would qualify as infidelity. To my surprise, he didn't. In fact, Khiru never looked happier. After months of agony, he only felt gratitude and relief, not only because I was unharmed and back in his arms, but also because he had eventually made up with Kalhan. The guilt and remorse that had been a constant cloud over his life had vanished. And, strangely, my affair with the man who was again his best friend contributed to his general satisfaction.

Khiru had another reason to be content.

When I told him about Vogh's baby plan, my contraceptive patch and my fake pregnancy, he looked like a treasure hunter who has been told there is a trunk of gold hidden in his backyard.

"It never occurred to me that you could get pregnant just from sex," he said, marveling at the possibility and, I'm sure, already dreaming of his own lineage.

The euphoria of the first weeks also stemmed from the gratifying developments on Gahra, and the happy endings all my friends enjoyed.

Although Vogh ran away from his palace as soon as the airborne squadron was announced, he didn't escape the Globals' extensive hunt on the island. He was sent to a full-time detention unit in the G-Zone where he would be under constant supervision. When the Global security department heard about the supply route at the bottom of the ocean, they expanded the magnetized belt underneath the water and improved surveillance radars around the island. After a thorough search, they confiscated all the merchandise, weapons and technological equipment that had been smuggled into Gahra.

When the militia took over Vogh's palace in the cave, they mostly walked into empty rooms. The only people they found were those who had been unable to escape.

In the gym, Lohrie hung from the ceiling like a piece of meat. Her back bore dozens of bleeding stripes, the result of a punishment derived from my escape. After intensive care in a Global hospital, Lohrie returned to her home territory.

Eeno was, as expected, confined to one of Vogh's infamous prison cells. She, too, was in sore physical condition, having suffered lashes and burns all over her body. However, her spirits were excellent. Because I was whisked away in a shuttle as soon as we reached the cave, I had no chance to celebrate our success on Gahra. But I met her later, in the Global city she had selected as her new home. Thanks to her involvement in my liberation, she obtained a full judicial pardon and established herself as a talented whip master in a scenemat.

"I will never be at the wrong end of the whip again," she vowed.

Following Kalhan's request, Leeham accompanied Khiru and me to Mhôakarta. His minor role in my kidnapping somehow eluded Global justice. Instead, he was welcomed as a hero who had largely contributed to my successful escape.

Faithful to his dream, and running from a world where his mentor could no longer help him, Leeham immediately applied to the Rhysh Academy. Thanks to Khiru's patronage, the Rhysh Board accepted his application without waiting for the end of the term, and my gentle Sweendi boy disappeared behind the inescapable walls of the reclusive realm where he would spend the next four years.

Leeham had entered Rhysh as a Northie candidate, but as Khiru pointed out, he would figure it all out during the first year. Rhysh trainers had a particular talent in revealing the true calling of a misplaced student.

When Leeham left, I envied the uncompromising path he had chosen. In comparison, my own future seemed full of questions and doubts. Although I loved Khiru deeply, my life was no longer complete. I felt like a war veteran, dismembered and lost. A sure sign that something was amiss in our lives, Khiru and I no longer engaged in erotic games beyond tender love bondage. Khiru insisted my body should heal first, and my mind needed to reconcile the idea of restraints and confinement with pleasure. The true reason, however, was that we were both wrapped up in what had become the trial of the year.

The Global troops had placed Kalhan in detention at the same time the rest of us flew away to freedom. Charges against him were heavy, but he benefited from a series of alleviating circumstances.

The social upheaval in favor of equal rights for NGAs shed an uncommon light on Kalhan's crimes. For many, he was a martyred hero to an honorable cause. Popular opinion, both in Free Territories and the G-Zone, called for clemency.

Khiru was confident that our testimonies had impressed the judges favorably. But the facts remained that Kalhan was guilty of association with criminals and kidnapping.

With the hearing of dozens of witnesses, including Kalhan's parents, members of the Rhysh Board, Sweendi freemen, and even Suri, who publicly owned up to her false accusations, the trial lasted five months, a long time by Khyrian standards.

By the time the verdict was due, I had bitten my nails to blood. Khyrian trials aren't public, and that morning, Khiru and I were anxiously waiting for the news to appear on the legal news page in the Data. It fell like the blade of a guillotine: three years of full-time servicing.

Khiru's shout of relief contrasted with my desperate silence. I knew the sentence was very moderate. Servicing was a civil condemnation, and Kalhan wouldn't be considered a criminal. There would be neither a location chip nor restraints. His confinement unit would resemble an adult camp more than a prison, and once his time was done, he would return to a normal life. But all I could think about was the "full-time" verdict. I wouldn't see him for the next three years.

Although I put on a brave face for Khiru's sake, my heart was still mourning when he announced we were moving out of Mhôakarta. He thought a change of air would benefit me; I seriously doubted it.

Our private shuttle was flying down on a cluster of dark buildings surrounded by a patchwork of greens hinting at forests and meadows. The lower we got, the more impressive the vision became. Encircling the city ahead of us was a wide wall that reminded me of medieval fortifications on Earth. Inside, I noticed hundreds of houses tightly grouped together and a number of large edifices that seemed to defy the passing of time itself.

"This must be a very old town," I said inquiringly.

"The oldest on Khyra, the only one that remained unscathed after the Gene War. But this is more than a city," Khiru explained. "It's an independent state, with houses, rules and traditions dating back centuries."

I only knew of one such place on Khyra.

"This is Rhysh," I whispered respectfully.

Khiru's silence confirmed my guess, and a heat wave spread through me.

"Did you ask the Council's permission?" I couldn't help asking, remembering with acute details how, on my first day, they had warned Khiru to take it easy on me.

Khiru grinned. "The Council immediately approved the idea. After all that happened, they agreed that this was the safest place for you on the planet."

"What about my DNA samplings?"

"We'll organize them from here."

He had obviously thought it through.

So this is how he's going to keep my mind off Kalhan, I reflected, unsure of what my feelings should be.

"I thought Rhysh was bigger," I commented. "Isn't there a harbor, an airport?"

Khiru pointed to a silver ribbon beyond the city wall, then followed it to the far left, where a small group of buildings was hardly visible.

"The harbor is over there, near the border," he said. "The airport is north of the city. The wall you see is a relic enclosing the ancient original town; it holds the administrative center and the various faculties. But it represents barely one-tenth of Rhysh. The realm extends over pastures and woods, and hundreds of scattered individual housings, all surrounded by an invisible magnetized belt that marks its perimeter."

While I frenetically conjectured about our new life and what it would involve, Khiru approached a small airport where a stylized "Rh" marked the main landing area. Calling in the air controllers, he requested a privileged spot near the "stables," a favor that was immediately approved.

After our smooth vertical landing, an airport official welcomed us and offered to take care of our luggage.

"Your mount is ready, Master," he told Khiru with obvious deference.

I had never heard anyone call Khiru "Master" before. Northies had long dropped the old usage, which was reserved to special historical scenes. These days, the title only served to qualify Rhysh graduates, but even they never required such obsequiousness when addressed.

But Rhysh was a timeless place where traditions still ruled.

Another shocking revelation came when we crossed the threshold to the stables. I had wrongly assumed the name was an old-fashioned way of describing a modern transportation facility. The large house did contain stables, with the most noble of mounts: argalis.

"Argalis are the most common way to get around Rhysh," Khiru explained as we neared one of the tall brown animals that uncannily reminded me of Pagis. "At least for Masters," he added, trying to provoke me. "Slaves usually walk."

But after a wink, Khiru helped me settle on the argali and jumped behind me with the same ease Kalhan had shown months before.

Leaving the airport and the city wall far behind us, we headed north and rode for a long time between fields and meadows. I spotted a few isolated houses along the way, as well as farms and craft shops. Even on Earth, this place would have been behind the times.

"We're almost there," Khiru announced.

The argali walked a few more steps and reached the top of a hill. Down below was a large wooden house with several annexes, built on the shore of a pond. The mid-afternoon sun reflected off the clear water where a family of web-footed birds searched for edible bugs.

While we made our way down, Khiru gave me instructions.

"I know you'll want to look around the house and check our surroundings, but that will have to wait."

His tone was unmistakably commanding; I warmed up instantly.

"There's something I've been dreaming of since the day I met you, something I was denied for a year, something I've been postponing for six months."

Faster than a computer, my mind was scanning all the possibilities. What was he talking about?

"My patience has worn thin, and I've decided that today was the day. And because I don't want you to argue about it…"

He strapped a lilk gag around my head, then cuffed my hands behind my back.

The argali had stopped in front of the door to the house, but when Khiru brought me to the floor, he directed me toward the main annex, almost as big as the central building.

When I walked in, I realized I was going to spend many hours in there. It was a fully equipped dungeon spread across three rooms. One contained an imposing poster-bed and a bathroom. The second room was the staging area, with enough devices to bind me in as many positions as anatomy would allow. The third room doubled as a storage area and a workshop where my presence was by no means recommended.

"Over there," Khiru ordered when we returned to the middle room. He was indicating a board I recognized to be the ultimate whipping support. I placed myself against the vertical kauchu-coated board, with my face poking through an adequate hole. After removing my cuffs and positioning my arms around the support, well away from my back, Khiru finger-locked an impressive series of straps to immobilize my limbs, hips and shoulders. When I was totally restrained, with my legs slightly apart, he lowered the board to a 30-degree angle, a position less strenuous to hold than the stand-up classic.

Then he stood behind me, placed his hands tenderly on my waist and kissed my neck.

This was an important moment for both of us. I was confident that I had breached the psychological barrier that made it impossible for me to yield to pain and find pleasure in it. Kalhan's whipping was a vivid memory that I constantly replayed. It fed my fantasies and inspired many dreams of future scenes to come. There was however a glitch. When I pictured the person holding the whip, I always thought of Kalhan, not Khiru. Because Khiru had witnessed the disastrous scene with Lodel, he acted as a catalyst to my fear. I could only hope I would be able to crack that other barrier.

"You're nervous," Khiru whispered while stroking my hips. "I'll be honest with you: I'm slightly fazed, too."

I didn't need to know that.

Khiru's hands became very subtle, hardly noticeable. He moved from my waist to my shoulders.

"But someone's here to help us break the spell."

I gave an imperceptible start. His voice came from the side; it didn't match the location of his hands. My eerie impression was confirmed when another man spoke behind me.

"There's no reason why you shouldn't enjoy now what you enjoyed months ago."

For a split second, I thought I was dreaming. This was simply impossible; the implications were unfathomable. Yet, the touch was real; the voice was inimitable.

Under the gag, I groaned something that I hoped resembled "Kalhan, what, by Plya, are you doing here and, please, can I turn around and kiss you?"

He laughed, and the cheerful sound sent a shockwave through my chest.

"We'll have time to kiss and tell, Earth girl," he teased. "Right now, Khiru and I have other intentions, whether you like it or not."

He took several steps back, and a silence full of promises and expectations filled the air.

My mind was so elated and my body so excited, my new concern was to reach ecstasy after a single whiplash. I was practically shaking from the thought itself.

But two Rhysh Masters know better than to nip desire in the bud.

The whipping started slowly, as soft as a caress, a whisper. Each flogger wrapped its straps around my skin like a cat taunts with its clawless paws. Striking left, than right, they warmed my body for long minutes. The implicit threat of a more severe blow soon, sooner, now, kept me on the edge. Wriggling, moaning, I was showing signs of impatience, but the floggers continued to strike mildly.

"She still requires a lot of training in the patience department," I heard Kalhan say on my left just as the whip he was holding landed on my bottom.

"I agree," Khiru admitted to my right, repeating Kalhan's hit on exactly the same spot. "Patience is not her best achievement."

Another precise blow, without the slightest deviation. My cheeks were becoming very sensitive.

"Your task wasn't easy," Kalhan went on, like a teacher commenting on a child's performances with a colleague. "Considering where she comes from, it was an extraordinary challenge."

Khiru mimicked a sigh deep enough for me to hear it over the whistle of his flogger. Center bottom again.

"You know me," he was saying. "I like a good challenge, but the Council tied my hands, if I may say so."

Kalhan's next blow stirred the incipient anger in me. Whether it was their idle banter about me or their precisely-aimed attack, my impatience became violent. I grunted and banged my brow in protest.

Kalhan walked behind me. He placed a large strap behind my head and secured it to the board, forcing my face to keep still inside the hole.

Khiru hit my cheeks before his friend resumed his position. He aimed for the same vulnerable spot and struck with similar intensity. Then Kalhan followed suit, as if my reaction had been nothing more than a minor technical interruption.

"The Council will have little to say now," Kalhan carried on. "And I doubt anyone in Rhysh will raise his eyes if we administer proper punishment."

"It's the whole point, isn't it?" Khiru commented, punctuating his rhetorical question with a very concrete strike.

I was getting thoroughly upset. My ass burned like hell, a pain that was insignificant compared to my wounded pride. At the same time, my sex contracted more fiercely with each whiplash and each sarcastic comment.

"I was wondering," Kalhan said. "Given our obviously evil intentions, could this be technically construed as a kidnapping?"

Khiru thought about it during a series of three blows.

"The Council and the Rhysh Board approved. The only person who could blame us for dragging her here is Megan herself."

"And we don't care if she complains."

I swore they would pay for their insolence. I had a vision of me running away, daring them to catch me, but had increasing trouble focusing on the idea. I felt myself drifting to a state where pleasure would overwhelm me, but only if I submitted to it, only if I submitted to them.

I resisted as long as I could, but the whips were tongues of passion, and the words, an expression of love. Desire enveloped me like a thick layer of mist. It twirled around me, brushed against me, urged me to let go.

My muscles unclenched; my mind stopped arguing. Like a female feline offering her defenseless neck to the victorious male, I surrendered.

I didn't register the different sensations until after the third strike. Khiru and Kalhan had swapped their floggers for whips. Aiming at the same target, they began to hit harder. They had stopped talking; the only sound in the room came from the lashes cleaving the air.

Even I was quiet. Subdued, bathing in blissful fervor, I received every stroke with gratitude. The pain magnified my needs. I would never have enough.

The hits fell more quickly, often simultaneously. Always one on my cheeks, another down my legs or on my shoulders. Tracing them became difficult. They landed and landed, marking my flesh, branding my soul. I was beyond myself, floating, dreaming. I had never felt so much love; there was nothing I wouldn't do for the men holding the whips.

Pain reached its peak, and so did pleasure. An avalanche of strikes rolled onto me, and I roared like thunder.

The silence and quiet that followed were surreal. Time stopped, but not for long.

The climax provoked by the whips hadn't satiated my longings for more carnal pleasures. My sex was still throbbing, and I was anxious to welcome my lovers inside me, let them possess me now that I had abandoned myself to them. My body was no longer mine, but it required a new master. Or two.

One of the men lowered the whipping board until I was lying horizontally. While I continued to enjoy post-climatic euphoria, all the restraints went loose, one by one. Then, four hands lifted me off the board and carried me to the bedroom.

Khiru and Kalhan lowered me on the bed and lay down by my sides. Both were naked and ready. For the first time, I noticed Kalhan's new bracelet partly concealing his scar. It was black, with the "Rh" embossed in silver.

Seeing them together brought me back to a limited level of consciousness. How often had I fantasized about this? How could this be true? My eyes were full of questions, but answers were limited to smiles and grins.

In one synchronized move, the two men grabbed my arms and locked them inside shackles connected to the headboard. Their unambiguous act of dominance made me swoon, and, once again, I glided down the delightful path of submission.

Khiru kissed my left nipple; Kalhan licked my right ear. Two tongues started to explore my body, from my ears to my navel. The dual sensation ignited fireworks inside me. I squirmed to escape the incessant rain of teasing kisses and gentle bites. I tried to kick sideways and hit a couple of calves, but my pathetic fight only served as a signal for increased bondage. Using their legs, both men caught mine and held them wide apart.

Helpless, I held my breath when two hands swiftly moved up my legs and stopped at their intersection. When two fingers pried my sex open, my instincts opposed the intrusion. I wasn't programmed for this. One man was right, two men were wrong.

Catching my apprehension, Khiru and Kalhan slowed their invasion and were staring at me, their expression one of challenge.

I shook my head, not very convincingly.

The men smiled, and their fingers dived deeper inside me.

"Yes, Megan."

Khiru kissed my temple, and Kalhan preyed on a nipple. Ignoring my feeble protests, they continued to spur my desire, their magic transforming my nervousness into more sexual craving. Their love, their unbending claim on me sent Earth and its rules light-years away. Thanks to them, I was free and powerful, and too dizzy for philosophical concerns.

When I thought I would faint, Kalhan slithered under my body while Khiru climbed on top of me. One held my waist down; the other spread my legs. The combination of their strength doubled my helplessness and desire. Khiru took possession of me, and Kalhan held my breasts in hostage. He would only release them when I'd given the prize he awaited.

Khiru came violently and exerted his pressure long enough for me to go limp underneath him. Even then, I hadn't reached the pinnacle of sexual bliss.

The two men swapped positions.

Under me, Khiru used his legs to stretch mine until they hurt. For him to offer me to another man was a symbol onto itself. His generosity humbled me; his trust touched my very soul. I warmed up again, ready to give as much as I received. When Kalhan entered me, my heart exploded.

I awoke under the evening sky.

Strange bird sounds filled the night; a few splashes flittered from the pond. A gentle breeze blew over my face, hardly perceptible through the blanket that covered my body.

Above me, millions of stars pierced the darkness. Lower, two large, dissimilar globes shone brightly, like the distorted eyes of a monstrous beast. Tonight, Mhô was smaller than Plya. With its white scar across its face, the female moon was smiling at me again. I returned her smile.

"Back among the living?" a tender voice asked.

Khiru and Kalhan lay by my sides, under the blanket, their hands underneath my breasts. Propped up on their elbows, they were also smiling.

As I emerged from the underworld, they made me drink and nibble on a biscuit. I was still too mesmerized to ask questions, but I could hear them forming at the back of my mind, ready to burst out.

"How?" I finally managed to ask.

As usual, they answered together. They spoke slowly, giving me time to absorb the truth, to believe in it.

Even before the Court announced its verdict in Kalhan's trial, Khiru had approached the Rhysh Board. He had little problem convincing the governing Masters who were always prone to defend one of theirs. The Board took longer to advocate the idea to the Council, but in the end, political prudence and fair justice prevailed. On the one hand, while he had committed crimes, Kalhan was not a criminal. He needed a lesson, but didn't deserve any harsh treatment. On the other hand, he had become an important social figure. A debate on rights in peaceful NGAs was now on the Council's agenda, and nobody wanted him to create, willingly or not, a cradle of opposition in his confinement unit. What Khyra's highest authority wanted was Kalhan's temporary disappearance. Where and how was hardly their concern.

The Court's sentence of three years of full-time servicing would be respected. However, the place of confinement was traditionally elected by local authorities, depending on their needs. On the Council's direct order, Kalhan was sent to Rhysh, where he would remain until his time was done. The Rhysh Board was directly responsible for him.

"Why didn't you tell me?" I asked Khiru, annoyed that he had let me despair for weeks when he knew of such a happy resolution.

"The Council didn't allow me," he explained. "Their decision was extremely confidential. Rhysh is often criticized for the privileges its members receive. Giving asylum to Kalhan could give rise to much envy and resentment. To avoid this, secrecy was a part of the deal. Nobody outside Rhysh should know about him living here."

I had never seen Kalhan look so radiant. He was even more handsome than in his troubled Sweendi days.

"Are we really going to stay here for three years?" I questioned both of them. "Khiru, what about your job at the Space Center?"

"I obtained a prolonged sabbatical," he said with a joking twist in his voice. "My new duty is to see that Kalhan serves his sentence properly."

"I doubt he will try to escape from here," I teased.

Fingers squeezed one of my nipples. It took me a second to link the source of the sensation to the man responsible for it, in this case Kalhan.

"Khiru means he will make sure I perform my task well."

"What task?" I asked, with the impression I was walking down a path the men wanted me to take.

Khiru answered instead of Kalhan. "You don't think the Rhysh Board will let him stay here without compensation? They've asked Kalhan to do what Masters are here for: train a new slave."

A severe pang of jealousy hit me, and without thinking, I growled.

"You're going to master another girl?"

My eyes darted from one man to the other, refusing to believe that…

A very long time ago on Earth, when I was about to turn six, I had undergone the same feeling. My father had casually mentioned that a young girl in the neighborhood was going to receive a brand-new bicycle for her birthday. I had automatically assumed the worst and let my envy explode in angry words until I saw my dad smile knowingly at me and I finally understood what he meant. I had felt utterly stupid and unworthy of the present he had bought for me.

That was exactly how I felt now.

But instead of hiding and blushing, I chose to play, too.

Khiru and Kalhan were acutely observing my face, waiting for a huge smile to spread across it.

I frowned. "Oh, I see," I said, immediately causing their brows to furrow. "You would like me to submit not to one, but two Rhysh Masters?"

They grinned uncertainly.

"We know it's against your Earth nature," Khiru said. "But please do consider it."

I didn't fake my surprise. "You've had me to yourself for over a year, and now you're ready to share me?"

"A Khyrian man cannot hope to keep a woman to himself," he said. "Even as children, we know we will share the one we love. We grow up dreaming that at least we'll share her with someone we trust and respect. A friend."

He looked at Kalhan, who confirmed: "A long time ago, Khiru and I promised each other that we would be partners to the same woman. It was a child's promise, of course, not very realistic, but today, we feel that, if you agree to try, we could make our dream come true."

"I'm not sure I'll be up to the challenge," I replied honestly.

"Neither are we," Khiru replied.

An angel passed.

Enjoying what was probably the last time I would make an important decision, I defied them.

"Will you at least give me some slack?" I asked. "Some independence, control over my life?"

They both fixed me intensely. They showed no trace of hesitation when they replied as one voice.

"No."

They were so arrogant, proud, self-assured.

"Then, Khiru, Kalhan—"

They were tender, generous, brave, smart and so much fun.

"I'm all yours."

Khyra's night sky disappeared behind them as they bent down on me, their lips half opened. However, I didn't need to see the moons to know that Mhô and Plya were still hovering above us. Both of them would forever watch over me, imposing their lights and their moods, turning the night into an ever-changing spectacle. Making it all worthwhile.

Finis

0-595-33084-3

Printed in the United States
22408LVS00002B/314

9 780595 330843